James H. Graff, George A. Lawrence

Sword and Gown

a novel

James H. Graff, George A. Lawrence

Sword and Gown
a novel

ISBN/EAN: 9783337349578

Printed in Europe, USA, Canada, Australia, Japan

Cover: Foto ©Andreas Hilbeck / pixelio.de

More available books at **www.hansebooks.com**

SWORD AND GOWN.

A Novel.

BY THE AUTHOR OF

"GUY LIVINGSTONE," "BARREN HONOUR,"

"BRAKESPEARE," ETC.

LONDON:

TINSLEY BROTHERS, 18, CATHERINE STREET, STRAND.

1868.

LONDON :

WYMAN AND SONS, PRINTERS, GREAT QUEEN STREET,

LINCOLN'S INN FIELDS, W.C.

SWORD AND GOWN.

CHAPTER I.

THERE *is* something in this climate, after all
I suppose there are. not many places where
one could lie on the shore in December, and enjoy
the air as much as I have done for the last two
hours.

Harry Molyneux turned his face seaward again
as he spoke, and drank in the soft breeze eagerly
he could scarcely help thanking it aloud, as i
stole freshly over his frame, and played gently
with his hair, and left a delicate caress on his
cheek—the cheek that was now always so pale
save in the one round scarlet spot where, month
ago, Consumption had hung out her flag of "No
surrender."

There is enough in the scene to justify an average
amount of enthusiasm. Those steep broken hills in
the background form the frontier fortress of the
maritime Alps, the last outwork of which is the

rocky spur on which Molyneux and his companion are lying. Fir woods feather the sky-line; and from among these, here and there, the tall stone pines stand up alone, like sentinels—steady, upright, aud unwearied, though their guard has not been relieved for centuries. All around, wild myrtle and heath and eglantine curl and creep up the stems of the olives, trying, from the contact of their fresh youth, to infuse new life and sap into the grey gnarled old trees, even as a fair Jewish maiden once strove to cherish her war-worn decrepit king. There are other flowers too left, though December has begun, enough to give a faint fragrance to the air and gay colours to the ground. Just below their feet is a narrow strip of dark ribbed sand, and then the tangle of weed, scarcely stirred by the water, that all along this coast fringes like a beard the languid lip of the Mediterranean Sea.

Molyneux appreciated and admired all this, after his simple fashion, and said so : his companion did not answer immediately; he only shrugged his shoulders and lifted his eyebrows, as if he could have disputed the point if it had not been too much trouble. An optimist in nothing, least of all was Royston Keene grateful or indulgent to the beauties and bounties of inanimate creation.

"Ah well!" Harry went on resignedly, "I know it's useless trying to get a compliment to Nature

out of you. I ought to have given you up that
night when we showed you the Alps from the
terrace at Berne. You had never seen the Jung-
frau before, and she had got her prettiest pink
evening-dress on, poor thing! and all you would
say was, 'There's not much tho matter with the
view.'"

"It was a concession to your wife's enthusiasm,"
Keene replied; "a sudden check might have been
dangerous just then, or I should have spoken
more bitterly, after being brought out to look at
mountains, when I was dusty and travel-stained,
wanting baths and dinners and other necessaries
of life."

The voice was deep-toned and melodious enough
that spoke these words, but too slow and deliberate
to be quite a pleasant one, though there was nothing
like a drawl in it. One could easily fancy such a
voice ironical or sarcastic, but hardly raised much
in anger; in the imperative mood it might be very
successful, but it seemed as if it could never have
pleaded or prayed. It matched the speaker's ex-
terior singularly well. Had you seen him for the
first time—couchant, as he was then—you would
have had only an impression of great length and
laziness; but as you gazed on, the vast deep chest
expanded under your eye; tho knotted muscles,
without an ounce of superfluous flesh to dull their
outline, developed themselves one by one; so that

gradually you began to realize the extent of his surpassing bodily powers, and wondered that you could have been deceived even for a moment. The face guarded its secret far more successfully. The features were bold and sharply cut, bronzed up to the roots of the crisp light-brown beard and hair, except where the upper brow retained its original fairness—presenting a startling contrast, like a wreath of snow lying late in spring-time high up on the side of a black Fell. You would hardly say that they were devoid of expression, any more than that a perfectly drilled soldier is incapable of activity; but you got puzzled in making out what their natural expression was: it was not sternness, far less ferocity—the face was much too impassible for either; and yet its listlessness could never be mistaken for languor. The thin short lips might be very pitiless when compressed, very contemptuous and provocative when curling; but the enormous moustache, sweeping over them like a wave, and ending in a clean stiff upward curve, made even this a matter of mere conjecture. The cold, steady, dark eyes seldom flashed or glittered; but when their pupils contracted, there came into them a sort of sullen, suppressed, inward light, like that of jet or cannel coal. One curious thing about them was that they never seemed to care about following you, and yet you felt you could not escape from them. The first hand-gripe, however, settled the

question with most people : few, after experiencing
the involuntary pressure, when he did not in the
least mean to be cordial, doubted that there were
passions in Royston Keene—difficult perhaps to
rouse, but yet more difficult to appease or subdue.

His profession was evident. Indeed, it must be
confessed that the Dragoon is not easily dissembled.
I know a very meritorious parish-priest, of fair
repute too as a preacher, who has striven for years
—hard, but unavailingly—to divest himself of the
martial air he brought with him out of the K.D.G.
He strides down the village street with a certain
swagger and roll, as if the steel scabbard were still
trailing at his heel, acknowledging rustic bows
with a slight quick motion of the finger, like
troopers' salutes; on the smooth shaven face is
shadowed forth the outline of a beard, nurtured and
trimmed in old days with more than horticultural
science; in the pulpit and reading-desk gown and
surplice hang uneasily, like a disguise, on the erect
soldierly figure ; and the effect of his ministrations
is thereby sadly marred; for apposite text, earnest
exhortation, and grave rebuke flow with a curious
inconsistency from the lips of that well-meaning
but unmitigated Plunger.

Royston Keene was no exception to this rule,
though he did not like to be told so, and rather
ignored the profession than otherwise. Perhaps he
had begun it early enough to have got tired of it ,

for he had now been for some little time on half-
pay, and a brevet-major, after doing good service in
the Indian wars, and was not yet thirty-four. Molyneux had served in the same light cavalry regiment
as his subaltern, and there the foundation was laid
of their close alliance. It was not a very fair or
well-balanced one, being made up of implicit
obedience, reliance, and reverence on the one other
side, and a sort of protecting condescension on the
other—much like the old Roman relation between
Client and Patron; nevertheless it had outlasted
many more sympathetic and better-looking friend-
ships.

They used to say of "The Cool Captain" (so he
was always called off parade), that "he could bring
a boy to his bearings sooner than any man in the
army." Yet he was a favourite with them all.
There was a regular ovation among those "Godless
horsemen" whenever he came into the Club, or into
their mess-rooms; they hung upon his simplest
words with a touchingly devout attention, and
thought it was their own stupidity when they could
see nothing in them to laugh at or admire; they
wrote off all that they could remember of his sarcasms and repartees—generally strangely traves-
tied and spoilt by carriage—to unlucky comrades,
martyrized on far-off detachments, or vegetating
with friends in the country; the more ambitious,
after much private practice, strove to imitate his

way of twisting his moustache as he stood before
the fire, though with some, to whom nature had
been niggard of hirsute honours, it was grasping
a shadow and fighting with the air.

Certainly, Molyneux never was so happy as in
that society. Fond as he was of his pretty wife,
her influence was as nothing in the scale. She
complained of this, half in earnest, soon after
they were married. The fever of post-nuptial
felicity was strong upon Harry just then, but he
did not attempt to deny the imputation. He
only said, "My pet, I have known him so much
the longest!" I wonder, now, how many brides
would have admitted that somewhat unsatisfactory
and illogical excuse? Fanny Molyneux did; she
was the best-natured little woman alive, and
wise too in her generation, for she never brought
matters to a crisis, or measured her strength
against the "heavy-weight."

Indeed, they got on together extremely well.
Whenever Keene happened to be with them—
which was not often—she gave up the manage-
ment of Harry's Foreign Affairs to him, reserving
to herself the control of the Home Department,
and, between the two, they ruled their vassal
right royally. After some months' acquaintance,
they became the greatest friends; on Royston's
side it was one of the few quite pure and unselfish
feelings he had ever cherished towards one of her

sex not nearly akin to him in blood. He always
seemed to look on her as a very nice, but rather
spoilt child, to be humoured and petted to any
amount, but very seldom to be reasoned with or
gravely consulted. Considering her numerous
fascinations, and the little practice he had had
in the paternal or fraternal line, he really did it
remarkably well: be it understood, it was only
en petite comité that all this went on; in general
society his manner was strictly formal and deferen-
tial. It provoked her though, sometimes, and
one day she ventured to say, " I wish you would
learn to treat me like a grown-up woman !"
Royston's eyes darkened strangely : and one
glance flashed out of the gloom that made her
shrink away from him then, and blush painfully
when she thought of it afterwards alone. He
was frowning, too, as he answered, in a voice
unusually harsh and constrained, " It seems to
me we go on very well as it is. But women
never *will* leave well alone." She did not like to
analyze his answer or her own feelings too closely,
so she tried to persuade herself it was a very rude
speech, and that she ought to be offended at
it. There was a coolness between those two for
some days, amounting to distant courtesy. But
the dignified style did not suite *ma mignonne*
(as Harry delighted to call her) at all, and was,

indeed, a lamentable failure; it made her look
as if she had been trying on one of her great-
grandmother's short-waisted dresses; so they soon
fell back into their old ways, and like the prince
and princess in all fairy tales, " lived very happily
ever afterwards."

CHAPTER II.

KEENE had spent some time with the Molyneuxs during the autumn and winter, and
had conducted himself so far with perfect propriety, certainly keeping Harry straighter than he
would have gone alone; for he was unluckily of a
convivial turn of mind wholly incompatible with
delicate health and a frail constitution. Being a
favourite with the world in general, he felt bound,
I suppose, to reciprocate; so, albeit strictly
enjoined to keep the earliest hours, he would
sit up till dawn if any one encouraged him, and
then come home, perfectly sober perhaps, but
staggering from mere weakness. He did not care
for deep drinking in the least, but the number
of magnums he had assisted in flooring, when
on a regimen of "three glasses of sherry," would
have made a double row of nails round the coffin of
a larger man. Nature, however, being a Dame,
won't stand being slighted, or having her admoni-
tions disregarded, and the way she asserted herself
on the morrow was retributive in the extreme.
Harry was always so *very* ill after one of those
nights "upon the war-path!" On such occasions,

his feelings, without being quite remorseful, were
beautifully and curiously penitent; they manifested
themselves chiefly by an extraordinary ebullition
of the domestic affections. "Bring me my children" (he had two tiny ones), he would cry, on
waking, just as another man would call for brandy
and soda; and, strange to say, the presence of
those innocents seemed to have a similarly in-
vigorating and refreshing effect: during all that
day he would make pilgrimages to their cribs,
and gaze upon them sleeping, with the reverence
of an old *dévote* kneeling before the shrine of
her most efficacious saint. Then he would go
forth, and return with a present for his wife,
bearing an exact proportion in value to the extent
and duration of the past misdemeanour; so that
her jewel-case and writing-table soon became as
prettily suggestive as the votive chapel of Nôtre-
Dame des Dunes. Very unnecessary were these
peace-offerings; for that dear little woman never
dreamt of "hitting him when he was down," or
taking any other low advantage of his weakness.
She would make his breakfast beamingly, at all
untimely hours, and otherwise pet and caress him,
so that he might have been a knight returning
wounded from some Holy War, instead of a discomfited scalp-hunter, bearing still evident traces
of the "war-paint." A stern old lady told her
once that such condonation of offences was

unprincipled and immoral. It may be so, but I cannot think the example is likely to be dangerously contagious. Whatever happens, there will always remain a sufficiency of matronly Dicæarchs, over whose judgment-seats the legend is very plainly inscribed, *Nescia flecti*.

These Ember days formed the only exceptions to the remarkably easy way in which Molyneux took everything: there seemed to be no rough places about his disposition for trouble or care to take hold of. Hunting four days a week through the winter—six weeks in town during the season, with incidentals of Epsom, Goodwood, *saumon à la Trafalgar*, bouquets, and opera-stalls—living all the rest of the year at a mess curious as to the quality of its dry champagne—these simple pleasures involve a certain expenditure hardly fairly 'warranted by our regimental rate of pay.' To accomplish all this on about £500 a year, and yet to steer clear of ruin, is an ingenious process doubtless, but a sum not to be wrought out (most soldiers will tell you) without some anxiety and travail of mind. Now, in the very tightest state of the money-market, Harry was never known to disquiet himself in vain. He would not borrow from any of his comrades, refusing all such proffers of assistance gratefully, but consistently. No Mussulman ever equalled his contented reli-

ance on the resources of Futurity, and his implicit
belief in the same. He would anchor his hopes
on some such improbability as "a long shot
coming off," or "his Aunt Agnes coming down"
(a proverbially awful widow, who had forgiven
him seven times already; and after each fresh
offence had sworn unrelenting enmity to him and
his heirs for ever). Strong in this faith, he met
condoling friends with a pleasant, reassuring smile:
with the same demeanour he confronted threatening creditors. He used no arts, and conde-
scended to no subterfuge, in dealing with these
last; but, as one of them observed, retreating from the barracks moneyless but gratified,
"Mr. Molyneux seems to *feel* for one, at all
events." So he did. He sympathized with his
tailor, not in the least because he owed him
money, but because he was a fellow-creature in
difficulties, regretting heartily it was not in his
own power to relieve them; just as a very
charitable but improvident person might feel on
reading a case of real distress in the *Times*.
Strange to say, hitherto he had always pulled
through. Either the outsider *did* win, or the
aunt, touched in the soft place of her heart
through her ruffled feathers, was brought down
by a "wild shot," when considered quite out of
distance, and "parted" freely. The last and
hardest trial of all—long debility and frequent

illness—had failed to shake this intense serenity.
He was never cross or unreasonable, and tried
to give as little trouble as possible; but was
grateful to a degree for everything that was done
for him: he could even manage to thank people
for their advice, whether he took it or not. So
far as one could make out, he was nearly as
much interested in the state of his own health
as one would be about that of any pleasant casual
acquaintance.

It must be confessed that poor Harry and his
like are by no means strong-minded, or large-
brained, or persevering men; they seldom or
never rise to eminence, and rarely have greatness
thrust upon them. They do not often volunteer
to lead the vanguard of any great movement,
shouting out, on the slightest provocation, the war-
cry of "Life is earnest!" for they are the natural
subalterns of the world's mighty battalia, and could
hardly manœuvre one of its companies, without
hopelessly entangling it, and exposing themselves: indeed, if they are useful at all in their
generation, it is in a singularly modest and un-
obtrusive way. Yet there is an attraction about
them, a power of attachment, that the great and
wise ones of the earth have appreciated and
envied, ere now. It is curious, too, to see what
an apparent contradiction to themselves the
extremes of, the class—those who exaggerate

nonchalance into insensibility, and softness into effeminacy—have shown when brought face to face with imminent peril or certain destruction. France held few more terrible *ferrailleurs* than the curled painted minions of her third Henry: the sun never looked down on a more desperate duel than that in which Quélus, Schomberg, and Maugiron did their *devoir* manfully to the last. Nay, though he came delicately to his doom, the King of Amalek met it, I fancy, gallantly and gracefully enough, when once he read his sentence in the eyes of the pitiless Seer, who ordained that he "should be hewn in pieces before the Lord in Gilgal."

R. I. P

There was silence for some minutes after the few words that opened this story; and then Royston Keene spoke again.

"Hal, do you remember that miserable impostor in Paris being enthusiastic about Dorade and its advantages, describing it as a sort of happy hunting-ground, and so deciding us on choosing it in preference to Nice?"

"Ah, he *did* drivel a good deal. I think he had been drinking," the other answered.

"No; I understand him now. He had been bored here into a sullen, vicious misanthropy;

and he wanted to take it out of the human race by getting others in the same mess. It's just like that zealous old Heathfield, who, when he is up to his girths in a squire-trap, never holloas ''ware-bog' till five or six more are in it. I can fancy the hoary-headed villain gloating hideously over us just now. I wish I had him here. I could be *so* unkind to him! He talked about the shooting and the society. Bah! there's about one cock to every thousand acres of forest; and as for women fair to look upon, I've not flushed once since we came. I don't think I can stand it much longer."

"I'm very sorry," Harry said; "I knew you were being bored to death, and it's all on my account; but I didn't like to ask you about it. I'm so horribly selfish!" The shadow of an imminent penitence began to steal over him, when Royston broke in—

"Don't be childish. I liked to stay—never mind why—or I should not have done so. Only now—you are getting better, and I realize the situation more. I hardly know where to go. Not back to England, certainly, yet. Besides the nuisance and chancework of picking up a stud in the middle of the season, it isn't pleasant to be consoled for a blank day by, 'You should have been here last month. Never was such scent; and heaps of straight-running foxes!' And then they indulge themselves in an imaginative 'cracker,' knowing you can't contradict them. Shall I go to Albania? I should like to kill *something* before I turn homewards."

Harry seemed musing. Suddenly he half started up, clapping his hands. " I knew I had forgotten !"

" Not such a singular circumstance as to warrant all that indecent exultation," was the reply. " Well, out with it."

" I never told you that Fan had a letter this morning from Cecil Tresilyan (they're immense friends, you know) to ask her to engage rooms for them. They are in Paris now, and will be here in three days."

Keene raised himself on his arm, regarding his comrade with a sort of admiration. " You're a natural curiosity, *mon cher*. None of us ever quite appreciated you. I don't believe there's another man in existence, situated as we are, who would have kept that intelligence at the back of his head so long. *The* Tresilyan, of course? I remember hearing about her in India. Annesley came back from sick leave, perfectly insane on the subject. She *must* be something extraordinary, for the recollection of her made even him poetical—when he was sober. I asked about her when I got to England, but her mother was taken very ill, or did something equally unjustifiable, so she left town before I saw her."

" The mother really *was* ill," Molyneux said, apo-
logetically; "at least she died soon after that. Miss
Tresilyan has never shown much since. But you've
no idea of the sensation she made during her season
and a half. They called her The Refuser, she had
such a fabulous number of offers, and wouldn't look
at any of them. By-the-bye, there's rather a good
story about that. You know Margate? He's going
to the bad very fast now, but he was the crack
puppy of that year's entry : good-looking, long
minority, careful guardians, leases falling in, mother
one of the best Christians in England, and all that
sort of thing. Well, Tom Cary took him in hand,
and brought him out in great form before long.
They were talking over their preparations for the
moors, for they were going to start the next day.
'I believe that's all,' Margate asked, ' or have we
forgotten anything ?' 'Wait a minute,' said Tom,
and reflected (provident man, Tom; fond of his comforts and proud of it)—'Ah, I thought there was
something. You haven't proposed to The Tresilyan.'
They say Margate's face was a study. He never
disputed the orders of his private trainer, so he only
said, piteously, ' But I don't want to marry any
one,' and looked as if he was going to cry. 'You
are " ower young," ' Cary said, encouragingly, ' and
it's about the last thing I should press upon you.
It wouldn't suit my book at all. But I don't see
how that affects the question. I can lay ten ponies

to one she won't have you. It's the thing to do,
depend upon it. All the other good men have had
a turn, and you have no right to be singular; it's
bad taste. Rank has its duties, my lord. *Noblesse
oblige*, and so forth. You understand?' Margate
didn't in the least, but he went and proposed quite
properly, and was rejected rather more decidedly
than his fellows. Then he went down into Perthshire, and missed his grouse and lost his salmon
with a comfortable consciousness of having dis-
charged his obligations to society.

Royston Keene actually groaned. "Why didn't
she come sooner?" he said. "What a luxury, in
this God-forgotten place, to talk to a clever, handsome woman who tramples on strawberry-leaves!"

"Perhaps she would have come if she had known
how much we wanted her," replied Harry. "They
say she is a model of charity, and several other
virtues too. She is coming here for the health of
some companion, or governess, who lives with her.
Yet she flirts outrageously at times, in her own
imperial way. Better late than never. I'm certain
you'll like her, and perhaps she'll like you."

"*Qui vivra verra*," Keene said, rising slowly.
"Let us go home now. Draw your plaid closer
round you; it's getting chilly."

CHAPTER III.

THERE is a terrace in Dorade, fenced in from
every wind that blows except the south, and
even that has to creep cautiously and cunningly
round a sharp corner to make its entrance good.
Four small stunted palms grow there; they look
painfully out of place, and conscious of it; for they
are always bowing their heads in a meek humiliation, and shiver in a strange unhealthy way at the
slightest breeze, just as you may see Asiatics
doing in our 'land of mist and snow.' But the
natives regard those unhappy exotics with a fana-
tical pride, pointing them out to all comers as living
witnesses to the perfection of the climate; they
would gladly stone any irreverent stranger who
should suggest a comparison between their sacred
shrubs and the giants of Indian seas. The only
inhabitant of the place who ever attained any eminence anywhere (he really was a good tailor),
bequeathed a certain sum for the beautifying of the
renowned *allée*, instead of endowing charitable
institutions, and his townsmen endorsed the act
by erecting a little mural tablet to commemorate
his public spirit.

The view is rather pretty, stretching over vine-
yards, and gardens, and olive-grounds down to the
shore, with the islands in the far foreground rearing
themselves against the sky, clear and blue, or if
the weather is misty to seaward, sleeping in an
aureole of golden haze; so that the whole effect
would be cheerful if it were not for the melancholy
invalids who haunt the spot perpetually. Faces
and figures are to be seen, sometimes, that would
send an uncomfortable shiver of revulsion through
you if you met them on the Boulevard des Italiens,
strengthened by your anteprandian *absinthe*. Here
the place belonged to them so completely, that a
man in rude health felt like an unwarrantable intruder, in which light I am sure the hypochon-
driacs always regarded him. As such a one
passed, you might see a glare, half-envious, half-
resentful, light up some hollow eyes; and thin
parched lips worked nervously, as though they
were uttering a very equivocal blessing.

Does the character gain much by the extermina-
tion of more impulsive passions, when their place
is possessed by the two devils that neither age
nor sickness can exorcise—Avarice and Envy?
It is with this last, perhaps, that we have most to
do; and the shadow of it, however indistinct and
distant, makes the landscape near the horizon look
somewhat dreary. The nature of many of us is
so faulty and ill-regulated, that it may be doubted

if even advancing years will make us much better
or wiser; but, when winter shall have closed in,
and our hot blood is more than cool, is there no
chance of an "open season"?   Must it come to
this—that the mere sight of the youth and strength
and beauty that have left us far behind, shall stir
our bile, as though it were an insolent parade—
that the choicest delicacies at our neighbour's
wedding breakfast shall not pique our palate like
the baked meats at his funeral?   Not so; if we
must give ground, let us retreat in good order,
leaving no shield behind us that our foe may build
into his trophy.   If we are rash enough to assail
Lady Violet Vavasour with petitions for a waltz,
and see her look doubtfully down her scribbled
tablets, till the "sweetest lips that ever were
kissed" can find no gentler answer than the terrible "Engaged," let us not gnash suicidally our
few remaining teeth, even though Brabazon Leslie
—all the handsomer for the scar on his smooth
forehead—should come up upon our traces, and
ride roughshod over those hieroglyphics, as he did
at Balaklava through Russian squadrons.   Rather
let us try to sympathize with his triumph, while
he carries off his beautiful prize from under the
enemy's guns, as Dundonald may have cut out a
frigate beneath the batteries of Vera Cruz.   *Non
omnia corripit ævum.*   Hath the savour departed
wholly from the Gascon wine, because the name of

no living love crowns the draught? Shall we stay
sullenly at home when all the world is flocking to
the tournament, because our limbs have stiffened
so that we may no longer sit saddle-fast, and hold
our own in the *mêlée*? A corner in the cushioned
gallery is left to us still. Come, comrade of mine
—*nate mecum Consule Manlio*—we will go up and
lounge there among the Chatelaines : some may
be found goodnatured enough to listen (in the
pauses of the tilting), while we tell how, not so
many years back, plume and pennon went down
before our lance.

I place no great reliance on the Pleasures of
Memory. But if pearls and bright shells be rarely
found there, surely waifs, better than *echini* and
sting-rays, are to be gathered on the "shores of
long ago." Ah, cynic! you are strong enough to
be merciful—just this once. Spare us the string
of examples that would overwhelm us utterly.
Does it not suffice that we confess the truth of
that saddest adage, tolled in our ears by every
passing bell—

> Those whom the gods love well die young ?

Royston and his companion were crossing the
terrace on their way home, when the former
stopped suddenly.

"Go on, Hal," he said; "it is too late for you
to be standing about; but I must speak to that

poor Châteaumesnil. I shall see you at dinner."
He went up to a wheeled chair that was being
drawn by at the time.

Its occupant was a man of large frame, as far as
could be made out through the thick wrappings
of furs; his head was bent forward and low, resting on his hands, that were crossed on a crutch
handle. He appeared profoundly unconscious of
all that was passing, and never moved till Keene
addressed him. Then, very slowly, he lifted up
his face. Few of us, fortunately for those who
have strong imaginations and weak nerves, see
its like twice in a lifetime, or there would be
wild work in dreamland.

It was not distorted in any way, nor deformed,
except by a ghastly livid pallor : gaunt and drawn
as the features were, they still bore evident traces
of a rare manly beauty, that even the neglected
beard of iron-grey could not conceal. But it was
the savage face of one who has wrestled with
physical pain, till it has assumed almost the visible
and tangible shape of a personal enemy—a mocking devil, that always is ready, with fresh ingenuity
of torture, to answer and punish the rebellious
question, "Art thou come to torment me before
my time ?" The lines on the forehead were so
strongly marked and dreadfully distinct, that, like
the markings of the locust, they seemed to form
characters that might be read, if it were given

to mortal cabalists to decipher the handwriting of God.

Look once more : it is worth while if you are curious in contrasts and comparisons. Five years ago, that bowed blasted cripple was the most reckless dare-devil, the most splendid Paladin, in all the army of Algiers ; the man for whom, after an unusually brilliant exploit, St. Arnaud, loving him as his own right hand, could find no higher praise than to write in his despatches—' *Les* 3me *Chasseurs se sont conduits en héros ; leur chef-d'escadron en—Châteaumesnil.*' And it was true that the annals of his house could boast of no nobler soldier, though they had been fighting hard since Clovis' day. His name is known very well in Africa. The *spahis* talk of it still over their watch-fires, and the wild Bedouins load it with guttural curses—their lips white with hatred and remembered fear; they do not forget how far and fast they fled into their desert strongholds, and never could shake off the light cloud of whirling dust, that told how Armand and his stanch gaze-hounds pressed hard upon their trail.

Rheumatic fever, coming close on a severe bullet wound, had brought him very near to death ; and the first thing he heard when he began to recover, was that he would never stand upright again.

He is answering Keene's salutation.

" My friend, you failed us last night at the

Cercle, and yet we waited for you long." A hoarse
hollow voice—very measured and slow, as if carefully disciplined to repress groans—yet every now
and then there will come a modulation, that shows
how rich and cheery it might have been when
trolling a *chanson à boire*—how clear and sonorous
when, over the stamping of hoofs and the rattle
of scabbards, it rang out the one word,
" Charge ! " — how winning and musical when
whispering into a small pink ear laid against his
lips lovingly.

The Vicomte de Châteaumesnil cares for but one
thing on earth now—play, as deep as he can make
or find it. It is not a pastime, or a distraction, or
an occasional fever-fit, but the sole interest of his
existence. A fearfully unworthy and unsatisfactory
one, you will say. Granted; but try and realize
his condition.

He is not forty yet. All the passions of mature
manhood were alive within him; not one desire or
impulse had been tamed by natural or even premature decay, at the time he was struck down and
cut off from every object and aim of his former
life, when it was too late to form or turn to others.
Imagine how eagerly his strong fiery nature must
have grasped at some of these—how it must have
appreciated the alternations of glory, pleasure, and
peril—all worse than blanks now. You dare not
speak to him of woman's love. Worse than all

other torments of the Titan's bed of pain, would
be wild dreams of impossible Oceanides!

Remember that his only change of scene is from
one of the waters of Marah to another, according
to his own or his physician's fancy about mineral
springs. Remember, too, that the cleverest or the
most sanguine of them all have only ventured to
promise an abatement of his agonies: of their
cessation they say no word; nor can they even
prophesy that the end will come quickly. He is
not allowed to read much, even if his taste lay that
way, which it does not; for a literary *Chasseur
d'Afrique* is such a whim as Nature never yet indulged herself in. So perhaps he caught at the
only resource that could have saved him from worse
things; under which, I presume, is to be included
the temptation to take laudanum in proportions
by no means prescribed or sanctioned by the
Faculty.

Every day about noon the servant helped him
into the card-room at the club, and settled him at
his own table, where, with the two hours' respite
of dinner, he sat till midnight, ready to give battle
to all comers at all weapons, just as the Knights of
Lyonnesse used to keep a bridge or a pass while
achieving their vows. It is needless to say that
the changes of good or bad luck affected him not
at all. Few men of his stamp indulge in the
weakness of railing at Fortune, which is the

privilege and consolation of the *roturier*. Neither
was he ever heard to reproach a partner, or
become bitter against an adversary. He seemed to
take a pleasure in disappointing those who were
always expecting from him some savage outbreak
of temper: they judged from his appearance, and
had some grounds for their anticipations ; for,
winning or losing, that strange look, half-weary,
half-defiant, never was off his face. But, with
Armand de Châteaumesnil, the *grand seigneur* had
not been merged in the soldier ; the *brusquerie* of
the camp had not overlaid the manner of the
courtly school in which he and all his race had
been trained—the school of those who would stab
their enemy to the heart with sarcasm or inuendo,
but scorned to stun him with blatant abuse—of
those who would never have dreamt of listening
to a woman with covered head, though they
might be deaf as the nether millstone to her
entreaties or her tears. It was with the Revolution that the rapier went out and the *savate*
came in.

Very few men came up to his standard of play ;
for he was hard to please in style as well as in
stakes. Keene did fully ; and this, with a certain
similarity of tastes, accounted for his liking the
latter so well. He had little regard to throw away,
and was chary of it in proportion. On the other
hand, Royston treated the invalid with an amount

of deference very unusual with him, in whom the
bump of Veneration was probably represented by
a cavity.

The two were still talking on the terrace, when
a man passed them, who lifted his hat slightly,
and then sighed audibly, looking upwards with an
ostentatious contrition, as though he apologized
to heaven for such a bowing-down to Rimmon.
This was the Rev. James Fullarton, British chaplain at Dorade. A difficult and anomalous position
—in which the unlucky divine, in addition to his
anxiety about the conscientious discharge of his
duties, has to cultivate the friendship of a vast
number of unrighteous Mammons, if he would be
allowed to perform his functions at all. Our
countrymen are popularly supposed to take out a
special licence for liberty of thought and action as
soon as they cross the Channel; and the pastor's
pulpit-cushion can hardly be stuffed with roses
when every other member of his congregation—
embracing devotees of about a dozen different
shades of High, Low, and Broad Church—thinks
it his or her daily duty to decide if the formula—
Quamdiu se bene gesserit—has been duly complied
with. Perhaps foreign air and warmer climates
develop, like a hotbed, our innate instinct of
destructiveness. Look at portly respectable fathers
of families—householders who, at home, have accepted their spiritual position without a murmur

for a quarter of a century, roused to revolt by no vexed question of copes, candles, or church-rates —even these cannot escape contagion. When once the game is afoot, they will open on the scent with the perseverance of the steadiest "line-hunter," and join in the "worry" as eagerly as the youngest hound. I remember seeing a similar case in Scotland, where a minister was preaching before "the Men" who were appointed to judge of his qualifications. Right in front of him, on a low bench, sat the awful Three, silent, stolid, and stern. His best-rounded periods, his neatest imagery, his aptest quotations, brought no light into their vacant grey eyes; perhaps they were looking beyond all these, straight at the doctrine. The breeze blew freshly from the German Ocean, over the purple hills; but it brought no coolness to that miserable Boanerges. How he *did* perspire! I could not wonder at it; and though he preached for ninety-five minutes, and wearied me even to death, I bore him no enmity, pitying him from my soul.

Mr. Fullarton, however, had steered through the reefs and quicksands with better skill or luck than his fellows, and judging from the ruddiness of his broad, beardless face, and the amplitude of his black waistcoat, the cares of office had not hitherto affected his health materially. He was a well-meaning, conscientious man, ready to work hard for his flock and his family; indeed, barring a certain frail leaning towards *gourmandise*, of which a full pendulous lip told tales, and an occasional infirmity of temper, he had as few outward failings as could be desired. For one of no extreme views, he could count an extraordinary number of adherents. Without being particularly agreeable or instructive, he possessed a rather imposing readiness and rotundity of speech, and had a knack of turning his arm-chair into a pulpit somewhat oftener than was quite in good taste. However, I suppose the best of us will talk "shop" when we see a fair opening. He had a large wife and several small children. No one admired him more devotedly than this truly excellent woman. As far as sharing in her husband's successes went, or partaking in any other advantages of society, she might as well have been a squaw of an Iowa brave; for her time was more than taken up in tending her offspring, and in providing for her lord the savoury meats in which he delighted; but she looked the picture of contentment, and so nobody thought it necessary to pity her.

From the first moment of their meeting, the chaplain had entertained a nervous dislike, approaching to a presentiment, toward Royston Keene. He regarded him as a brand likely to inflame others, but itself by no means to be plucked from the burning. The latter saw his gesture as he passed, and smiled—not pleasantly. "Remark the shepherd, M. le Vicomte," he said; "he sees the wolves prowling, and trembles for his lambs."

"One wolf, at least, is toothless," answered Châteaumesnil. "What have we to do with lambs, except *en suprême*? But the sun is down; I must go home, or these cursed pains will avenge themselves. Till this evening."

"I will not fail; but you will permit me to accompany you so far," said Keene, bending over the invalid with the grand courteous air that became him well; and he walked by the other's side till they reached his door, talking over the varying fortunes of last night's play.

CHAPTER IV.

YOU have found out already that you are only looking at a chaplet of cameos, with just enough of story to string them together. Under these circumstances, the right thing of course to do is to work out each character by the rules of metaphysical mathematics, and then to reverse the process and "prove" the result. But I never tried to extract the square-root out of *anything* without failing miserably, and one can only speak, and act, and write, according to one's light. After all, it seems a more uncertain science than astronomy. Comets *will* appear, now and then, at abnormal times, and in places where they have no heavenly business; and people are still to be found so very ill-regulated as to go right or wrong in opposition to all rules and precedents. Where the variations are so infinite, it is difficult to argue safely from one singular example to another; and if you miss one step, your whole deduction is apt to come to grief. Some one said, that "there were corners in the nature of the simplest peasant-girl to which the cleverest man alive could never find a key." Perhaps, too, those who fancy, rightly or wrongly, that they have mesmerized the heart even of one fellow-creature so completely that the poor thing could not, if it would, keep back a single secret, think it hardly fair to give the world in general the full benefit of their discoveries. Practically, does all this help one much ? It is possible that some who have passed for the deepest observers of human nature, owed their renown more to an acute observation of the phenomena of feeling, an intuitive knowledge of what people like and dislike, a retentive memory, and a happy knack of making all these available at the right moment, than to any profound reasoning on abstract principles. Like some untaught arithmeticians, their calculations came out correct, but they could not have gone through the steps of the process.

There lives, even now, a sublime theorist, who professes to have made feminine physiology his peculiar study. Sitting at his desk, or in his arm-chair, he will trace the motives, impulses, and sensations which a woman must *necessarily* have experienced under any given circumstances, as lucidly as a skilful pathologist, scalpel in hand, may lecture on the material mysteries of the blood or brain : he will analyze for you the waters of the *Fons Lacry-marum*, just as Letheby or Taylor might do those of a new chalybeate spring. A fearful power, is it not, and fatal, if used tyrannously ? Well I re-member hearing a very beautiful and charming

person speak of an evening she had spent in the
society of The Adept, during which she was
conscious of being subjected to the action of his
microscope, stethoscope, and other engines of
science. She said, "it did not hurt her much,"
and on the whole seemed by no means so impressed with awe and admiration as could be
wished. Indeed, before they parted, if any one
was disquieted, discomfited, or otherwise damaged,
I fancy it was—*not* the loveliest Margaret. From
my slight acquaintance with that tremendous
philosopher, supposing that he were turned loose
among a bevy of perfectly well-educated women, and
meant mischief, I should be disposed to lay longer
odds against his chances than I would against
those of many men who have never read one word
of Balzac, Michelet, or Kant.

Still, as was aforesaid, in the days of high art
and high farming, high physiology is clearly the
thing to go for. So, for my shortcomings, to all
critics—ethic, dialectic, æsthetic, and ascetic—I say
mea culpa, thus audibly.

Nevertheless, while they are waiting for her at
Dorade, we will try to sketch Cecil Tresilyan.

Her father died when she was too young to remember him, and the first fourteen years of her
life were spent almost entirely in the old Cornish
manor-house from which her family took its name.
That great rambling pile stood at the head of a

glen, terraced at first into gardens, and then thickly
wooded, and stretching down to the shore. There
was a small bay just here, the mouth of which
curved inwards abruptly. It seemed as if the
black cliffs had caught the sea in a trap, and stood
forward to keep the outlet fast for ever: the waves
were free to come and go for a certain distance,
but never to rave or rebel any more; when their
brethren of the open main went out to war, the
captives inside might hear the din, but not break
out to join them; they could only leap up weakly
against their prison-bars. There was nothing at all
remarkable in the house itself, except its furniture
and panellings of black oak, and two pictures, to
which was attached a story bearing on the hereditary failing which had made the family proverbial.
The first was the likeness of a lovely girl, in the
court dress of James the Second's time, with beautiful hazel eyes, half timid, half trusting, like a pet
doe's. The second represented a woman, perhaps
of middle age: in this the hood of a dark grey robe
was drawn far forward, and under it the eyes shone
out of the colourless face with a fixed expression of
helpless agonized terror, as of one fascinated by
some ghastly apparition. You were sorry when
you realized that they were portraits of the same
person.

Sir Ewes Tresilyan was a man of strong passions
and rather weak brain—of few words and fewer

sympathies ; he never made a companion of Mabel, his daughter, though his love for her was the feeling next his heart, after his almost insane pride ; but he trusted her implicitly—less because he had faith in her truth and goodness, than because he held it as impossible for a Tresilyan to disgrace herself or otherwise derogate, as for the moon to fall from heaven. He was no classic, you see, and had never read of Endymion.

In her solitary rides Mabel met the son of a neighbouring squire, and they soon began to love each other after the good old fashion. Neither had one thought that was not honest and pure ; but they were so afraid of her father that they dared not ask his consent to their marriage as yet. They were prudent, but not prudent or patient enough. So there came about meetings—first at noon in the woods, then at twilight in the park, then at midnight in tho garden; and at last Sir Ewes Tresilyan heard of it all ; and heard too that his daughter's name was abroad in the country-side, and more than lightly spoken of. That day, as the sun was setting, two men stood foot to foot, with their doublets off, on the very spot of smooth turf where the lovers parted last ; and Arthur Bampfylde had to hold his own, as best he might, with the deadliest rapier in the western shires. Poor boy !—he would scarcely have had the heart to do his uttermost against

Mabel's father; but better will and skill would have availed little against the thirsty point that came creeping along his blade and leaping over his guard like a viper's tongue. At the sixth pass his enemy shook him heavily off his sword, wounded to the death. He had tried explanation before, utterly in vain; but the true heart would make one effort more to get justice done, before it ceased to beat. He gasped out these words through the rush of blood that was choking him— " Mabel—I swear, she is as pure as the Mother of God; and I—what had I done?"

Sir Ewes knelt down and lifted Arthur's head upon his knee—not in pity, but that he might hear the more distinctly. "I will tell you," he said; " you have wooed a Tresilyan like a yeoman's daughter." The homicide wrote in his confession of all this that, as he laid the head gently down, a smile came upon the lips before they set. Was it that the parting spirit—standing on the threshold of Eternity, and almost within the light of the grand secret—fathomed the earthworm's miserable vanity, and could not refrain its scorn?

Mabel was sitting alone when her father returned. She had no idea that anything had been discovered; but the instant she saw his face, she cast herself on her knees, crying—"I am innocent indeed I have done no wrong!"

He griped her arm and raised her up, gazing

straight and steadfastly at her for some moments : then he gave his verdict—"Guilty of having brought shame on your house; not guilty of sin, I know, or *this* should only half atone,"—and he drew out the blade that had never been wiped since it drank her lover's blood.

She slid slowly down out óf his grasp, never speaking, but bearing in her eyes the awful look of horror that settled there for ever. The second picture might have been taken then, though it was not painted till long afterward. She never thenceforth, while her father lived, left the wing of the Manor-house in which her rooms lay; neither did he, or any one else, except the two servants who attended her, look upon her face. People pitied her very much at first, and then forgot her entirely. Once the superior of a Belgian convent, a relation of the family, offered to admit Mabel, if she chose to take the vows. Perhaps Sir Ewes Tresilyan was more gratified than he liked to show, for the best blood in Europe was to be found in that sisterhood; but his reply was not a gracious one :—

" I thank the Abbess," he wrote, " but *we* are used to choose for our gifts the most precious thing we have—not the most worthless. I will not lighten my house from a heavy burden, by offering it to God."

He relented, however, when he was dying, and sent for his daughter. Very reluctantly she came.

He had prepared, I believe, a pompous and proper oration, wherein he was to pardon her and even bestow a sort of qualified blessing; but the wan face and wild hollow eyes, not seen for twelve years, frightened all his grandeur out of his head; and the obstinate, narrow-minded tyrant collapsed all at once into a foolish, fond old man. Something too late (that's one comfort) to avail him much. In Mabel's nature, soft and yielding as it appeared, there was the black spot that nothing but harsh-ness and cruelty could have brought out—the utter incapacity of relenting, which had given rise to the rude rhyme known through three counties—

> In Tresilyan's face
> Fault finds no grace.

So, when the sick man cried out to her, through his sobs, to kiss him and forgive him, the dreary monotonous voice only answered—" I can kiss you, father;" and when she had laid her icicles of lips on his forehead, she glided out of the room like a ghost that has accomplished its mission and hastens away to its own place. Sir Ewes never tried to call her back; he scarcely spoke at all intelligibly after that; but lay, for the few remaining hours of life, moaning to himself, his face turned to the wall.

For a very short time after her father's death, Mabel seemed to take a pleasure in roaming about the gardens and woods from which she had been debarred so long; but the walks grew gradually shorter, and she soon shut herself up in the house entirely, seeing only a few of her near relatives. It was one of these who, at her own request, painted the second portrait—a rude performance, but it must have been a likeness. She seemed to feel an odd sort of satisfaction in looking at the two and comparing them. Her brain was somewhat clouded and unsteady; but I fancy she was counting up all the harm and wrong the hard world had done to her, and calculating what amends would be made in the next. I doubt not they were kind and pitiful and indulgent enough there; but on earth she found no source of comfort strong enough to banish from her eyes that terrible look which haunted them within five minutes of her end.

When spirits assemble from the four corners of heaven, how many thousand companions, think you, will greet the Gileadite's daughter?

Before you saw Cecil Tresilyan's face, the curve of her neck, and the way her head was set on it, told you that she was by no means exempt from the family failing which had laid its hand so heavily on her ancestress. Yet it was not a hard or habitually haughty, or even a very decided face. There was nothing alarmingly severe about the slight aquiline of the nose; the chin did not look as if it were "carved in marble," or "clasped in steel," or as if it were made of anything but

soft flesh prettily dimpled; the delicate scarlet
lip, when it curled, rarely went beyond sauciness;
though the splendid violet eyes could well express
disdain, this was not their favourite expression—
and they had many. The head would certainly
have been too small had it not been for the
glossy masses of dark chestnut hair sweeping down
low all round it, smooth and unbroken as a deep
river in its first curl over a cataract. Candid
friends said her complexion was not bright enough;
perhaps they were right; but the colour had not
forgotten how to come and go there at fitting
seasons : at any rate, the grand clear white could
never be mistaken for an unhealthy pallor. An
extraordinarily good constitution was ever part of a
Tresilyan's inheritance; and if you doubted whether
her blood circulated freely, you had only to compare her cheek, on a bitter March day, with some
red-and-white ones, when a sharp east wind had
forced these last to mount *all* the stripes of the
tricolor. By the way, are not the "roses dipped
in milk" going out of fashion just now? A
humble but stanch adherent of the House of
York, I like to think—how many battlefields, since
Towton, our flower has won!

But if Cecil's face was not faultless, her figure
was. Had one single proportion been exaggerated or deficient, she could never have carried off
her height so lithely and gracefully. She might

take twenty *poses* in a morning, and people always thought they would choose the last one to have her painted in. Here, she was quite inimitable. For instance, women, I believe, used to practise in their own rooms for hours to catch her peculiar way of half-reclining in an arm-chair; but the most painstaking of them all never achieved anything beyond a caricature. Yet no one could accuse her of studying stage-effects. If a trifle of the *Incedo Regina* marked her walk and carriage, it was *à l'Eugénie*, not *à la Statira*.

Indeed, she was thoroughly natural all over; cleverer and more fascinating, certainly, than ninety-nine women out of every hundred; but not one bit more strong-minded, or heroic, or self-denying. She had been very well brought up, and had undeniably good principles; but she would yield to occasional small temptations with perfect grace and facility. Great ones she had never yet encountered; for Cecil, if not quite fancy-free, had only read and perhaps dreamt of passions. She had known one remorse, of which you may hear hereafter (not a heavy allowance considering her opportunities), and one grief—the death of her mother. She entertained a remarkable reverence for all ministers of the Established Church; yet she was about the last woman alive to have married a clergyman, and would have considered the charge of the old women and schools of a country

parish as a lingering and unsatisfactory martyr-
dom.   There never was a more constant attendant
at all sorts of divine service; though perhaps the
most casual of worshippers had never been more
bored than she was by some of the discourses to
which she listened so patiently.   She would confess this to you at luncheon, and then start for the
same church in the afternoon, with an edifying but
rather comic expression of resignation.   I am sure
she would not deliberately have vexed the smallest
child; and yet the number of athletic men who
ascribed the loss of their peace of mind to her,
was, as the Yankees have it, "a caution."   Some
of the "regulars," wary adventuresses of three
seasons' standing, had brought off several pretty
good things by following her, and picking up the
victims fluttering about helpless in their first
despair, just as the keepers after a battue go
round the covers with the retrievers.

If there were any more antitheses in her character, they had better speak for themselves hereafter; nor is there much that need be told about
her companions.

Mrs. Danvers, or "Bessie," as she liked to be
called, had been Cecil's last governess, and was retired on full-pay, which, she flattered herself, she
earned in the capacity of travelling chaperone and
censor; but, inasmuch as when she really held
some tutelar authority her pupil had never taken

the slightest notice of her prohibitions, she could hardly be expected now to exercise any very salutary influence or control.

Dick Tresilyan was absurdly proud and fond of his sister, and performed all her behests with a blind obedience; but when he heard that he was to attend her during a whole winter's residence abroad, he did think that it was stretching her prerogative to the verge of tyranny. No wonder. A dragoon who has lost his horse, a goose on a turnpike-road, or any other popular type of help-lessness, does not present so lamentable a picture as a Briton in a foreign land, without resources in himself, and with a rooted aversion to the use of any language except his own. In this case, the victim actually attempted some feeble remonstrance and argument on the subject. Cecil was almost as much astonished as the Prophet was under similar circumstances; but she considered that habits of discussion in beasts of burden and the lower order of animals generally were inconvenient, and rather to be discouraged; so she cut it short, now, some-what imperiously. Thereupon, Dick Tresilyan slid into a slough of despond in which he had been wallowing ever since. A faint gleam of sunshine broke in when one of his intimates, hearing he was going to France, suggested, " That's where the brandy comes from ; " but it was instantly over-clouded by the remark which followed : " I suppose, though, you won't be able to drink much more of it than you do here;" on realizing which crushing fact, his melancholy became, if possible, more profound than ever. Indeed, since he crossed the Channel, he had spent most of his leisure moments in a sort of chronic blasphemy, which, it is to be hoped, afforded him some slight relief and consolation, as it was wholly unintelligible to his audience; for, to do Dick justice, in his sister's presence the door of his lips was always strictly guarded.

However, to Dorade they came—hours after their time, of course, but perfectly safe; no accident ever does happen in France to anything properly booked, except to luggage sent by *Roulage*, to which there attaches the romantic uncertainty of Vanderdecken's correspondence. Cecil rather liked travelling; it never tired her; so, by midnight she had seen Mrs. Danvers, weary and querulous, to bed—gone through a variety of gymnastics in the way of *accolades*, with Fanny Molyneux—taken some trouble in inquiring about shooting and other amusements likely to divert her brother from his sorrows—and yet did not feel very sleepy.

They ignore shutters in these climes; and her reflection was still flitting backward and forward across the white window-blinds as Royston Keene came home from the Cercle. He knew the room, or guessed who the shadow belonged to; and as he moved away, after pausing a minute or two, he waved, his hand towards it with a gesture so unwarrantably like a salute, that, were *silhouettes* sensitive or prudish, it might have proved an offence not easily forgiven.

CHAPTER V

THE next morning was so soft and sunny that it tempted Miss Tresilyan out on the terrace of their hotel very soon after breakfast. She was waiting for her brother on the top of the steps leading down into the road, when Major Keene passed by again. If he had never heard of her before, the smooth sweeping outline of her magnificent form, and the careless grace of her attitude, as she stood leaning against the stone balustrade, were not likely to escape an eye that was wont to light on every point of feminine perfection, as a poacher's does on a sitting hare. But he never got so far as her face then; and hardly had time to criticise her figure; for at that moment, a brisk gust of the *mistral* swept round the corner and revealed a foot and ankle so marvellously exquisite, that they attracted his eyes, as long as he dared to fix them without risking a stare; and kept his thoughts busy till he saw her again. "*Caramba!*" he muttered, half aloud; "I don't wonder at any one who has seen *that*, not looking at a nautch-girl afterward." And he quickened his pace toward the

Molyneux's house. He met them before he reached the door.

"I am going to Miss Tresilyan," Fanny said. "Isn't it lucky, her first morning hero being such a delicious one?"

"Ah, I thought that was your point," answered Keene. "There must be a tremendous amount of 'gushing' to be got through still; the accumulation of—how many months? I suppose you only took the rough edge off last night. Don't hurt her, please, that's all. And, Hal, you were actually going to preside over the meeting of two young hearts, and gloat over their emotions, and spoil their innocent amusements? I wonder at you. Means well, Mrs. Molyneux; but he's *so* thoughtless."

Fanny laughed. "I think I could do without him. But we mean to walk this afternoon, and he may come then; and you, too, Major Keene, if you are good."

"I'll enter into all sorts of recognizances to keep the peace," was the reply; "but I should have thought you might trust me by this time. It's that excitable husband of yours that wants disciplining. I'll give him some soda-water by way of a precaution. Then, when you have sacrificed to friendship sufficiently, you will lionize Miss Tresilyan? The Castle first, of course. Shall we meet you there at two?"

Harry did not quite see the thing in this light, and looked slightly disappointed; but he yielded the point, as he always did, and went away dutifully with his superior officer.

"Describe the brother," the latter said, abruptly, when they had gone a few steps.

" Well, I believe he's the most ignorant man in Great Britain," answered Molyneux: "that's his *spécialité*. He never had much education; and he has been trying to forget that little, ' hard all,' ever since he was eighteen. You remember how our fellows used to laugh at me about my epistles? I could give him 21 lb., and a beating, any day. They say, two men have to stand over him whenever he tries to write a letter, for no *one* is strong enough to keep him straight in his spelling and grammar. If he tries it on alone, he gets bewildered in the second sentence, and wanders up and down, knocking his head against particles and parts of speech, like the man in the Maze; and throws up the sponge at last, utterly beat. Helplessly devoted to his sister, but rather obstinate with other people, and apt to be sulky sometimes; but goodnatured on the whole; and drinks *very* fair."

"Oh, he drinks fair, does he?" Royston said, meditatively. " Has that anything to do with his brotherly affection? Everybody who is fond of Miss Tresilyan seems to take to liquor. Annesley was pretty sober till he knew her. It's rather odd. I don't suppose she encourages them."

"Certainly not; at least, I know she has tried to stint Dick in his brandy, very often. It's the only point she has never been able to carry."

"A man must be firm about some one thing," the other remarked, "or there's an end of free-agency altogether. He has no intellects to be affected by it apparently; and I dare say his health does not suffer much yet. It's a question of constitution, after all."

He dropped the subject then, and was very silent all the rest of the morning, till they came to the place of meeting. Somehow or another, it did not occur to him to mention to Harry what he had seen on the terrace.

They had not waited long, before the three women came slowly up the zigzags of the path that wound round the Castle-hill. Dick Tresilyan had "got his pass signed" for the day, and had started off, with his courier, to make the lives of several natives a burden to them, on the subject of *bécasses* and *bécassines*.

Cecil might have been known by her walk among ten thousand. She seemed to float along without any visible exertion, as if her dress were buoyant and bore her up in some mysterious fashion; but looking closer, and marking how straight and firmly and lightly every footfall was planted, you gave the narrow arched instep and the slender rounded ankle the credit they well deserved, marvelling only that so delicate a symmetry could conceal so much sinewy power. Upon this occasion, she was evidently accommodating her pace to that of Mrs. Danvers; and no racing man could have seen the two, without thinking of one of the Flyers of the turf walking down by the side of the trainer's pony.

Miss Tresilyan's hat, of soft black felt, shaded by a blackcock's feather, was decidedly in advance of her age: for that very provocative headgear, with the many-coloured *panaches*, had not then become so common; and even the Passionate Pilgrim might hope (with luck) to walk along a pier or a parade without meeting a succession of Red Rovers—each capable of boarding him at a minute's notice, and making all his affections walk the plank. Her tunic of iron-grey velvet, without fitting tightly to her figure, still did it fair justice; and from the tie of her neck ribbon, down to the wonderful boots that slid in and out from under the striped scarlet kirtle over which her dress was looped up, there was not the minutest detail that might not have challenged and baffled criticism.

Royston Keene appreciated all this thoroughly. No man alive held the stale old adage of " Beauty when unadorned," &c., in profounder scorn. A

pair of badly-fitting gloves, a soiled *collerette*, or
a tumbled dress, had cured more than one of the
fever-fits of his younger days; and he was ten
times as fastidious now. He drew a long slow
breath of intense enjoyment, as a thirsty cricketer
may do after the first deep draught of claret-cup
that rewards a two hours' innings.

"It's very refreshing, after weeks of total ab-
stinence, to see a woman who goes in for dress,
and does it thoroughly well." He had no time for
more, for the others were almost within hearing.

When the introductions were over, Mrs. Danvers said she was tired, and must rest a little.
Very few words will do justice to her personal
appearance. Brevity, and breadth, and bluntness
were her chief characteristics, which applied
equally to her figure, her face, and her extremities;
and, not unfrequently, to her speech too. Her
health was really infirm, but she never could
attain the object of many an invalid's harmless
ambition—looking interesting. Illness made her
cheeks look pasty, but not pale; it could not fine
down the coarsely-moulded features, or purify
their ignoble outline. Her voice was against her,
certainly: perhaps this was the reason why, when
she bemoaned herself, so many irreverent and
hard-hearted reprobates called it "whining." It
was very unfortunate; for few could be found,
even in the somewhat exacting class to which

she belonged, more anxious and active in
enlisting sympathy. She was looking especially
ill-tempered just then, but Major Keene was not
easily daunted, and he went in at her straight and
gallantly—about the weather, it is needless to say,
both being English. While Mrs. Danvers was
disagreeing with him, Cecil took her turn at in-
spection. Royston's name was familiar to her, of
course, for no one ever talked to Mrs. Molyneux
for ten minutes without hearing it. Though she
had scarcely glanced at him in the morning, she
had decided that the tall erect figure and the
enormous moustache with its *crocs à la mousquetaire*, could only belong to Fanny's Household
Word. It was very odd—she had not a shade of
a reason for it—but neither had *she* mentioned that
rencontre to her friend. Perhaps they had so many
other things to talk about. She could scan him
now more narrowly, for his face was turned away
from her. The result was satisfactory : when
Major Keene stood up on his feet, not even his
habitual laziness could disguise the fair proportions
and trained vigour of a stalwart man-at-arms ; and
be it known that Cecil's eye, though not so professional as that of Good Queen Bess, loved to
light upon such dearly.

"Harry," Mrs. Molyneux observed, "Mr. Fullarton called while I was at the *Lion d'Or* this
morning, and stayed half an hour. He is so very

anxious to get Cecil to lead the singing in church."

" Yes; he has been, so to speak, throwing his hat up, ever since he heard you were coming, Miss Tresilyan," was the reply. " I supposo he calculated on your vocal talents; there's the nuisance of having a European reputation; you are always expected to do something for somebody's benefit. I hope you'll indulge him, in charity to us. You have no idea what it has been. Two Sundays ago, for instance, a Mr. Rolleston and his wife volunteered to give us a lead. He didn't look like a racing man, and yet he must have been. I never saw anything more artistically done. He went off at score, and made the pace so strong, that he cut them all down in the first two verses; and then the wife who had waited very patiently, came and won as she liked—nothing else near her."

Cecil thought the illustration rather irreverent, and did not smile. Keene saw this as he turned round.

" The turf slang has got into your constitution, I think, since you won that Garrison Cup. It's very wrong of you not to cure yourself, when you know how it annoys Mrs. Molyneux. He is right, though, Miss Tresilyan; it is a case of real distress: our vocal destitution is pitiable; so, if you have any benevolence to spare, do bestow it upon us, and your petitioners will ever pray, &c."

Now it so happened that Fanny valued that same cup above all her earthly possessions, as a mark of her husband's prowess. No testimonial ever gave so much satisfaction to a popular rector's wife as that little ugly mug afforded her, albeit it was the very wooden spoon of racing plate. So she first smiled consolingly at the culprit, who was already contrite, and then looked up at the last speaker with amusement and wonder glittering in her pretty brown eyes. She did not see what interest the subject could have for Keene, who had only darkened the chapel doors once since they came. Mr. Fullarton, indeed, was supposed to have alluded to him several times—his discourses were apt to take a personal and individualizing turn—but he had never had the satisfaction of a " shot in the open " at that stout-hearted sinner.

Royston caught *la mignonne's* glance, and understood it perfectly; but not a line of his face moved. He was waiting for Cecil's reply very anxiously: he had not heard her speak yet.

"Mr. Fullarton is rather rash," she said, " for our acquaintance is slight, and I don't think he ever heard me sing. But I shall do my best next Sunday. Every one ought to help, in such a case, as much as they can."

"Yes, and you will do it so beautifully, Dearest!" Cecil bit her lip, and coloured angrily.

Nothing annoyed her like Mrs. Danvers' obtrusive partisanship and uncouth flattery.

The gleam of pleasure that shone out on Keene's dark face for a moment, only Harry interpreted rightly He had scarcely listened to tho words, but he thought, " I knew I was right; I knew tho voice would match tho rest ! " When they moved on again, he walked by Miss Tresilyan's side, and " still their speech was song."

His first remark was, " I hope you condescend to ballads sometimes ? I confess to not deriving much pleasure from those elaborate performances where the voice tries dangerous feats of strength and agility: even at the Opera they make one rather uncomfortable. Some of the very scientific pieces suggest ideas of homicide or suicide, as the case may be, according to my temper at the moment. Of course, I know less than nothing about music ; but I don't think this quite accounts for it. I really believe that unso-phisticated human nature revolts at the *bravura*."

It was rare good fortune, so early in their acquaintance, to tempt forth the brilliant smile that always betrayed when Cecil was well pleased.

" Mrs. Molyneux has told you what my tastes are ? " she said. " I have never tried *bravuras* since I left off masters, and even then I only attempted them under protest. But there are some quiet songs I like so much that I sing them

to myself when I am out of spirits, and it does me
good.   Don't you like the old-fashioned ones best?
I fancy, in those days, people felt more what they
wrote, and did not consider only how the words
would suit the composer."

"Probably," Keene replied.   "If Charles Edward
was of no other use, some good strong lines were
written about him.   I do not think he lived in
vain.   There are no partisans now.   The only songs
of the sort that I ever saw with any *verve* in them,
were some seditious Irish ones : rather spirited—
only they had not grammar enough to ballast them.
The writer either was, or wanted to be, transported.
We are *all* very fond of the Guelphs—at least everybody in decent society is—and that is just the
reason why we are not enthusiastic.   We are all
ready to 'die for the Throne,' &c., but we don't
see any immediate probability of our devotion being
tested.   So the Laureate only rhymes loyally, and
he at stated seasons, and in a temperate professional style."

"Please don't laugh at Tennyson," she inter-
rupted; "I suppose it is very easy to do so, for so
many people try it; but I never listen to them if I
can help it."

"A premature warning," was the grave reply;
"I had no such idea.   I admire Tennyson fully as
much as you can do, and read him, I dare say,
much oftener.   I was only speaking of his per-

formances in the *manège*; indeed, there is not
enough of these to make a fair illustration, so I
was wrong to bring them in. When he settles to
his stride, few of the 'cracks' of last century
seem able to live with him. They have not set all
his best things to music. A clever composer might
do great things, I fancy, with 'The Sisters,' and
the *refrain* of 'the wind in turret and tree.' "

"It would never bo a very general favourite,"
Miss Tresilyan observed. "It seems hardly right
to set to music even an imaginary story of great
sin and sorrow. I saw a sketch of it some time
ago. The murderess was sitting on a cushion, close
to the Earl's body, with her head bent so low that
one of her black tresses almost touched his smooth
golden curls; you could just see tho hilt of the
dagger under her left hand. That, and the corpse's
quiet pale face were the only two objects that stood
out in relief, for the storm outside was stirring the
window curtains, and making the one lamp flare
irregularly. Her features were in the shadow, and
you had to fancy how hard and rigid and dreary
they must be. It was the merest sketch; but if it
had been worked out, it would have made a very
terrible picture."

"A good conception," Royston said; "well,
perhaps it would not be a pleasant song to sing;
but better, I should think, than some of those
dreadful sentimental ones. They are not much

worse than the Strephon and Chloe class, in which
our ancestors delighted; still they are indefensible.
If our Lauras find Petrarchs now, they are usually
very beardless ones, and the green morocco cover,
with its golden lock, covers their indiscretions.
Those who write love ditties for the piano *must*
celebrate a shadow who can't be critical. Imagine
any man insulting a real woman of average intellect
with ' Will you love me then as now ? ' "

" Yes," she assented, "they are too absurd,
as a rule. They make our cheeks burn, as if we
were performing some very ridiculous part in low
comedy; but they do not warm one's heart like
' Annie Laurie.' "

" Ah, it's curious how that always suggests itself
as the standard to compare others with : not fair,
though, for it makes most of them sound so feeble
and effeminate. Douglas of Finland wrote it, you
know, in the campaign which finished him. Long
before that the charming Annie had given her
promise true to Craigdarroch ; and she had to keep
it, *tant bien que mal,* for it was pronounced in the
Tron Church, instead of on the braes of Maxwellton.
I wonder if she inscribed those verses in her scrap-
book. I dare say she did ; and sang them to her
grandchildren in a cracked treble."

" I am so sorry you have told me that," Cecil
exclaimed ; " my romance was quite a different one,
and not nearly so sad. I always fancied the man

who wrote those lines must have ended so happily! One would despise her thoroughly if she could ever have forgiven herself or forgotten him."

Her eyes brightened and her cheek flushed as she spoke. The momentary excitement made her look so handsome that Keene's glance could not withhold admiration; but there was no sympathy in it, any more than in his cold quiet tones.

"No, don't despise her," he said. "She could scarcely be expected to wait for a corporal in the Scottish Regiment. When the Cavaliers sailed from home, they knew they were leaving every-thing but honour behind them: of course, their mistresses went with the other luxuries. They had not many of these in the Brigade, if we can believe history. Fortunately for us (or we should have missed the song), Finland never knew of the 'fresh fere' who dried the bright blue eyes so soon. He would not have carried his pike so cheerily, either, if his eyes had been good enough to see across the German Ocean. Well, perhaps the story isn't true; very few melodramatic legends ever are."

"I shall try not to believe it; but I am afraid you have destroyed an illusion."

"You don't say so!" was the reply. "I regret it extremely. If I had but known you carried such things about with you! Indeed, I will be more careful for the future. We are outwalking the main-guard, I see. Shall we wait for them here? It is a good point of view. One forgets that there are two invalids to be considered."

Did Royston Keene speak thus purposely, on the principle of those practised periodical writers who always leave their hero in extreme peril, or their heroine on the verge of a moral precipice, in order to keep our curiosity tense till the next number? If not, chance favoured him by producing the very effect he would have desired.

His companion's fair cheek flushed again; and this time a little vexation had something to say to it. It was incontestably correct to wait for the rest of the party, but she would have preferred originating the suggestion. Besides, the conversation had begun to interest her; and she liked being amused too well not to be sorry for its being cut short abruptly. She thought Major Keene talked epigrammatically; and the undercurrent of irony that ran through all he said was not so obtrusive as to seriously offend her.

It was no light ordeal he had just passed through. First impressions are not made on women of Cecil Tresilyan's class so easily as they are upon guileless *débutantes*; but they are far more important and lasting. It is useless attempting to pass off counterfeit coin on those expert money-changers; but they value the pure

gold all the more when it rings sharp and true.
It is always so with those who have once been
Queens of Beauty. A certain imperial dignity
attaches to them long after they have ceased to
reign : over the brows that have worn worthily
the diadem there still hangs the phantasm of a
shadowy crown. There need be nothing of repellant haughtiness, or, what is worse, of evident
condescension ; but, though they are perfectly
gentle and goodnatured, we risk our little sallies
and sarcasms with timidity, or at least diffidence;
feeling especially that a commonplace compliment
would be an inexcusable profanation. Our sword
may be ready and keen enough against others ;
but before *them* we lower its point, as the robber
did to Queen Margaret in the lonely wood. We
are conscious of treading on ground where
stronger and wiser and better men have knelt
before us ; and own that the altar on which
things so rare and precious have been laid, has
a right to be fastidious as to the quality of in-
cense.

Not the less did such glory of past royalty sur-
round the Tresilyan, because she had abdicated,
and never been dethroned.

CHAPTER VI.

THERE is something singularly refreshing in
the enthusiasm that one pretty and fascinating woman will display when speaking of
another highly gifted as herself—perhaps even
more so. It seems to me there is more honesty
here, and less stage-trick and conventionality, than
is to be found in most manifestations of sentiment
that take place in polite society. A perfectly plain
and unattractive female may, of course, be sincerely attached to her beautiful friend; but her
partisanship must be somewhat theoretical; it has
not the *esprit de corps* which characterizes the
other class. These last can count victories enough
of their own to be able to sympathize heartily with
the triumphs of their fellows without envying or
grudging them one. What does it matter if Rose
has slain her thousands, and Lilian her tens of
thousands? It is always "so much scored up to
our side."

Would you like to assist, invisibly, at one of
those two-handed "free-and-easys" where notes
are compared and confidences exchanged, where the
fair warriors "shoulder their fans, and show how

fields were won "? Perhaps our vanity would
suffer though our curiosity were gratified. The
proverb about listeners has come in since the time
of Gyges, it is true ; but his luck was exceptional,
and would not often follow his Ring. Campaspe
en déshabille is not invariably kind. It is a popular
superstition that men are apt at certain seasons to
speak rather lightly, if not superciliously, of the
beings whom they ought to delight to honour.
If so, be sure the medal has its reverse. When
you secured that gardenia from Amy's bouquet,
or that ribbon from Helen's glove-trimming, you
went home with a placid sense of self-gratulation,
flattering yourself you had done it rather diplo-
matically, without compromising your boasted freedom by word or sign. Perhaps two hours later
you figured conspicuously in a train of shadowy
captives adorning the conqueror's ideal ovation.
A change of colour of which you were unconscious
—a tremulous pressure of fingers that you risked
involuntarily—a sentence that was meant to be
careless and indifferent, but ended by being earnest
and imploring,—all these were commented upon in
the select committee, and estimated at their proper
value.

Very keen-sighted are those soft almond eyes
ambushed behind their trailing lashes, and from
them the sternest stoic may not long conceal his
wound. The Knight of Persia never groaned, or

shrank, or drooped his crest when the quarrel
struck him; but Amala needed only to look down,
to see his blood red upon the waters of the ford.
Some penalty must attach itself to unauthorized in-
truders, even in thought, upon the *Cerealia*. I don't
wish to be disagreeable, or to suggest unpleasant
misgivings to the masculine mind, but—do you
think we are always compassionated as much as we
deserve? I own to a horrible suspicion that our
betrayals of weakness form matter of exultation,
and that our tenderest emotions are not unfrequently derided.

Clearly this delightful sympathy can only exist
where fancies, and ambitions, and interests do not
clash. They seldom need do so: there is room
enough for all. So much disposable devotion is
abroad in this world, that no one woman can monopolize it. It is a tolerably fair handicap, on the
whole; and even the second horse may land a very
satisfactory stake. Never was night when the
moon shone so dazzlingly as to blind us to the
brilliancy of "a star or two beside." Bothwell,
and Châtelet, and Rizzio were not the only love-
stricken ones in Holyrood. Had the Queen of
Scots been thrice as charming, glances and sighs
and words enough would still have been found to
satisfy the most exacting of her Maries.

Fanny Molyneux was a capital specimen of the
thoroughpaced partisan. She was terribly indig-

nant at dinner on that first day of their meeting
when Major Keene would not endorse *all* her rap-
tures about her favourite. He assented to everything, certainly; but though his approbation was
decided, it was perfectly calm. He entrenched
himself behind his natural and acquired *sang-
froid*, and the fair assailant could not force those
lines.

"Don't be unreasonable," Royston said at last;
"as Macdonough always says when he has lost the
first two rubbers, ' The night is young and drink is
plenty ' Admiration will develop itself if you only
give it time. I have serious thoughts already of
adding another to the many little poems that must
have been written about Miss Tresilyan. Shall I
send it to the *United Service Gazette?* It would
be a great credit to our branch of the profession.
No dragoon has published a rhyme since Lovelace,
I believe. I've got as far as the first line :—

Ah, Cecil! hide those eyes of blue."

"I think I've heard something very like that
before," Fanny answered, laughing. "She deserves
a prettier compliment than a *réchauffé.*"

"Have you heard it before? Well, I shouldn't
wonder. You don't expect one to be original and
enthusiastic at the same moment, when both are
out of one's line. I own it, though. Your princess
merits all the vassalage she has found—better than

she will meet with here—if only for the perfection
of her costume. That *is* a triumph. Honour to
the artist who built her hat. I drink to him now,
and I wish the Burgundy were worthier of the toast.
(Hal, this Corton does not improve.) I should
advise you to secure the address of her *bottier*.
You know her well enough to ask for it, perhaps?
It must be a secret."

"Then you have not found out how very clever
she is?"

"Pardon me," was the reply; "I can imagine
Miss Tresilyan perfectly well educated; so well,
that she might dispense with carrying about a
living voucher in the shape of that dreadful *ex-
institutrice*. I never knew what makes very nice
women cling so to very disagreeable governesses.
Perhaps there is a satisfaction in patronizing
where you have been ruled, and in conferring
favours where you have only received 'impositions'
—a pleasant consciousness of returning good for
evil. There is no other rational way of accounting
for it."

La mignonne was not indignant now, as might
have been expected; but she gazed at the speaker
long and more searchingly than was her wont, with
something very like pity in her kind, earnest eyes.

"I suppose you would not sneer so at everything
if you could help it," she said. "I am not wise
enough to do so; but I don't envy you."

Royston's hard cold face changed for an instant, and the faintest flush lingered there, about as long as your breath would upon polished steel. It was not the first time that one of her random shafts had struck him home. All the sarcasm had died out of his voice as he answered slowly,

"Don't you envy me? You are right there. And you think you are not wise enough to be cynical? If there was any school to teach us how to turn our talents to the best account, I know which of us two would have most to learn." When he spoke again it was in his usual manner, but upon another and perfectly indifferent subject.

Harry had taken no part in the discussion. Always languid, towards night he generally felt especially disinclined to any bodily or mental exertion. At such times there was nothing he liked so well as to lie on his sofa, and assist at a passage-of-arms between his wife and Keene, encouraging either party occasionally with an approving smile, but preserving a cautious and complete neutrality. On the present occasion, he had his own reasons for not being disappointed about the latter's appreciation of Miss Tresilyan. Had he felt any such misgivings, they would have vanished later in the evening.

The doctor was a stern man; but he must have been more than human to have stood fast against the entreaties and cajolement with which his patient backed up the petition, "to be allowed just one cigar before going to roost." The prospect of this compensating weed had supported poor Harry through the dulness and privations of many monotonous days. As the appointed time drew nigh, he would freshen up visibly, just like the camels, when, staggering fetlock-deep through the sand-wastes, they scent the water or sight the clump of palms. Was there more in all this than could be traced to the mere soothing influence of the nicotine and flavour of the tobacco? Might not this one old habit, still indulged, have been the only link that sensibly connected the invalid with those pleasant days when he enjoyed life so heartily, with so many cheery comrades to keep him in countenance—when he would have laughed at the idea of anything short of a sabre-cut, a shot-wound, or a rattling fall over an "oxer," bringing him down to that state of helpless dependence, when our conception of womankind resolves itself into the ministering angel? Harry certainly could not have told you if this were so: for an inquiry into the precise nature of his sensations would have posed him at any time quite as completely as a question in hydrostatics or plane trigonometry. At any rate, the consumption of The Cigar was a very important ceremony with him; not conducted in the thoughtless and improvident spirit of men who smoke a dozen or so a day but partaking rather of the character of a sacrifice, at once festal and solemn. There were times, as we have said before, when he would break out of bounds recklessly ; but upon such occasions he gave himself no time to reflect ; so there was nothing then of calm and deliberate enjoyment; and these escapades grew more and more rare as the warnings of his constitution spoke more imperiously.

Among the very few traits of amiability that Major Keene had ever displayed, were the sacrifices of personal convenience he would make for Harry Molyneux. He had given up a good many engagements to see his comrade through that especial hour ; and if the day had left any available geniality in him, it was sure to come out then. Upon this occasion, however, he was remarkably silent, and answered several times at random, as if his thoughts were roving elsewhere : they were not unpleasant ones, apparently, for he smiled twice or thrice to himself, much less icily than usual. At last he spoke abruptly, after a long pause—Miss Tresilyan's name had not once been mentioned—"Hal, you know that old hackneyed phrase about 'a woman to die for' ? I think we have seen one to-day who is worth living for ; which is saying a good deal more."

"You like her, then ? " Molyneux asked.

" Yes—I—like—her." The words came out as if each one had been weighed to a grain ; and his lip put on that curious smile once more.

Harry did not feel quite satisfied. He would have preferred hearing more, and inferring less; but acting upon his invariable rose-coloured principle, he would not admit any disagreeable surmises, and went to bed under the impression that "it was all right," and that Royston was in a fair way towards being repaid for the sacrifices he had made to friendship.

CHAPTER VII

THE Saturday night is waning, but Molyneux shows no signs of moving yet from Keene's apartments. He has been a model of prudence though, so far, as to his drinks, and, in good truth, their companion is not amusing, or instructive, or convivial enough to tempt or to excuse transgression.

Dick Tresilyan looks about twenty-five, strongly and somewhat heavily built; rather over the middle height, even with the decided stoop of his broad round shoulders. He carries far too much flesh to please a professional eye, and by the time he is fifty will be very unwieldy; but there is more activity in him than might be supposed, and he walks strongly and well, as you would find if you tried to keep pace with him through the turnips on a sultry September day. His face, without a pretension to beauty in itself, suggests it—just the face that makes you say, " That man must have a handsome sister;" indeed, it bears an absurdly strong family likeness to Cecil's, amounting to a parody. But the outline of feature which in her is so fine and clear, is dull and filled out even to

coarseness. It reminded one of looking at the
same landscape, first through the medium of a
bright blue sky, and then through driving mist,
when crag, and cliff, and wood still show themselves, but blurred and dimly. His hair and eyes
are, by several shades, the lighter of the two. The
great difference is in the mouth. Cecil's is so
delicately chiselled, so apt at all expressions, from
tender to provocative, that many consider it one
of her best points; her brother's is so weak and
undecided in its character (or rather want of
character), that it would make a more intellectual
face vacuous and inane.

The " Tresilyan constitution " holds its own gallantly against the inroads of hardish living, and
Dick looks the picture of rude health. Men endowed with an invincible obtuseness of intellect and
feeling have no mental wear and tear, and if the
machine starts in good order, it seems as if it might
last out indefinitely; so it would, I dare say, if
it were not for a propensity to drink, and otherwise
to abuse their bodily advantages, peculiar to this
class. But for this neutralizing element in their
composition perhaps they would live as long as
crows or elephants, and we should be visited by a
succession of stupid Old Parrs; which would be a
very dreadful dispensation indeed. The present
subject takes a good deal of exercise to be sure,
and naturally few cares have ever troubled him;

he has always had more money than ho know what
to do with, and as for serious annoyances, a certain
train of thought is necessary to form them, while
our poor Dick's brain is utterly incapable of holding
more than one idea at a time. Whatever may
happen to be the dominant thought, reigns with an
undivided empire, and will not endure a rival even
near its throne, till it is violently trust out and
annihilated by its successor, on the principle of

> The priest that slays the slayer,
> And shall himself be slain.

He never originates a conception, of course, but
is always open to a fair offer in the way of a suggestion from anybody, and adopts it with the blind
zeal of a proselyte. It follows that chance occur-
rences may bother him for the moment, but he is
saved an infinity of trouble by being independent
of foresight and memory. To this last defect there
is one exception. If he is crossed, or vexed, or
injured, he cherishes against the offender a dull,
misty, purposeless sort of resentment, scarcely
amounting to animosity, but cannot explain, either
to you or to himself, *why* he does so. Fortunately,
he is tolerably harmless and unsuspicious, for to
reconcile him would be simply impossible.

Not one *mésalliance* could be detected in the main
line of the Tresilyans ; but there must have been a
blot somewhere, a link of base metal in the golden

chain, of which an adulteress and her confessor could have told. Perhaps the son of transgression bore no stigma on his forehead, and ruffled it among his peers as bravely as the best of them, never witting of his mother's dishonour; but the stain had come out in this generation. Even the faults and vices of that strong stubborn race were curiously distorted and caricatured in their representative. His pride, for instance, chiefly displayed itself in a taste for low company, where he could safely lord it over his inferiors. He did this whenever he had a chance, but, to do him justice, by no means in an illnatured or bullying way. He had resided almost entirely on his own estates; and, during his rare visits to London, had not extended his knowledge of the world beyond the experience that may be picked up by frequenting divers equivocal places of public resort, and from occasional forays on the extreme frontier of the *demi-monde.* The result was, that in general society, he felt himself in a false position, and was evidently anxious to escape into a more congenial atmosphere.

Can you guess why I have lingered so long over a portrait that might well have been despatched in three lines? It is because, in the eyes of those who knew Cecil Tresilyan, some interest must attach itself to the basest thing that bears her name: it is because there are men alive who think that the broidery of her skirt, or the trimming of her mantle, deserve describing better than the shield of Pelides; who hold that one of her dark chestnut tresses is worthier of a place among the stars than imperial Berenice's hair. A lame excuse, I admit, to the many that never saw her—even in their dreams.

On this particular evening Dick was supremely happy Keene had got him upon shooting—the only subject on which that unlucky man could talk without committing himself; and, by the time he was well into his fourth tumbler of iced cognac and water, he was achieving a rare conversational triumph; for he had left off answering monosyllabically, had volunteered an observation or two, and even ventured to banter his companions about their not availing themselves sufficiently of the sporting resources in the neighbourhood.

"There are several boars near here," he was saying; "they shoot them sometimes, and you can go, if you manage properly. I wonder you men never found that out."

"Ah, they *did* talk a good deal about pigs," Royston remarked indifferently. "But, you see, we used to stick them in the Deccan. The first time I heard of their way of doing it here, I felt very like Deering when they asked him to shoot a fox in Scotland,—Tom Deering, you know, the old boy that has hunted with the Warwickshire

and Atherstone for thirty seasons, and could tell
you the names, ages, and colours of the hounds
better than he could those of his own small family
—pedigrees too, I shouldn't wonder."

Dick tried to look as if he had known the
man from his childhood, and succeeded but very
moderately.

"Well," the other went on, "they were beating
a cover for roe, and the gillie suggested a particular pass, as the most likely to get a shot at
what he called a 'tod.' It was some time before
Tom realized the full horror of the proposition;
when he did, he shut his eyes like a bull that is
going to charge, and literally *fell* upon the duinhe-
wassal, bellowing savagely. He had no more idea
of using his hands than a fractious baby; but it
is rather a serious thing when sixteen stone of
solid flesh becomes possessed by a devil. Robin
Oig was overborne by the onset, and did not
forget the effects of it that season."

Tresliyan laughed applaudingly, as he always
did when he could understand more than half a
story.

"I suppose it's pretty good fun hunting them
out there?" he said, going off at score, as usual,
on the fresh theme.

"Not bad," Keene replied; "sharp going while
it lasts, and a little knack wanted to stick them
scientifically. Some say it's more exciting than

fox-hunting, but that's childish; I never heard a man assert it whose liver was not on the wane. It is more dangerous, certainly. A header into the Smite or the Whissendine, is nothing to a fall backwards into a nullah, with a beaten horse on the top of you."

Molyneux woke up from a reverie. The familiar word stirred his blood like a trumpet, and it flashed up brightly in his pale cheek as he spoke. "Ah! we have had a brushing gallop or two in the gay old times, before we got married and invalided, and all that sort of thing. Dick, I should like to tell you how I got my first spear."

"Of course you would," the Major said, re-signedly; "it's my fault for starting the subject. Get over it quickly then, please." He did not stop him, though, as he would have done on another occasion—*pour cause.*

"I had been entered some time at boar," Harry began, "before I had any luck at all. Ride as hard as I would at the start, the old hands *would* creep up at the finish, just in time to get 'first blood.' I gave long prices for my Arabs, too, and didn't spare them. I own I got discouraged, and thought the whole thing a robbery, a delusion, and a snare. One day, however, we had a good deal of deep marshy ground at first, and a quick gallop afterwards, which served my light weight

well. I had it all to myself when he came to bay;
so I went in full of confidence, and gave point, as
I thought, well behind the shoulder-blade. I did
not calculate on the pace we were going, and I
was just three inches too forward. My horse was
as young and hot as I was; and though he had
no idea of flinching, didn't know how to take
care of himself. The instant the brute felt the
steel he wheeled short round, and cut The Em-
peror's forelegs clean from under him. We all
came down in a heap; my spear flew yards away;
and there I was on my face, clear of my horse,
with my right wrist badly sprained. Would you
have fancied the position? *I* didn't. The devil
was too blown to begin offensive operations at
once, for we had burst him along pretty sharply;
but he stood right over me, champing and rasping
his tusks, and getting his wind for a good vicious
rip. I felt his boiling foam dropping upon me,
as I lay quite still. I thought that was the best
thing to do. All at once hoofs came up at a hard
gallop; something swept above me with a rush;
there was a short smothered sound like a tap on
a padded door; and then the beast stretched himself slowly out across my legs, and shivered, and
died. That man, opposite you, had leapt his horse
over us both, and, while he was in the air, speared
the boar through the spinal marrow. If he had
been struck anywhere else, he might still have torn

me badly, before the life was out of him. Neatly done, wasn't it?"

Harry drank off the remains of his sherry and seltzer rather excitedly, and then sighed. He was thinking how often in other days, when health and nerves were to the fore, he had drained a stronger and deeper draught to "Snaffle, spur, and spear!"

"A mere stage trick," Keene remarked; "effective, but not in the least dangerous, with a horse under you as steady as poor old Mahmoud. May his rest be glorious! Gilbert killed a tiger that had got loose in the same way, which *was* something to talk about, for even clean-bred Arabs don't like facing tigers. You made rather better time than usual over that story to-night, Hal; it's practice, I suppose."

Tresilyan's eyes fastened on the speaker, full of a heavy pertinacious admiration. You might have told him of the noblest action of generosity or self-denial that ever constituted the stock in trade of a Moral hero, and he would have listened patiently, but without one responsive emotion. Bodily prowess and daring he could appreciate. Keene's physical *prestige* was just the thing to captivate his limited imagination; besides which, the ground was prepared for the seed-time. He had some soldier-friends; and dining with these at the " Swashing Buckler," he had heard some of those club chronicles in which the Cool Captain's name figured prominently.

The latter interpreted perfectly well the gaze that was riveted upon him, without being in the least flattered by it. He felt, perhaps, the same sort of satisfaction that one experiences when, fighting for the odd trick, the first card in our hand is a heavy trump. Dick's thorough and undivided allegiance, once secured, was a good card in the game he was playing at the moment. Whatever his thoughts might have been, his face told no tales. He had been flooring glass for glass with his guest, till the liquor began to work its way into the cracks even of such a seasoned vessel; but, for any outward or visible sign in feature, speech, or manner, he might have been assisting at a tee-totaler's *soirée*.

Very often—late on guest-nights, or other tour-naments of deep drinking, where Trojan and Tyrian met to do battle for the credit of their respective corps—the calm, rigid face, never flushing beyond a clear swarthy brown, and the cold, bright, inevi-table eyes, had stricken terror into the hearts of bacchanalian Heavies, and given consolation, if not confidence, to the Hussars, who were failing fast: these knew that, though their own brains might be reeling, and their legs rebelliously independent, their single champion was invincible. As the last of the Enōmotæ went down, he saw Othryades standing steadfastly, with never a trace of wound or weakness, ready and willing to write NIKH on his shield.

When our poor Dick was once thoroughly impressed, for the first time, with awe or admiration either for man or woman, he generally fell into a species of trance, from which it was exceedingly difficult to bring him round. He would have sat there, staring stupidly till morning, with perfect satisfaction to himself, if Molyneux had not attacked him with a direct question—"How long do you think of staying at Dorade? And have you made any plans afterwards?"

Le mouton qui rêvait roused himself with an effort, and searched the bottom of his empty glass narrowly for a reply. Eventually he succeeded in finding one :—

"Cecil talks about two months; then we are to go on by Nice, Genoa, Florence, Rome, and Naples, and so come back by—Italy." He had got up the first names by rote, and run them off glibly enough; but was evidently at fault about the last one. I fancy he had some vague idea of Austrian troops being quartered in these regions, and looked upon Hesperia in the light of an obscure state or moderate-sized town somewhere in the north of Europe.

Harry was balked in his inclination to laugh : the rising smile was checked upon his lip, just in time, by a glance from his chief, severely authoritative.

"Italy?" the latter said, without a muscle moving; "well, I shouldn't advise you to stay long there. It's rather a small place, and very stupid; no society whatever. The others will amuse you, as you have never seen them."

He rose as he spoke the last words. Perhaps he thought he had done, that night, "enough for profit and more than enough for glory." The Cool Captain seldom suffered himself to be bored without an adequate object very clearly in view.

"Hal, I am going to turn you out. It is far too late for you to be sitting up, and we have a good deal to do to-morrow."

Molyneux did not quite comprehend what extraordinary labours were before any of them, but he rose without making an objection, and Tresilyan prepared to accompany him. Dick considered that, individually, he had been remarkably brilliant, and had left a favourable impression behind him. But all this newly-acquired confidence, and much strong drink, were not sufficient to embolden him to risk, as yet, a *tête-à-tête* with Royston Keene.

Long after they had departed, the Major sat, gazing steadfastly at the logs burning on the hearth. If he had gone straight to bed, the enormous dulness of one of the party would have weighed him down like a nightmare.

Is there one of us who cannot remember having seen prettier pictures in a flame-coloured setting than the Royal Academy has ever shown him? What earthly painter could emulate or imitate the coquettish caprice of light and shadow, that enhances the charms, and dissembles all possible defects in those fair fleeting Fiamminas? Something like this effect was to be found in the miniatures that were in fashion a dozen years ago; where part only of a sweet face and a dangerously eloquent eye looked at you out of a wreath of dusky cloud, that shrouded all the rest and gave your imagination play. Truly it was not so utterly wrong, the ancient legend that wedded Hephæstus to Aphrodite. The Minnesingers and their coevals spoke fairly enough about Love, and probably had studied their subject; but, rely upon it, passionate Romance died in Germany when once the close stoves prevailed. Don't you envy the imagination of the dreamer who could trace a shape of loveliness in those dreadful glazed tiles?

Being rather a *Guebre* myself, I once got enthusiastic on the subject in the company of an eccentric character, who very soon made me repent my expansiveness. If he had committed any atrocious crime (he was a small sandy-haired creature, and wore coloured spectacles), no one knew of it, and he never hinted at its nature; but his whole ideas seemed tinged with a vague gloomy remorse that made him a sadder, but scarcely a wiser or better man. Perhaps it was a monomania; let us hope so. On that occasion he heard me out quite patiently; then the blue glasses raised themselves to the level of my eyes, and I felt convinced their owner was staring spectrally behind them. Considering that he measured about thirty-four inches round the chest, his voice was extraordinarily deep and solemn : it sounded preternaturally so as he said very slowly, "There is one face that does not often leave me alone here, and will follow me, I think, when I go to my appointed place; I see it now—as I shall see it throughout all ages—always *by firelight.*"

I felt very wroth, for surely to suggest a new and unpleasant train of ideas is an infamous abuse of a *tête-à-tête.* I told my friend so; and as he declined to retract or apologize, or in anywise explain himself, departed with the conviction that, though a clever man and an original thinker, he was by no means an exhilarating or instructive companion. I should have borne him a grudge to this day, but as I was walking home, decidedly disconsolate (there's no such bore as having a pet fancy spoiled, it is like having your favourite hunter sent home with two broken knees), it suddenly occurred to me that if the Penitent was in the habit of looking at the fire through those blue barnacles, it was not likely there would be much rose-colour in his visions. In great triumph I retraced my steps, and knocked the culprit up to put in this "demurrer." I flatter myself it floored him. He did attempt some lame excuse about "taking his spectacles off at such times," but I refused to listen to a word, and marched out of the place with drums beating and colours flying, first exasperating him by the assurance of my complete forgiveness. Since then, if, sitting alone, *ligna super foco largè reponens,* I involuntarily recur to that ill-favoured conception, it suffices to contrast with it the grotesque appearance of its originator, and the pale phantom evanisheth.

I have no excuse to offer for this long and egotistical anecdote, except the pendant which Maloney used to attach to his ultra-*marine* stories—"The point of it is, that—it's strictly true."

CHAPTER VIII.

ANOTHER and a much more reputable Council of Three sat that night in Miss Tresilyan's apartments. Mr. Fullarton represented the male element there, and was in great force. The late accession to his flock had decidedly raised his spirits : he knew how materially it would strengthen his hands; but, independently of all politic consideration, Cecil's grace and beauty exercised a powerful influence over him. Do not misconstrue this. I believe a thought had never crossed his mind relating to any living woman that his own wife might not have known and approved; nevertheless was it true that Mr. Fullarton liked his penitents to be fair: not a very eccentric or unaccountable taste either. It is a necessity of our nature to take more delight in the welfare and training of a beautiful and refined being than in that of one who is coarse and awkward and ugly. Even with the merely animal creation we should experience this; and not above one divine in fifty is *more* than human, after all.

So, gazing on the fair face and queenly figure that were then before him, and feeling a sort of

vested interest in their possessor, the heart of the
Pastor was merry within him ; and he, so to
speak, caroused over the profusely-sugared tea
and well-buttered *galette* with a decorous and
regulated joviality ; ever as he drank casting
down the wreaths of his florid eloquence at the
feet of his entertainers. In any atmosphere whatsoever, no matter how uncongenial, those garlands
were sure to bloom. His zeal was such a hardy
perennial that the most chilling reception could
not damage its vitality. Principle and intention
were both all right, of course, but they were clumsily
carried out, and the whole effect was to remind
one unpleasantly of the Clockmaker puffing his
wares. At the most unreasonable times, and in
the most incongruous places, Mr. Fullarton always
had an eye to business, introducing and inculcating
his tenets with an assurance and complacency
peculiar to himself. Sometimes he would adopt
the familiarly conversational, sometimes the theatrically effective style ; but it never seemed to
cross his mind that either could appear ridiculous
or grotesque. Some absurd stories were told of
his performances in this line. On one occasion,
they say, he addressed his neighbour at dinner,
to whom he had just been introduced, abruptly
thus : " You see, what we want is—more Faith,"
in precisely the manner and tone of a *gourmet*
suggesting that " the soup would be all the better

for a little more seasoning;" or of Mr. Chouler asserting, "The farmers must be protected, sir." On another, meeting for the first time a very pious and wealthy old man (I believe a joint-stock bank director), he proceeded to sound him as to his " experiences." The unsuspecting elder, rather flattered by the interest taken in his welfare, and never dreaming that such communications could be anything but privileged and confidential, parted with his information pretty freely. Mr. Fullarton was so delighted at what he heard that he turned suddenly round to the mixed assembly and cried out, " Why, here's a blesséd old Barzillai ! " His face was beaming like that of an enthusiastic numismatist who stumbles upon a rare Commodus or an authentic Domitian. There were several people present of his own way of thinking ; but some, even among these, felt very ill afterwards from their efforts to repress their laughter. The miserable individual thus endued with the " robe of honour " would have infinitely preferred the most scandalously abusive epithet to that fervid compliment. He would have parted with half his bank shares at a discount (they were paying about 14 per cent. then—you can get them tolerably cheap now) to have been able to sink into his shoes on the spot ; indeed these were almost large enough to form convenient places of refuge. It had a very bad effect on him : he never again unbosomed himself on any subject to man, woman, or child. Even in his last illness—though he must have had one or two troublesome things on his mind, unless he had peculiar ideas as to the propriety of ruining widows and orphans—he declined to commit himself,

> But locked the secret in his breast,
> And died in silence, unconfessed.

On that Saturday night, to one of the party at all events, Mr. Fullarton's presence was very welcome. Mrs. Danvers was somewhat of a hard-drinker in theology, and, like other intemperate people, was not over-particular as to the quality of the liquors set before her, provided only that they were hot and strong, and unstinted. The succulent and highly-flavoured eloquence to which she was listening suited her palate exactly, besides which, the chaplain's peculiar opinions happened to coincide perfectly with her own. As the evening progressed she got more and more exhilarated; and at length could not forbear intimating "how sincerely she valued the privilege of sitting under so eminent a divine."

The latter made a scientific little bow, elaborated evidently by long practice, expressive at once of gratification and humility.

"A privilege, if such it be, dear Mrs. Danvers,

that some of my congregation estimate but very
lightly. You would hardly believe how many
members of my flock I scarcely know, except by
name. It is a sore temptation to discouragement.
I fear that Major Keene's pernicious example is
indeed contagious, and that his evil communications have corrupted many—alas! too many."
He rounded off the period with a ponderous professional sigh.

Miss Tresilyan was leaning back in her arm-
chair: as the wood-fire sprang up brightly and
sank again suddenly, her great deep eyes seemed
to flash back the fitful gleams. It was long since
she had spoken. In truth, she had been drawing
largely upon her piety, at first, to make herself feel
interested, and, when this failed, upon her courtesy,
to appear so; but she was conscious of relapses
more and more frequent into the dreary regions of
Boredom. Everybody *would* agree with everybody
else so completely! A bold contradiction, a sting-
ing sarcasm, or a caustic retort, would have been
worth anything just then to take off the cloying
taste of the everlasting honey. She roused herself
at these last words enough to ask languidly, "What
has he done?"

There could not be a simpler question, nor one
put more carelessly; but it was rather a "facer"
to Mr. Fullarton, who dealt in generalities as a
rule, and objected to being brought to book about

particulars—considering, indeed, such a line of argument as indicativo of a cavilling and narrow-minded disposition in his interlocutor.

" Well," he said, not without hesitation, " Major Keene has only once been to church : and, I believe, has spoken scoffingly since of tho discourse ho heard delivered there. Yet I may say I was more than usually ' supported' on that occasion." The man's thorough air of conviction softened somewhat the absurd effect of his childish vanity.

Cecil would have been sorry to confess how much excuse she felt inclined to admit just then for the sins both of commission and omission—sins that at another time, when her faculties were fresh and her judgment unbiassed, she might have looked upon as anything but venial. Ah, Mr. Fullarton, the seed you have scattered so profusely to-night is beginning to bear fruit already you never dreamt of. Beetroot and turnips will not succeed on *every* soil. It must be long before a remunerative crop of these can be gathered from the breezy upland which for centuries, till the heather was burned, has worn a robo of uncommercial but imperial purple.

Nevertheless, Miss Tresilyan frowned perceptibly. It looked very much as if Keeno had been amusing himself at her expense when he affected an interest in her leading the choir. Unwittingly, to " make

sport for the men of war in Gath," by no means
suited the fancy of that haughty ladye.

"It is very wrong of him not to come to church,"
she observed after a pause (for the sin of sarcasm
disapproval was not so ready, and she made the
most of scanty means of condemnation). "Yet I
scarcely think he can be actively hostile. You
know he almost lives with the Molyneuxs, and has
great influence with them. Do they not attend
regularly?"

Mr. Fullarton admitted that they did. "But,"
said he, "constant intercourse with such a man
must ere long have its injurious effect. Indeed, I
felt it my bounden duty to warn Mrs. Molyneux on
the subject. I grieve to say she treated my admo-
nition with a very unwarrantable levity."

Mrs. Danvers' sympathetic groan was promptly
at the service of the speaker; fortunately, turning
to thank her for it by a look, he missed detecting
her pupil's smile. She could fancy so well Fanny's
little *moue*, combining amusement, vexation, and
impertinence, while undergoing the ecclesiastical
censure.

"You must be merciful to Mrs. Molyneux," she
remarked, with a demure gravity that did her credit
under the circumstances. "She is my greatest
friend, you know. When a wife is so very fond of
her husband, surely there is some excuse for her
adopting his prejudices for and against people?"

The Pastor brightened up suddenly: he had just recollected another fact to fire off against the *bête-noir*.

"I forgot to tell you that Major Keene is much addicted to play, and besides is intimate with the Vicomte de Châteaumesnil. *Noscitur a sociis.*" The reverend man was an indifferent classic; but he had a way of flashing scraps out of grammars and *Analecta Minora* before women and others unlikely to be down upon him, as if they were quotations from some recondite author.

"You cannot mean that cripple who is drawn about in a wheel-chair?" Cecil asked. "We saw him to-day, only for a moment, for he drew his cloak over his face as we passed. I never saw such a melancholy wreck; and I pitied him so much that I fear he will haunt me."

Far deeper would have been the compassion, had she guessed at the pang that shot straight to Armand's heart, as he veiled his blasted features and haggard eyes, feeling bitterly that such as he were not worthy to look upon her in the glory of her brilliant beauty.

"A notorious atheist and profligate," was the reply. "We cannot regard his sore affliction in any other light than a judgment—a manifest judgment, dear Miss Tresilyan."

There was grave disapproval and just a shade of contempt in the face of one of his hearers as she

said, " The hand of God is laid so heavily there,
that man may surely forbear him." But Mrs.
Danvers struck in to her favourite's rescue, re-
joicing in an opportunity of displaying her partisanship.

" A judgment, of course. It would be sinful to
doubt it. Besides, do not *others* suffer ? " (She
cast up her eyes here pointedly, as though she said,
" There may be more perfect saints; but if you
want a fair specimen of the fine old English martyr
—*me voici.*") " Cecil, my love, I wonder you did
not perceive Major Keene's true character at once.
You were talking to him a good deal the other
day."

" He did not favour me with any remarkably
heretical opinions," Miss Tresilyan replied, carelessly. " Perhaps they have been exaggerated. At
all events, he is not likely to do us much harm.
Don't you think *we* are safe, Bessie ? Dick does
not care much for play ; and his ideas on religious
subjects are so very simple, that it would be hard to
unsettle them."

Clearly she thought the topic was exhausted, but
it had a strange fascination for Mr. Fullarton.
One of the many goodnatured people who especially abound in those semi-English continental
towns, had been kind enough to quote, or mis-
quote, to him a remark of Royston's about that
sermon ; and on this topic the Chaplain was very

vulnerable. He would have forgiven a real substantial injury far sooner than a depreciation of his
discourses.

Was he one whit weaker or more susceptible than
his fellows? I think not. All the philosophy on
earth will not teach us to endure without wincing
a mosquito's bite. The hardiest hero bears about
him one spot where an ivy leaf clinging intercepted
the petrifying water—a tiny out-of-the-way spot,
not very far from the head or heart, but palpable
enough to be stricken by Paris' arrow or Hagen's
spear. Cæsar is very sensitive about that bald
crown of his, and fears lest even the laurel wreath
should cover it but meagrely. Many wars, since
that which brought Ilium to the dust, might have
been traced to slighted vanity; and many excellent
Christians have waxed quite as wroth as the Queen
of heathenish heaven, about the *spretæ injuriæ
formæ*. (Do you think this is a peculiarly feminine
failing? I have seen a First-Class man and Ire-
land Scholar look massacres at the child of his
bosom-friend, when the unconscious innocent made
disagreeable remarks on his personal appearance,
alluding particularly to the shape of his nose,
which was *not* Phidian. He has since been heard
to speak of that terrible deed in Bethlehem as a
painful but justifiable measure of political expediency; and is inclined, on many grounds, to
excuse and sympathize with the stern Idumean.)

The insult offered to the ambassador in Tarentum was only the outbreak of a single drunkard's brutality; but all the wealth of the fair City of Phalanthus did not suffice to pay the account for washing the soiled robe white again: and blood enough ran down her streets to have quenched some blazing temples, before the Romans would give her a receipt in full.

Arguing from these *data*, we may conclude that Mr. Fullarton was labouring under a slight delusion in believing (which he did sincerely) that only a pure and disinterested zeal for the welfare of his flock impelled him to say—"I shall make it my business to inquire more fully into Major Keene's antecedents. I am convinced there is something discreditable in the background, and it may be well to be armed with proofs in case of need."

Though *he* may have deceived himself completely as to the nature of the spirit that possessed him, Cecil Tresilyan was more clear-sighted. She had not failed to remark a certain vicious twinkle in the speaker's eye, and a deeper flush on his ruddy countenance, betokening rather a mundane resentment. Her lip began to curl.

"How very disagreeable some of your duties must be. No doubt you interpret them correctly; but in this case perhaps it would be well to be *quite* sure before acting on the offensive. If I

were a man—even a clergyman—I don't think
I should like to have Major Keene for my declared
enemy"

The text with which the Chaplain enforced his
reply—expressive of a determination to keep his
own line at all hazards, strong in the rectitude
of his cause—had better not be quoted here,
especially as it was not apposite enough to "lay"
the contradictory spirit that was alive in his fair
opponent. (How very angry Cecil would have
been, if she had been told, ten minutes ago, that
such an expression would apply to her!) The
temptation to answer sharply was so powerful, that
she took refuge in distant coldness.

" You quite misunderstand me, Mr. Fullarton.
I never dreamt of offering advice; it would have
been excessively presumptuous in me, especially
as I have not the faintest interest in the subject
we have been talking about. Need we discuss
it any longer? I think Major Keene has been
too highly honoured already."

That weary look was so manifest now on the
beautiful face that even the Chaplain, albeit tena-
cious of his position as a sea-anemone, felt that,
for once, he had overstayed his time and was
perilling his popularity So, after an expansive
benediction, and an entreaty that they would be
early at church on the morrow, he went "to his
own place."

With a sigh of admiration—" What an excellent man, and how well he talks!" said Bessie Danvers.

With a sigh of relief—" He talks a great deal, and it is very late," said Cecil Tresilyan.

CHAPTER IX.

FROM his "coign of vantage" in the reading-desk the next morning, Mr. Fullarton surveyed a crowded congregation, serenely complacent and hopeful, as a farmer in August looking down from the hillside on golden billows of waving grain. Visitors had been pouring in rather fast during the week; and there was a vague general impression, which no individual would have owned, that they were to hear something unusually good. For once expectation was not to be disappointed—a remarkable fact, when one considers how much dissatisfaction is created, as a rule, in the popular mind, by the shortcomings of eclipses, processions, Vesuvian eruptions, new operas, and other advertised attractions, natural and artificial. The singing was really a success. Miss Tresilyan's magnificent voice did its duty nobly, and did no more. Without overpowering or singling itself out from the others, it lured them on to follow where they could never have gone alone: the choir was kept in perfect order without even knowing that it was disciplined.

There was an elderly Englishman who had

resided at Dorade, ever since he had a slight difference of opinion with the Bankruptcy Court, a quarter of a century back. Drifting helplessly and aimlessly about Europe in search of employment, he had taken root where he came ashore, and vegetated, as floating weeds will do. He picked up rather a precarious livelihood by acting as a species of factotum to his countrymen in the season, ministering, not injudiciously, to their myriad whims and necessities. Amongst his multifarious functions, perhaps the most respectable and permanent was that of clerk to the English Chapel. He was by no means a very religious man, nor were his morals quite unexceptionable; but he had completely identified himself with the fortunes and interests of that modest building. A sneer at its capabilities, or a doubt as to its prospects, would exasperate him at any time far more than a direct insult to himself (to be sure there was little self-respect left to be offended). When disguised in drink, which was the case tolerably often, he generally proposed to settle the question by the ordeal of battle, and was only to be appeased by an apology or a great deal more liquor.

On this occasion the success and the singing combined—for excess and hardship had not quite deadened a good ear for music—moved the old castaway strangely. His thoughts wandered back

to the misused days when he had friends and a
position and character; when he was a householder
and vestryman, and even dreamt ambitiously of a
churchwardenship. He could see distinctly his own
pew, with the grey worm-eaten panels, where he
had sat many and many a warm afternoon, resisting
sternly, as became a man of mark in the parish,
treacherous inclinations to slumber. He saw the
ponderous brown gallery—eyesore to archæologists
—which held the village choir: there they were,
with the sun streaming in on their heads through
the western window, till even the faded red cushion
in front deepened into rich crimson, chanting their
quaint old anthems with right good courage,
though every one got lost in the second line, and,
after much independent exertion of the lungs, just
came up in time to join in the grand final rally. He
saw the mild-faced, grey-haired parson mounting
slowly the pulpit-stairs, adjusting and manœuvring
the refractory gown that *would* come off his
shoulders with the nervous gesture which, beginning in timidity, had grown into a habit that was
part of the man. More plainly than all—he saw a
low green mound just beyond the chancel walls,
where One was sleeping who had lavished on him
all the treasures of a rare unselfish trusting love;
the dear meek little wife, who was so proud of her
husband's few poor talents, so indulgent to his
many failings, who ever had an excuse ready to

answer his self-reproaches, whose weak thin hand
was always strong enough to pluck him back from
ruin and dishonour, till it grew stiff and cold. She
knew it, too, for he remembered the wail that burst
from her lips when she thought she was alone, the
night before she died—" Ah, who will save him
now that I am gone ? " How miserable and lonely
he was, long after they buried her! How incessantly he used to repeat those last words, meant to
be comforting, that she spoke, with her arm wound
round his neck—" Darling, you have been so very,
very kind to me ! " So it went on, till the devil of
drink, choosing his time cunningly, entered into
him and battled with and drove out the angel ! A
strange resurrection ! Memories that had died
years ago, withering from very shame, began to
curl and twine themselves round the hard battered
heart as tenderly as ever. These pictures of the
past were still vivid and clear, when he became
aware of a dimness in his eyes that blinded them
to all real surrounding objects ; he felt so surprised
that it broke the spell : tears had almost forgotten
the way to his eyes.

Not very probable, is it, that a prosaic elderly
clerk should dream all this during the three last
verses of a hymn ? Well, the steadiest imagination
is apt to disregard sometimes the proprieties of
place ; and as for space—of course the visions of
the night are quicker on the wing than their rivals

of the day; yet there must be some analogy;
and, they say, we pass through the vicissitudes
of half a lifetime in the few seconds before we
wake.

Cecil was really pleased with the result of the
singing. She would have been even more so had
it not been for the marked expression of approval
on the face of Royston Keene. It was evident she
had been on her trial. The cool, appreciative smile
was very provoking. It made her feel, for the
moment, like a *prima donna* on her first appearance
at a new theatre.

Unusually eloquent and verbose was the sermon
that day; for not only was the preacher aware that
bright eyes looked upon his deeds, but he saw his
enemy in the front of the battle. Surely all extem-
poraneous speakers, in court, pulpit, or senate,
must be accessible to such external influences. It
ought not to be so, of course, but I fancy it *is*.
Would John Knox have been so fiery in denuncia-
tion if those wicked maids of honour had not derided him? I doubt, if a discourse delivered in a
Union would ever soar to sublimity, even if the
excellent paupers could be supposed to understand
it. So, with every sentence more plaintive grew
Mr. Fullarton's lamentations over worldlings and
their vanities, more bitter his invectives against
those who, having themselves broken out of the
fold, seek to lead others astray. An occasional

gesture — something tco expressive — was not needed to point his animadversions. The object of them sat, with his head slightly bent, neither by frown nor smile betraying that a single allusion had gone home. The simple truth was, that he scarcely caught one word. The last cadence of sweeter tones was still lingering in his ears, and had locked them fast against all other sounds. The energetic divine might have poured out upon his guilty head yet stormier vials, and he would never have heard one roll of the thunder. However, the dearest friends must part; and all orations must come to an end, except those of the much-desiderated Chisholm Anstey, of whom an old-world Parliament was not worthy; so, after "a burst of forty-five minutes without a check," the Chaplain dismissed his beloved hearers to their digestion.

The stream, as it flowed out, divided, and broke up into small pools of conversation. Miss Tresilyan and her chaperone joined the Molyneux party, just as Fanny was saying to Keene that "she hoped he would profit by much in the sermon that was evidently meant for him."

"Was he personal?" the lattter asked so indifferently!—"I didn't notice it. Well, I suppose it amuses him, and it certainly does not hurt me." (Mrs. Danvers sniffed indignantly—a form of protest to which her nose, from its construction, was eminently adapted; but he went on before she

could speak)—"Miss Tresilyan, will you allow,
perhaps the unworthiest member of the congregation, to express an opinion that the singing went
off superbly ? "

Her beautiful eyes glittered somewhat disdain-
fully. "Thank you, you are very good. But I
think you have hardly a right to be critical. I
should like to have some one's opinion who is
really interested in the chapel. It was scarcely
worth taking so much trouble to appear so the
other day. You know what Liston said about the
penny? ' It is not the value of the thing, but one
hates to be imposed upon.' Delusions are not so
agreeable as illusions, Major Keene."

Royston was very much pleased. He liked
above all things to see a woman stand up to him
defiantly; indeed, if they were worth "setting to
with," he always tried to get them to spar as
soon as possible, to find out if they had any idea
of hitting straight. He did not betray his satisfaction, though, as he answered quite calmly,
"Pardon me, I could not be so impertinent, as to
attempt a ' delusion ' on so short an acquaintance.
I deny the charge distinctly. I believe that
residence in Dorade, and a certain amount
of subscription, constitute a member of Mr.
Fullarton's congregation, and give one a fran-
chise. He has not thought fit to excommunicate
me publicly as yet. I really was interested in the

subject, for I fully meant to go to church this morning, and I mean to go again."

Insensibly they had walked on in advance of the others. She shook her head with a saucy incredulity — " I am no believer in sudden conversions."

" Nor I; I was not speaking of such; but I am very fond of good singing, and I would go anywhere to hear it. Did our Chaplain include hypocrisy among my other disqualifications for decent society last night ? 'I understand he is good enough to furnish a catalogue of them to all new comers."

Cecil certainly had not abused him then ; so there was not the slightest necessity for her looking guilty and conscious, both of which she felt she was doing as she replied—" I am sure Mr. Fullarton would not asperse any one's character knowingly. He could only speak from a sense of duty, perhaps not a pleasant one."

" Quite so," said Royston ; " I don't quarrel with him for any fair professional move. If he thinks it necessary or expedient to prejudice indifferent people against me, he is clearly right to do so. Ah! I see you think I dislike him. I don't indeed. Morally and physically, he seems a little too unctuous, that's all. Capital clergyman for a cold climate ! Fancy how useful he would be in an Arctic expedition. They might save his salary in Arnott's stoves : I'm certain he *radiates*."

Miss Tresilyan knew that it was wrong to smile. But she had an unfortunately quick perception of the ridiculous, and the struggles of principle against a sense of humour were not always successful. She would not give up her point, though. "I cannot think that you judge him fairly," she persisted.

"Perhaps not ; but there is a large class who would scarcely be much moved by stronger and abler words than, I suppose, we heard to-day— spoken as they were spoken. These preachers won't study the fitness of things ; that's the worst of it. I have known a garrison-chaplain deliver a discourse that, I am convinced, was composed for a visitation. It seems absurd to hear a man warning us against a particular sin, and threatening us with all sorts of penalties if we indulge in it, when it is impossible that he himself should ever have felt the temptation. We want some one who can find out the harmless side of our character, as well as the diseased part, and work upon it. Such a person may be as strict and harsh as he pleases, but he is listened to." He paused for a moment, and went on in a graver tone—"I think it might have done even *me* some good, when I was younger, to have talked for half an hour with the man who wrote 'How Amyas threw his sword away'"

Cecil could not disagree with him now, nor did she wish to do so. She liked those last words of his better than any he had spoken. Remember, she was born and bred in the honest West country, where one, at least, of their own prophets hath honour. If you want to indulge your enthusiasm for the Rector of Eversley, let your next walking tour turn thitherwards; for, on all the seaboard from Portsmouth to Penzance, there is never a woman—maid, wife, or widow—that will say you nay.

Keene saw his advantage, but was far too wise to follow it up then. The weaker sex, as a rule, are acute but not very close reasoners : they mix up their majors and minors with a charming recklessness; and if innocent of nothing else, are generally guiltless of a syllogism. It follows that, in the course of an argument, it is easy enough to entangle them in their talk. When such a chance occurs, don't come down upon your pretty antagonists with, "I thought you said so and so;" but be politic as well as generous, and pass it by. They will do more justice to your self-denial than they would have done to your dialectic talents. Corinna loves to be contradicted, but hates to be convinced, and dreads no monster so much as a short-horned—dilemma. She may forgive the first offence as inadvertent, but "one more such victory and you are lost." Think how often clemency has succeeded where severity would have failed. What did that discreet Eastern emir, when he found his fair young wife sleeping in a garden, where she had no earthly business to be? He laid his drawn sabre softly across her neck, and retired without breaking her slumbers. The cold blade was the first thing Zuleika felt when she awoke; I cannot guess what her sensations were; but when she gave the weapon back to her solemn lord, she pressed her rosy lips thrice on the blue steel, and made a vow that she most probably kept; and Hussein Bey never was happier than when he drew her back to his broad breast, looking into her face, silently, with his calm, grave smile.

I fancy our sisters enter into an argument with more simple good faith and eagerness then we are wont to indulge in; so that it is probably easier to tease and exasperate them, which is amusing enough while it lasts. But no doubt it hurts them sometimes more than we are aware of; and, after all, breaking a butterfly on the wheel is poor pastime, and not a very athletic sport. The glory, too, to be won is so small, that it scarcely compensates for the pain we inflict, and may, perchance, eventually *feel.* Is Achilles inclined to be proud of the strength of his arm, or the keenness of his falchion, as he grovels in the dust at the slain Amazon's side? Nay, he would give half his laurels to be able to close that awful gaping wound

—to see the proud lips soften for a moment from their immutable scorn—to detect the faintest tremor in the long white limbs that never will stir again.

The solemnity of these illustrations, in which battles, murders, and sudden deaths are mingled, will prove that I regard the subject as by no means trivial, but am sincerely anxious to warn my comrades against yielding to a temptation which assails us daily.

On these principles the Cool Captain acted, then. His gay laugh opened a bridge to the retreating enemy as he said, " How my poor character must have been worried last night ! I wish Mrs. Molyneux had been there. She is good enough to stand up for her old friend sometimes. I could hardly expect *you* to take so much trouble for a very recent acquaintance."

" Of course not," replied Cecil. " I was not in a position to contradict anything, even if I had wished to do so. But, I remember, I thought I would speak to you about my brother. You know enough of him already, to guess why I am nervous about him. I almost forced him to take me abroad; and he is exposed to so many more dangers here than at home. Please, don't encourage him to play, or tempt him into anything wrong. Indeed, I don't mean to speak harshly or uncourteously, so you need not be angry."

She raised her eyes to her companion's with a

pretty pleading. He met them fairly. Whatever his intentions might be, no one could say that the Major ever shrank from looking friend or foe in the face.

"I am sorry that you should think the warning necessary. Supposing that it were so—on my honour, he is safe from me. I should like to alter your opinion of me, if it were possible. Will you give me a chance?" The others joined them before she could reply; but more than once that day Cecil wondered whether, even during their short acquaintance, she had not sometimes dealt scanty justice to Royston Keene.

CHAPTER X.

THERE is a pleasant theory—That every woman may be loved, once at least in her life, if she so wills it. It must be true, how otherwise can you account for the number of hard-featured visages—lighted up by no redeeming ray of intellect—that preside at " good men's feasts," and confront them at their firesides ? How do the husbands manage ? Do they, from constantly contemplating an inferior type of creation, lose their comparing and discriminating powers ; so that like the Australian and Pacific aborigines, they come to regard as points of beauty, peculiarities that a more advanced civilization shrinks from ? Or do their visual organs become gradually impaired, like those of captives, who can see clearly only in their own dungeon's twilight, and flinch before the full glare of day ? If neither of these is the case, they must sometimes sympathize with that dreary dilemma of Bias, which the adust Aldrich quotes in grim irony—'Εἰ μὲν κάλην, ἕξεις κοίνην, εἰ δ' αἰσχραν, ποίνην. (Whether of the two horns impaled the sage of Priēne ?) Some, of course, are fully alive to the outward defects of

their partners; but few are so candid as the old
Berkshire squire, who, looking after his spouse as
she left the room, said pensively — " Excellent
creature, that ! I've liked her better every day for
twenty years, but I've always thought she's the
plainest-headed woman in England ! " Fewer still
would wish to emulate the sturdy plain-speaking
of the "gudeman" in the Scottish ballad, who,
when his witch-wife boasted how she bloomed into
beauty after drinking the " wild flower wine,"
replied undauntedly—

> ' Ye lee, ye lee, ye ill womyn,
> Sae loud I hear ye lee ;
> The ill-faured'st wife i' the kingdom of Fife,
> Is comely compared wi' thee.'

He could stand all the other marvels of the
Sabbat, but *that* was too much for his credulity

No doubt many of these Ugly Princesses are
endowed with excellent sterling qualities. The
old Border legend says there never was a happier match than that of " Muckle-mou'ed Meg,"
though her husband married her reluctantly, with
a halter tightening round his neck. But such
advantages lie below the surface, and take some
time in being appreciated. The first process of
captivation is what I don't understand ; unless,
indeed, there are sparkles in the quartz, invisible
to common eyes, that tell the experienced gold-
seeker of a rich vein near.

Well, we will allow the proposition with which
we started; but do you suppose its converse would
hold equally good—That every woman could *love*
once, if she wished it? Nine out of ten of them
would, I daresay, answer boldly in the affirma-
tive ; but in a few rather sad and weary faces
you might read something more than a doubt
about this ; and lips, not so red and full as they
once were, on which the wintry smile comes but
rarely, could tell perhaps a different story. The
precise mould that will fit *some* fancies is as hard
to find as the slipper of Cendrillon ; and so, in
default of the fairy *chaussure*, the small white foot
goes on its road unshod, and the stones and briers
gall it cruelly.

With men it does not so much matter. They
have always the counteracting resources of bodily
and mental exertion, against which the affections
can make but little head. Indeed, some of the
most distinguished in arts, in arms, if not in song,
seem to have gone down to their graves without
ever giving themselves time to indulge in any one
of these. Perhaps they never missed a sentiment
which would have been very much in their way if
they had felt it. If all tales are true, mathematics
are a very effectual Nénuphar. But with women it
is different. They can't be always clambering up
unexplored peaks, or inventing improvements in
gunnery, or commanding Irregular corps, or

bringing in faultless Reform bills, or finding out
constellations, or shooting big game, or resorting
to any of *our* thousand and one safety-valves to
superfluous excitement. Are crochet, or crossed
letters, or charity schools, or even Cochins and
Crève-cœurs, so entirely engrossing as to drown
for ever the reproaches of Nature, that will make
herself heard ? If not, surely the most phlegmati-
cally proper of her sex does sometimes feel sad
and dissatisfied when she thinks that she has never
been able to care for any one more than for her
own brother. It must seem hard that, when the
frost of old age comes on, she shall not have even
a memory to look back upon, to warm her. But
in the world here, such temptations to discontent
abound; but the most guileless votary of the *Sacré
Cœur* might confess regrets and misgivings like
these, without meriting any extra allowance of
fast and scourge.

If we were to reckon up the cases we have
heard, of women who have "gone wrong," and
made, if not *mésalliances*, at least marriages inex-
plicable on any rational grounds, it would fill up a
long summer's day, even without drawing on
darker recollections of post-nuptial transgression.
In these last cases, perhaps, the utter and absolute
indifference was a more dangerous element than
Mrs. Malaprop's "little aversion," which is, at all
events, a *positive* thing to work upon. Lethargies

are harder to cure, they say, than fevers. Certainly they have the warning examples of others who have so erred, and paid for it by a life-long repentance; but that never has stopped them yet, and never will. Remember the reply of the *débutante* to her austere parent, when the latter refused to take her to a ball, saying that "*she* had seen the folly of such things"—"I want to see the folly of them too." Few of us men can realize the feeling that with our sisters may account for, though not excuse, much folly and sin. They see others happy all round them: it is hard to fast when so many are feasting. So there comes a shameful sense of ignorance—a vague, eager desire for knowledge—a terror of an isolation deepening and darkening upon them, and a determination, at any risks, to baulk, at least, *that* enemy—and so, like the poor Lady of Shalott, they grow restless, and reckless, and rebellious, at last. They are safe where they are, but the days have so much of dull sameness that there is a sore temptation in the unknown peril. "Better," they say, "than the close atmosphere of the guarded castle, and the phantasms of fairy-land, one draught of the fresh outer air—one glimpse of real life and nature—one taste of substantial joys and sorrows that shall wake all the pulses of womanhood; even though the experience be brief and dearly bought; though the web woven while we sat dreaming must surely be rent in twain; ay, even though the curse, too, may follow very swiftly, and the swans be waiting at the gate that shall bear us down to our burying."

If staid and cold-blooded virgins and matrons are not exempt from these disagreeable self-reproaches, how did it fare with Cecil Tresilyan, in whom the energy of a strong temperament was stirring like the spring-sap in a young oak-tree? Should she die, conscious of the possession of such a wealth of love, with none to share or inherit it? She had seen such numbers of her friends and acquaintance "pair off," that she began to envy at last the facility of attachment that she had been wont to hold in scorn. Very many reflections of "lovers lately wed" had been cast upon her mirror, and yet the One knightly shadow was long in coming. Can it be that yonder gleam through the trees is the flash of his distant armour?

I hope this illustrated edition of rather an old theory has not bored you much; because it would have been just as simple to have said at once that, as the days went on in Dorade, and they were thrown constantly into each other's society, Major Keene began to monopolize much more of Cecil Tresilyan's thoughts than she would have allowed, if she could have helped it; for, though she considered Mr. Fullarton's testimony unfairly biased by prejudice, she could not doubt that Royston was by no means the most eligible object to centre her young affections upon. He carefully avoided discussion or display of any of his peculiar opinions in her presence; and, on such occasions, seemed inclined to soften his habitually sardonic and depreciatory tone. Once or twice, when they did disagree, she observed that he contrived to make some one else take her side, and then argued the point, as long as he thought it worth while, with the last opponent. Beyond the courtesy which invariably marked his demeanour towards her sex, this was the only sign of especial deference that he had shown. She never could detect the faintest approach to the adulation that hundreds had paid her, and which she had wearied of long ago. Nevertheless, she knew perfectly that on many subjects, generally considered all-important, they differed as widely as the poles.

Perpetual struggles between the spirit and the flesh made Cecil's heart an odd sort of debateable land : if she could not always insure success and supremacy to the right side, she certainly did endeavour to preserve the balance of power. Personally, she rather disliked Mr. Fullarton, but she seemed to look upon him as the embodiment of a principle, and the symbol of an abstraction. He represented there the Establishment which she had always been taught to venerate; and so she felt bound, as far as possible, to favour and support

him ; just as Goring and Wilmot, and many more
wild Cavaliers, fearing neither God nor devil,
mingled in their war-cry Church as well as King.
(Rather a rough comparison to apply to a well-in-
tentioned demoiselle of the nineteenth century, but,
I fancy, a correct one.) Thus, if she indulged herself
in a long *tête-à-tête* with Keene, she was sure to be
extraordinarily civil to the Chaplain soon after ; and
if she devoted herself for a whole evening to the
society of the Priest and his family, the Soldier
was likely to benefit by it on the morrow. Unluckily, the sacrifice of inclination was all on *one*
side.

The antagonists had never, as yet, come into
open collision. It was not respect or fear that made
them shy of the conflict, but rather a feeling, which
neither could have explained to himself, resembling
that of leaders of parties in the House, who decline
measuring their strength against each other on
questions of minor importance, reserving themselves for the final crisis, when the want-of-con-
fidence vote shall come on. Once only there was a
chance of a skirmish—the merest affair of out-
posts.

Keene had been calling on the Tresilyans one
evening, in the official capacity of bearer of a verbal
message from Mrs. Molyneux. It was the simplest
one imaginable ; but, as graver ambassadors have
done before him, liking his quarters, he dallied over

his mission. (If Geneva, instead of Paris, were chosen for the meeting of a Congress, would not several knotty points be decided much more speedily?) When, at last, all was settled, it seemed very natural that he should petition Cecil for "just one song;" and you know what that always comes to. Royston never would "turn over" if he could possibly avoid it; he considered it a wilful waste of advantages, for the strain on his attention, slight as it may be, quite spoilt his appreciation of the melody. Perhaps he was right. As a rule, if one wanted to discover the one person about whose approval the fair *cantatrice* is most solicitous, it would be well to look, *not* immediately behind her ivory shoulder. At all events, he had made his peace with Miss Tresilyan on this point long ago. So he drew his arm-chair up near the piano, but out of her sight as she sang, and sat watching her intently through his half-closed eyelids.

I marvel not that in so many legends of witchery and seduction since the *Odyssey* the θεσπεσίη ἀοίδη has borne its part. "But," the Wanderer might say, replying against Circè's warning, "have we not learnt prudence and self-command from Athenè, the chaste Tritonid? Have not ten years under shield before Troy, and a thousand leagues of seafaring, made our hearts as hard as our hands, and our ears deaf to the charms of song? Thus

much of wisdom, at least, hath come with grizzled
hair, that we may mock at temptations that might
have won us when our cheeks were in their down.
O most divinely fair of goddesses! have we not
resisted your own enchantments? Shall we go
forth scathless from Ææa, to perish on the Isle
of the Sirens?" But the low green hills are
already on the weather-beam, and we are aware of
a sweet weird chant that steals over the water like
a living thing, and smooths the ripple where it
passes. How fares it with our philosophic Laer-
tiades? Those signs look strangely unlike incite-
ments to greater speed; and what mean those
struggles to get loose? Well, perhaps, for the
hero that the good hemp holds firm, and that
Peribates and Eurylochus spring up to strengthen
his bonds; well that the wax seals fast the ears
of those sturdy old sea-dogs, who stretch to their
oars till Ocean grows hoary behind the blades; or
nobler bones might soon be added to the myriads
that lie bleaching in the meadow, half hidden by
its flowers. It was not, then, so very trivial the
counsel that she gave in parting kindness—

Κίρκη ἰϋπλόκαμος, δεινὴ θεὸς αὐδήεσσα.

Are we in our generation wiser than the "man
of many wiles"? Dinner is over, and every one
is going out into the pleasance, to listen to the
nightingales.

"It will be delicious; there is nothing I should like so much; but I—I sprained my ankle in jumping that gate; and Amy " (that's ' my cousin who happens to sing'), " I heard you cough three times this morning. You won't be so imprudent as to risk the night air ? Ah, they are gone at last; and now, dear, good, kindest Amy !—open the especial crimson book quickly, and give me first your own pet song, and then mine, and then 'The Three Fishers,' and then ' Maud,' and then I suppose, they will be coming back again ; but by that time, they may be as enthusiastic as they please, we shall be able to meet them fairly."

Things have changed since David's day; spirits are raised sometimes now, as well as laid, by harp and song. In good truth, they are not always evil ones.

On that night, Royston Keene listened to the sweet voice that seemed to knock at the gates of his heart—gates shut so long that the bars had rusted in their staples—not loudly or imperiously, but powerful in its plaintive appeal, like that of some one dearly loved, standing without in the bitter cold, and pleading—" Ah, let me in !" He listened till a pleasant, dreamy feeling of *domesticity* began to creep over him, that he had never known before. He could realize, then, that there were circumstances under which a man might easily dispense with high play and hard riding, and hard

flirting (to give it a mild name), and hard drinking, and other excitements which habit had almost
turned into necessities, without missing any one
of them. There were two words which ought to
have put all these fancies to flight, as the writing
on the wall scattered the guests of Belshazzar—
"Too late." But he turned his head away, and
would not read them. He had actually succeeded in
ignoring another disenchanting reality—the presence of Mrs. Danvers. That estimable person
seemed more than usually fidgetty, and disposed
to make herself, as well as others, uncomfortable.
There was evidently something on her mind from
her glancing so often and nervously at the door.
It opened at last softly, just as Cecil had finished
" The Swallow," and revealed Mr. Fullarton standing on the threshold. The latter was not well
pleased with the scene before him. There was an
air of comfort about it which, under the circumstances, he thought decidedly wrong; besides
which he could not get rid of a vague misgiving
(the rarest thing with him!) that his visit was
scarcely welcome or well-timed.

Miss Tresilayn rose instantly to greet the intruder
(yes, that's the right word) with her usual calm
courtesy. Very few words had been exchanged
for the last hour, but she was perfectly aware—
what woman is not?—of the influence she had
exercised over her listener. That consciousness

had made her strangely happy. So, *she* certainly could have survived the Chaplain's absence. Royston Keene rose too, quite slowly. There are compounds, you know, that always remain soft and ductile in a certain temperature, but harden into stone at the first contact with the outer air. It was just so with him. Even as he moved, all gentle feelings were struck dead in his heart, and he stood up a harder man than ever, with no kinder emotion left than bitter anger at the interruption. He could not always command his eyes, he knew; and if he had not passed his hand quickly over his face just then, their expression might have thrilled through the new comer disagreeably.

" Cecil, dearest," Mrs. Danvers said, with rather an awkward assumption of being perfectly at her ease, " Mr. Fullarton was good enough to say he would come and read to us this evening, and explain some passages. I don't know why I forgot to tell you. I meant to do so; but—" Her look finished the sentence. Royston, like the others, guessed what she meant; and *you* may guess how he thanked her.

Cecil coloured with vexation. She was so anxious to prevent Mrs. Danvers from feeling dependent that she allowed her to take all sorts of liberties, and the amiable woman was not disposed to let the privilege fall into disuse. On the present occasion there was such an absurd incongruity of time and place, that she might possibly have tried to evade the "exposition," but she happened just then to meet Keene's eye. The sarcasm there was not so carefully veiled as it usually was in her presence. Never yet was born Tresilyan who blenched from a challenge: so she answered at once, to express "her sense of Mr. Fullarton's kindness, and her regret that he had not come earlier in tho evening." If Royston had known how bitterly she despised herself for disingenuousness he would have been amply avenged.

Even while she was speaking he closed the piano very slowly and softly. It did not take him long to put on his impenetrable face, for when he turned round there was not a trace of anger there; the scarce suppressed taunt in Cecil's last words, moved him apparently no more than Mrs. Danvers's glance of triumph.

"I owe you a thousand apologies," he said, "for staying such an unwarrantable time, and quite as many thanks for the pleasantest two hours I have spent in Dorade. Don't think I would detain you one moment from Mr. Fullarton and your devotional exercises. You know—no, you *don't* know—the verse in the ballad:

> Amundeville may be lord by day,
> But the monk is lord by night;
> Nor wine nor wassail would stir a vassal
> To question that Friar's right."

He went away then without another word
beyond the ordinary adieu. Royston had a way
of repeating poetry peculiar to himself—rather
monotonous perhaps, but effective from the depth
and volume of his voice. You gained in rhythm
what you lost in rhyme. The sound seemed to
linger in their ears after he had closed the door.

As the echo of the firm strong footstep died
away, a virtuous indignation possessed the broad
visage of the divine.

"It is like Major Keene," said he, "to select
as his text-book the most godless work of the
satanic school; but I should have thought that
even he would have paused before venturing, in
this presence, on a quotation from *Don Juan.*"

At that awful word Mrs. Danvers gave a little
shriek, as if "a bee had stung her newly." Had
she been a Catholic she would have crossed herself
an indefinite number of times : will you be good
enough to imagine her protracted look of holy
horror ? Cecil's eyes were glittering with scornful
humour as she answered, very demurely,

"What an advantage it is to be a large general
reader ! It enables one to impart so much information. Now, Bessie and I should never have
guessed where those lines came from if you had
not enlightened us. They seemed harmless enough
in themselves; and Major Keene was considerate
enough to leave us in our ignorance. So Byron

comes within the scope of your studies, Mr.
Fullarton. I thought you seldom indulged in
such secular authors?"

The Chaplain was quite right in making his
reply inaudible: it would have been difficult to
find a perfectly satisfactory one. However, the
hour was late enough to excuse his beginning the
reading without further delay. It was *not* a
success. There was a stoppage somewhere in the
current of his mellifluous eloquence; and the exposition was concluded so soon, and indeed abruptly, that Mrs. Danvers retired to rest with a
feeling of disappointment and inanition, such as
one may have experienced when, expecting a
" sit-down " supper, we are obliged to content
ourselves with a meagrely-furnished *buffet*. For
some minutes after Mr. Fullarton had departed
Miss Tresilyan sat silent, leaning her head upon
her hand. At last she said,

" Bessie, dear, you know I would not interfere
with your comforts or your arrangements for the
world; but, the next time you wish to have a
repetition of this, would you be so very good as
to tell me beforehand? I think I shall spend
that evening with Fanny Molyneux. I do not
quite like it, and I am sure it does me no real
good."

She spoke so gently that Mrs. Danvers was going
to attempt one of her querulous remonstrances,

K

but she happened to look at the face of her patroness. It wore an expression not often seen there; but she was wise enough to interpret it aright, and to guess that she had gone far enough. It was ever a dangerous experiment to trifle with the Tresilyans, when their brows were bent. So she launched into some of her affectionate platitudes, and profuse excuses, and under cover of these retreated to her rest. It is a comfort to reflect that she slept very soundly, though she monopolized all the slumber that night that ought to have fallen to Cecil's share.

What did Royston Keene think of the events of the evening? As he went down the stairs I am afraid he cursed the Chaplain once heartily; but on the whole he was not dissatisfied. At all events, the short walk down to the club completely restored his *sang-froid*, and the last trace of vexation vanished as he entered the card-room, and saw the " light of battle " gleam on the haggard face of Armand de Châteaumesnil.

CHAPTER XI.

THERE was in Dorade a stout and meritorious elderly widow, who formed a sort of connecting link between the natives and the settlers. English by birth, she had married a Frenchman of fair family and fortune: so that her habits and sympathies attached themselves about equally to the two countries. You do not often find so good a specimen of the hybrid. She gave frequent little *soirées*, which were as pleasant and exciting as such assemblages of heterogeneous elements usually are; that is to say—very moderately so. The two streams flowed on in the same channel, without mingling, or losing their peculiar characteristics. I fancy the fault was most on our side.

We no longer, perhaps, parade Europe with "pride in our port, defiance in our eye;" but still, in our travels, we lose no opportunity of maintaining and asserting our well-beloved dignity, which, if rather a myth and vestige of the past at home, abroad—is a very stern reality. Have you not seen, at a crowded *table-d'hôte*, the British mother encompass her daughters with the

K 2

double bulwark of herself and their staid governess
on either flank, so as to avert the contamination
which must otherwise have certainly ensued from
the close proximity of a courteous white-bearded
Graf, or a *fringante* Vicomtesse whose eyes out-
shone her diamonds? May it ever remain so!
Each nation has its vanity and its own peculiar
glory, as it has its especial produce. O cotton-
mills of Manchester! envy not nor emulate the
velvet-looms of Genoa or Lyons: you are ten times
as useful, and a hundredfold more remunerating.
What matters it if Damascus guard jealously the
secret of her fragrant clouded steel, when Sheffield
can turn out efficient sword-blades at the rate of
a thousand per hour? *Suum cuique tribuito*. Let
others aspire to be popular: be it ours, to remain
irreproachably and unapproachably respectable.

So poor Mdme. de Verzenay's efforts to promote
an *entente cordiale* were lamentably foiled. When
the English mustered strong, they would immediately form themselves into a hollow square, the
weakest in the centre, and so defy the assaults of
the enemy. Now and then a daring Gaul would
attempt the adventure of the Enchanted Castle,
determined, if not to deliver the imprisoned
maidens, at least to enliven their solitude. See
how gaily and gallantly he starts, glancing a saucy
adieu to Adolphe and Eugène, who admire his
audacity, but augur ill for its success. *Allons, je*

me risque. *Montjoie St. Denis!* *France à la rescousse!* He winds, as it were, the bugle at the gate, with a well-turned compliment or a brilliant bit of *badinage.* Slowly the jealous valves unclose; he stands within the magic precinct — an eerie silence all around. Suppose that one of the Seven condescends to parley with him : she does so nervously and under protest, glancing ever over her shoulder, as if she expected the austere Fairy momentarily to appear; while her companions sit without winking or moving, cowering together like a covey of birds when the hawk is circling over the turnip-field. How can you expect a man to make himself agreeable under such appalling circumstances ? The heart of the adventurer sinks within him. Lo! there is a rustling of robes near; what if Calyba or Urganda were at hand ? *Fuyons!* And the knight-errant retreats, with drooping crest and smirched armour — a melancholy contrast to the *preux chevalier* who went forth but now chanting his war-song, conquering and to conquer. The remarks of the discomfited one, after such a failure, were, I fear, the reverse of complimentary; and the unpleasant word, *bégueule,* figured in them a great deal too often.

Cecil and Fanny Molyneux were certainly exceptions to the rule of unsociability ; but the general dulness of those *réunions* infected them, and made the atmosphere oppressive; it required a vast amount of leaven to make such a large heavy lump light or palatable. Beside, it is not pleasant to carry on a conversation with twenty or thirty people looking on and listening, as if it were some theatrical performance that they had paid money to see, and consequently had a right to criticise. The fair friends had held counsel together as to the expediency of gratifying others at a great expense to themselves on the present occasion, and had made their election—not to go.

Early the next morning, Miss Tresilyan encountered Keene : their conversation was very brief; but, just as he was quitting her, the latter remarked, in a matter-of-course way, " We shall meet this evening at Madame de Verzenay's ? "

She looked at him in some surprise ; for she knew he must have heard, from Mrs. Molyneux, of their intention to absent themselves. She told him as much.

" Ah! last night she did not mean to go," replied Royston; " but she changed her mind this morning, while I was with them. When I left them, ten minutes ago, there was a consultation going on with Harry as to what she should wear. I don't think it will last more than half an hour; and then she was coming to try to persuade you to keep her fickleness in countenance."

Now, the one point upon which Cecil had been most severe on *la mignonne,* was the way in

which the latter suffered herself to bo guided by
her husband's friend. It is strange, how prone
is the unconverted and unmated feminine nature
to instigate revolt against the Old Dominion;
never more so, than when the beautiful *Carbonara*
feels that its shadow is creeping fast over the
frontier of her own freedom. Nay, suppose the
conquest achieved, and that they themselves are
reduced to the veriest serfdom, none the less will
they strive to goad other hereditary bondswomen
into striking the blow. Is it not known that
steady old "machiners," broken for years to
double harness, will encourage and countenance
their "flippant" progeny in kicking over the
traces? How otherwise could the name of mother-
in-law, on the stage and in divers domestic circles,
have become a synonym for firebrand? Look at
your wife's maid, for instance. She will spend
two-thirds of her wages and the product of many
silk dresses ("scarcely soiled") in furnishing
that objectionable and disreputable suitor of hers
with funds for his extravagance. He has beggared
two or three of her acquaintance already, under
the same flimsy pretence of intended marriage
that scarcely deludes poor Abigail: she has sore
misgivings as to her own fate. Alternately he
bullies and cajoles; but all the while she knows
that he is lying, deliberately and incessantly: yet
she never remonstrates or complains. It is true

that, if you pass the door of her little room late
into the night, you will probably go to bed haunted
by the sound of low, dreary weeping. But it would
be worse than useless to argue with her about her
folly; she cherishes her noisome and ill-favoured
weed, as if it were the fairest of fragrant flowers,
and will not be persuaded to throw it aside. Well
—if you could listen to that same long-suffering
and soft-hearted young female, in her place in
the subterranean Upper House, when the conduct
of " Master " (especially as regards Foreign Affairs)
is being canvassed, the fluency and virulence of her
anathemas would almost take your breath away.
Even that dear old housekeeper — who nursed
you, and loves you better than any of her own
children—when she would suggest an excuse or
denial of the alleged peccadilloes, is borne away
and overwhelmed by the abusive torrent, and can
at last only grumble her dissent. Very few women,
of good birth and education, make *confidantes*
nowadays of their personal attendants; and the
race of " Miggs " is chiefly confined to the class in
which Dickens has placed it, if it is not extinct
utterly. But there is a season—while the brush
passes lightly and lingeringly over the long trailing
" back-hair "—when a hint, an allusion, or an
insinuation, cleverly placed, may go far towards
fanning into flame the embers of matrimonial
rebellion. I know no case where such serious

consequences may be produced, with so little danger of implication to the prime mover of the discontent, except it be the system of the patriotic and intrepid Mazzini. Many outbreaks, perhaps— quelled after much loss on both sides, in which the monarchy was only saved by the judicious expenditure of much *mitraille*—might have been traced to the covert influence of that mild-eyed, melancholy *camériste*.

Cecil, who was not exempt from these revolutionary tendencies, any more than from other weaknesses of her sex, was especially provoked by this fresh instance of Fanny's subordination.

" Mrs. Molyneux is perfectly at liberty to form her own plans," she said, very haughtily. " Beyond a certain point, I should no more dream of interfering with them than she would with mine. She is quite right to change her mind as often as she thinks proper; only in this instance I should have thought it was hardly worth while."

" Well," Keene answered, in his cool, slow way, " Mrs. Molyneux has got that unfortunate habit of consulting other people's wishes and convenience in preference to her own; it's very foolish and weak; but it is so confirmed, that I doubt even *your* being able to break her of it. This time I am sure you won't. It is a pity you are so determined on disappointing the public. I know of more than one person who has put off other engagements in anticipation of hearing you sing."

He was perfectly careless about provoking her now, or he would have been more cautious. That particular card was the very last in his hand to have played. Miss Tresilyan was goodnature itself, in placing her talents at the service of any man, woman, or child who could appreciate them. She would go through half her *répertoire* to amuse a sick friend any day; neither was she averse to displaying them before the world in general at proper seasons; but she liked the "boards" to be worthy of the prima donna, and had no idea of "starring it in the provinces." All the pride of her race gathered on her brow just then like a thunder-cloud, and her eyes flashed no summer lightning.

"Madame de Verzenay was wrong to advertise a performer who does not belong to her *troupe.* I hope the audience will be patient under their disappointment, and not break up the benches. If not, she must excuse herself as best she may. I have signed no engagement, so my conscience is clear. I certainly shall not go."

The bolt struck the granite fairly; but it did not shiver off one splinter, nor even leave a stain. Royston only remarked, "Then, for to-day, it is useless to say *au revoir;*" and so, raising his cap, passed on.

The poor *mignonne* had a very rough time of it soon afterwards. Cecil was morally and physically incapable of scolding any one; but she was very severe on the sin of vacillation, and yielding to unauthorized interference. The culprit did not attempt to justify herself; she only said—"They both wanted me to go so much, and I did not like to vex Harry." Then she began to coax and pet her monitress in the pretty, childish way which interfered so much with matronly dignity, till the latter was brought to think that she had been cruelly harsh and stern; at last she got so penitent that she offered to accompany her friend, and lend the light of her countenance to Madame de Verzenay. For this infirmity of purpose many female Dracos would have ordered her off to instant execution—very justly. That silly little Fanny only kissed her, and said "she was a dear, kind darling." What can you expect of such irreclaimably weak-minded offenders? They ought to be sentenced to six months' hard labour, supervised by Miss Martineau : perhaps even this would not work a permanent cure. Still, on The Tresilyan's part, it was an immense effort of self-denial. She was well aware how she laid herself open to Royston Keene's satire, and how unlikely he was, this time, to spare her. Only perfect trust, or perfect indifference, can make one careless about giving such a chance to a known bitter tongue.

However, having made up her mind to the self-immolation, she proceeded to consider how best she should adorn herself for the sacrifice. Others have done so in sadder seriousness. Doubtless, Curtius rode at his last leap without a speck on his burnished mail; purple and gold and gems flamed all round Sardanapalus when he fired the holocaust in Nineveh; even that miserable, dastardly Nero was solicitous about the marble fragments that were to line his felon's grave. So it befell that, on this particular evening, Cecil went through a very careful toilette, though it was as simple as usual; for the ultra-gorgeous style she utterly eschewed. The lilac trimmings of her dress broke the dead white sufficiently, but not glaringly, with the subdued effect of colour that you may see in a campanula. The *coiffure* was not decided on till several had been rejected. She chose at last a chaplet of those soft, silvery Venetian shells—such as her bridesmaids may have woven into the night of Amphitrite's hair when they crowned her Queen of the Mediterranean.

It was a very artistic picture. So Madame de Verzenay said, in the midst of a rather too rapturous greeting; so the Frenchmen thought, as a low murmur of admiration ran through their circle when she entered. Fanny, too, had her modest success. There were not wanting eyes, that turned for a moment from the brilliant beauty of her companion, to repose themselves on the sweet girlish face shaded by silky brown tresses, and on the perfect little figure, floating so lightly and gracefully along amidst its draperies of pale cloudy blue.

Miss Tresilyan felt that there might be *one* glance that it would be a trial to meet unconcernedly, and she had been schooling herself sedulously for the encounter. She might have spared herself some trouble; for Royston Keene was not there when they arrived. She knew that Mrs. Molyneux had told him of the change in their plans; but the latter did not choose to confess how she had been puzzled by the very peculiar smile with which the Major greeted the intelligence: it was the only notice he took of it. So the evening went on, with nothing to raise it above the dead level of average *soirées*. Cecil delayed going to the piano till she was ashamed of making more excuses, and was obliged to "execute herself" with the best grace she could manage. Even while she was singing, her glance turned more than once toward the door; but the stalwart figure, beside which all others seemed dwarfed and insignificant, never showed itself. It was clear *he* was not among those who had given up other engagements to hear her songs. If we have been at some trouble and mental expense in getting ourselves into any one frame of mind—whether it be enthusiasm, or self-control, or fortitude, or heroism—it is an undeniable nuisance to find out suddenly that there is to be no scope for its exercise.

Take a very practical instance. Here is Lieutenant-Colonel Asahel, ready on the ground; looking, as his conscience and his backers tell him, " as fine as a star, and fit to run for his life :" at the last moment his opponent pays forfeit. Just ascertain the sentiments of that gallant Fusilier. Does the result at all recompense him for the futile privations and wasted asceticism of those long weary months of training—when pastry was, as it were, an abomination unto him—when his lips kept themselves undefiled from driest champagne or soundest claret—when he fled, fast as Cinderella, from the pleasantest company, at the stroke of the midnight chimes ? Of course he feels deeply injured, and would have forgiven the absentee far more easily if the latter had beaten him fairly, on his merits, breasting the handkerchief first by half a dozen yards.

On this principle, Miss Tresilyan laboured all that evening under an impression that Keene had treated her very ill, and was prepared to resent it accordingly. Another there besides herself felt puzzled and uncomfortable. Harry Molyneux could not understand it at all. Royston had seemed so very anxious in the morning to induce Fanny to go—a proceeding which would probably involve the presence of her "inseparable;" and disinterested persuasion was by no means in the Cool Captain's line. So Harry went wandering about in a purposeless, disconsolate fashion for some time, till he found himself near Cecil. I fancy he had an indistinct idea that some apology was owing to her for his chief's unaccountable absence; at all events, he began to confide his misgivings on the subject, as soon as the men who surrounded her moved away. They soon did so; for The Tresilyan had a way, quite peculiar to herself, of conveying to those whom she wished to get rid of that their audience was ended, without speaking one word. There was a very unusual element of impatient pettishness in her reply.

"What a curious fascination Major Keene appears to exercise over his friends! I suppose you would think it quite wrong to be amused anywhere, unless he were present to sanction it. Do you become a free-agent again, when you are given up entirely to your own devices? And do *all* subalterns keep up that veneration for their senior officers after they have left the service? It seems to be carrying the *esprit de corps* rather far."

Harry laughed out his own musical laugh; even the imputation of dependency and helplessness, which is apt to ruffle most people, fell back harmlessly from his impenetrable good humour. "I dare say it does look very absurd. But you ought to have lived with him as long as I have done to understand how naturally Royston gains his influence, and makes us do what he chooses."

"Certainly I cannot understand it. The *pococurante* style is so very common just now that one gets rather tired of it. I do not like the affectation at all, but I dislike the reality still more. I believe it *is* a reality with Major Keene. I cannot fancy him betraying any unrestrained excitement, however strong the passion that moved him might be. You have never known him do so, now? Confess it!"

"Yes I have, once," he answered, gravely, "and I never wish to see it again."

Cecil always liked talking to Harry Molyneux. On the present occasion the mere sound of his voice seemed to go far towards soothing her irritation; many others have experienced the same effect from those kindly gentle tones. Perhaps, too, the subject had an interest for her that she would not own. "Would it tire you to tell me about it? I am not particularly curious, but I have been so much bored to-night that a very little would amuse me."

He hesitated for an instant. "It is not *that;* but I don't know if I am right in telling you. Perhaps you would not like him the better for it; though he could not help it. Shall I? Well, it was in the second of our Indian battles, and the first time we had really been under fire: before, it was only nominal. Wo had been sitting idle for two hours or more, watching the infantry and the gunners do their work; and right well they did it. The Sikhs were giving ground in all directions; but they began to gather again on our right, and at last we were told to send out three squadrons and break them at three different points. Keeno was in command of mine. I never saw him look so enchanted as he did when the orders came down. I heard the chief warning him to be cautious, not to go too far (for there was a good deal of broken ground ahead), but to wheel about as soon as we had got through their lines, and to fall back immediately on our position. Royston listened and saluted, but I know he didn't catch one word: he kept looking over his shoulder all the time the Colonel was speaking, as if he grudged every second. We were very soon off: and almost before I realized the situation, we were closing in on the enemy, wrapped up in our own dust and in their smoke, for the firing became heavy directly we got within range. Now, I don't think I ought to be telling you all this: it is not quite a woman's story."

"Please go on. I like it." How grandly it flashed up in her cheek as she spoke—the fiery Tresilyan blood that had boiled in the veins of so many brilliant soldiers, but through twenty generations had never cooled down enough to breed one statesman!

He had taken breath by this time. "I won't make it longer than I can help; but it is difficult to tell some things very briefly. It was my first real charge you know: I suppose every man's sensations are rather peculiar under such circumstances. I did not feel much alarmed—there wasn't time for that—but the smoke, and the noise, and the excitement, made me so dizzy that I could hardly sit straight in my saddle. When we got within a hundred and fifty yards of the Sikhs their fire began to tell. I heard a bubbling smothered sort of cry close behind me, and I looked back just in time to see a trooper fall forward over his horse's shoulder, shot through the throat. Several more were hit, and our fellows began to waver a little—not much. Just then Royston's voice broke in; it was so clear and strong that it set my nerves right directly, and the dizzy stifling feeling went away, as it might have done before a draught of fresh pure air. 'Close up there, the rear rank. Keep cool, men! Steady with your bridle-hands, and strike fairly with the edge. *Now!*'

"He was three lengths ahead of his squadron, and well in amongst the enemy, when that last word came out. It was sharp work while it lasted, for the Sikhs fought like wounded wild cats: one fixed his teeth in my boot, and was dragged there till my covering sergeant cut him loose; but we were soon through them. When we had wheeled, and were dressing into line, I caught sight of Keene's face. It was so changed that I should hardly have known it: every fibre was quivering with passion, and his eyes, I've not forgotten them yet. We ought to have fallen back immediately on our old ground, but it was so evident he did not mean this, that I ventured to suggest to him what our orders had been. I was not second in command; but, of my two seniors, one was helpless (the stupidest man you ever saw), and the other hard hit. Royston faced round on me with a savage oath—'How dare you interfere, sir! Are you in command of this squadron?' Then he turned to the troopers: 'Have you had half enough yet, men? *I haven't.*' I am very sure he had lost his head, or he would never have spoken to me so, still less have made that last appeal, for he was the strictest disciplinarian, and looked upon his men as the merest machines. It seemed as if the devil that possessed him had gone out into the others too, for they all shouted in reply—not a cheery honest hurrah! but a hoarse hungry roar, such as you hear in wild beasts' dens before feeding-time. An old troop-sergeant, a rigid pious Presbyterian, spoke for the rest, grinding and gnashing his teeth: " We'll follow the captain anywhere—follow him to hell! " (Harry's voice had all along been subdued, but it was almost a whisper now.) " I do hope those words were not reckoned against poor Donald

Macpherson ; for, when we got back, his was one
of thirteen empty saddles. So we broke up, and
went in again at the Sikhs, who were collecting
in black-looking knots and irregular squares all
round. It was an indescribable sort of a *mêlée*,
every man for himself, and—I dare not say—God
for us all. I suppose I was as bad as the rest when
once fairly launched, and we all thought we were
doing our duty; but I should not like to have so
many lives on my head and hand as Royston could
count that night. Remember, *we* suffered rather
severely.

" As we took up our position again I saw the
Colonel was not well pleased. He had little of the
romance of war about him, and did not understand
his officers acting much on their own discretion.
Without hearing the words, I could guess, from the
expression of his hard old face, that he came down
on the squadron-leader heavily. When I ranged
up by Keene's side soon afterwards, he looked up
at me absently. 'I was thinking,' he said (now,
one naturally expected a sentiment about the scene
we had just gone through, or a reflection on the in-
justice of chiefs in general)—'I was thinking—
what rubbish those army-cutlers sell, and call it a
sword-blade.' He held up a sort of apology for a
sabre, all notched and bent and blunted ; then he
began to inquire if I had been hit at all. I had
escaped with hardly a scratch ; but I saw an ugly

cut above his knee, and blood stealing down his bridle-arm. 'Bah! it's nothing,' Royston observed, answering the direction of my eyes; 'but —if the tulwar and the reprimand had both been sharper—confess, Hal, that this time, *Le jeu valait bien la chandelle?*'

"We never had a real rattling charge after that day, at least none exciting enough to warm him thoroughly. Now, I am very sorry I have told you all this : it is not a nice story ; but it is your own fault if I have bored you. Besides, Madame de Verzenay will never forgive me for monopolizing you so long. I do think she does me the honour to believe in a flirtation."

Cecil's heightened colour and sparkling eyes might have justified such a suspicion in a distant and unprejudiced observer. Does not this show us how very cautious we ought to be in forming hasty conclusions from appearances, which are proverbially deceptive ? I protest I am filled with remorse and contrition while I reflect how often, in thought, I may have wronged and misjudged the innocent. I dare say in many outwardly flagrant cases the offenders were only expatiating on the merits or demerits of absent friends. Such a subject is quite engrossing enough to excuse a certain amount of "sitting out," and some people *always* blush when they are at all interested. The selection of the staircase, the balcony, or the conservatory for the discussion is the merest atmospheric question. I subscribe to Mr. Weller's idea—only "turnips" are incredulous. *Vive la charité!*

After a minute or two Miss Tresilyan spoke : "No; I don't think worse of Major Keene. As you say, I suppose he could not help it; but it must be terrible, when passions that are habitually restrained do break loose. No wonder that you do not wish to see such a sight again. It is very different, reading of battles and hearing of them from one who was an actor. Do you know, I think you have an undeveloped talent for narration. There, that ought to console you, even if Madame de Verzenay should asperse your character."

At this moment Harry was contemplating the proceedings of his pretty little wife at the opposite side of the room, with an intense satisfaction and pride.

"If I *had* yielded to temptation," he said, "I am sure Fan could not reproach me. She would keep a much greater sinner in countenance. Miss Myrtle is a thousand times worse since she married. Just remark that byplay with the handkerchief. You don't suppose M. de Riberac cares one straw about Valenciennes lace? It makes one feel *Moorish* all over. You need not be surprised if she is found smothered or strangled in the morning. I am 'not easily moved to jealousy, but being moved——' "

"Don't be too murderous," laughed Cecil; "you

are certain to regret it afterwards. We will reproach her as she deserves on our way home. Is it not very late?"

She wanted to be alone, to think over what she had heard; and in good truth, waking or sleeping, the watches of that night were crowded with dreams.

All this time, where was Royston Keene? He had been really anxious to induce Miss Tresilyan to present herself at Madame de Verzenay's, for he liked her well enough already to feel a personal interest in her triumphs: but after their interview in the morning (though he thought it probable that Fanny's persuasive powers might prevail), he had determined himself not to go; and he did not change his resolutions lightly. Still, he could not resist the temptation of getting one glimpse at her in " review order." If Cecil had been very observant when she went down to her carriage, she must have noticed a tall figure standing back, half masked by a pillar, whose eyes literally flashed in the darkness as they fastened on her in her passage through the lighted hall, and drank in every item of her loveliness. He stood still for some moments after she was gone, and then walked slowly down to the Cercle. While they were talking about him at Madame de Verzenay's, Royston was holding his own gallantly at *écarté* with Armand de Châteaumesnil, for the honour of England and—ten napo-

leons aside. As was his wont, he played superbly;
but he spoke seldom, and hardly seemed to hear
the comments of the crowded *galerie*. In truth, at
some most critical points—when the game was in
abeyance at *quatre à*—a delicate proud face, and a
shell wreath glistening in velvet hair, *would* rise
before him, and dethrone, in his thoughts, the
painted kings and queens. His adversary did not
fail to observe this; but he said nothing till the
play was ended, and most of the others had left the
room. Then he laid his hand on Keene's arm, and
drew his head down to the level of his own lips,
and spoke low:—

"Mon camarade, je me rappelle, d'avoir vu, il y
a quelques ans, au Café de la Régence, un homme
qui tenait tête, aux échecs, à quatre concurrens.
Les habitués en disaient des merveilles. Mais ce
n'était qu'un bon bourgeois après tout; et, nous
autres, nous sommes plus forts que les bourgeois.
Vous avez joué ce soir les deux parties que, dit le
proverbe, c'est presque impossible de remporter
simultanément; et je ne me tiens pas pour le seul
perdant."

Royston did not seem in the least inclined to
smile; had he done so, Armand would have been
bitterly disappointed. As it was, he answered very
coldly, without a shade of consciousness on his
face,

"Un compliment mérite toujours des remer-

cîmens, M. le Vicomte, même quand on ne le com-
prend pas. Pardon, si je vous engage, de ne pas
expliquer plus clairement vôtre allégorie."

The other looked up at him with an expression
that might almost have been mistaken for
sympathy.

" Parbleu ! " he muttered, " si beau joueur mérite
bien de gagner ! "

CHAPTER XII.

SOMETIMES, lying on the cliffs of Kerry or Clare, on a cloudless autumn day, when not a breath of wind is stirring, you may see rank after rank of heavy purple billows rolling sullenly in from the offing : these are messengers coming to tell us of battles fought a thousand leagues to the westward, in which they too have borne their part. Before the mail comes in we are prepared to hear of a storm that has worked its wicked will for nights and days, thundering among the granite boulders of Labrador, or tearing through the fog banks of Newfoundland. This is perhaps the most common-place of all ancient comparisons ; but where will you find so apt a parallel for the vagaries of the human heart as the phases of the deep, false, beautiful sea?

On the morning after Madame de Verzenay's party, Cecil rose in a very troubled frame of mind. She had no feeling of irritation left against Royston Keene; but she was uneasy and uncomfortable, and loth to meet him. What she had felt, and what she had heard, had moved her too deeply for her to resume at once her wonted composure. So it was

that sho accepted very readily an invitation from
Mrs. Fullarton to accompany herself and children
on a mild botanizing excursion among the hills.
These small *fêtes* went a long way with that hard-
working and meritorious woman; what with anticipation and retrospect, each lasted her about two
months. Miss Tresilyan was prevented from starting with the rest of tho party; but tho Chaplain
himself was to escort her to the placo of rendezvous; his little daughter, Katie, being retained, to
bo invested with the temporary and local rank of
chaperone—a formality which, in these days of
scanty faith, even married divines are not allowed
to dispense with. The quartette was completed by
the mule-driver—ono of those remarkable boys who
converse invariably in a tongue which the beasts of
burden seem to understand and sympathize with,
but which, to any other creature whatsoever, is
absolutely destitute of meaning. They had some
way to go; so Cecil had taken up Katie before her
on her mule; the Pastor walked by her side,
glozing (for tho road was not very steep) on all
sorts of subjects, gravely and smoothly, as was his
wont. They had crossed the first line of hills, and
were descending into the valley beyond, when,
turning a sharp corner, where a projecting rock
almost barred the path, they camo suddenly on
Royston Keene. He was lying at full length; his
head resting against the knotted root of an olive,

with eyes half closed, and the cigar between his lips that seldom left them when he was alone. It *was* odd that he should have selected that especial spot for the scene of his *siesta*. Cecil did her very utmost to look unconcerned : it was too provoking that she could not help blushing ! Mr. Fullarton evidently looked upon it in the light of an ambush. Had he ventured to give his thoughts utterance, certainly the ready text would have sprung to his lips—" Hast thou found me, O mine enemy ? " If there was " malice prepense " there, the " enemy " deserved some credit for the perfectly natural air of surprise with which he rose and greeted them.

" Are you recruiting after last night's triumphs, or escaping from popular enthusiasm, Miss Tresilyan ? I have met several Frenchmen already who are quite childish about your singing. I should not advise you to venture on the Terrace to-day. There might be temptations to vanity, which Mr. Fullarton will tell you are dangerous."

She had so completely made up her mind to some allusion to her change of purpose, or to his own absence, that it was rather aggravating to find him ignore both utterly. But she rallied well.

" Nothing half so imaginative, Major Keene. It was a very stupid party, and I only sang once; as, I dare say, you have heard. We are only going to help Mrs. Fullarton to find some wild-flowers. I hope you have not anticipated us ? "

He *fixed* her with the cool penetrative look that was harder to meet than even his sneer.

"No; the flowers are safe from me. I don't care enough about them to keep them; and it is a pity to pick them and throw them away to wither. But I would have asked to be allowed to help you in your search, only—I don't like to spoil a picture. You brought a very good one to my mind as you turned the corner—a 'Descent into Egypt' that I saw long ago. The blot *there*, I remember, was a very stout rubicund Joseph, not at all worthy of the imperial Madonna."

While he was speaking he drew back, and leant lazily against the stem of the olive, with the evident intention of resuming his original posture as soon as courtesy would allow. Miss Tresilyan could not restrain a quick gesture of impatience.

"As we did not come out to *poser*, Mr. Fullarton, don't you think we had better not delay any longer? We are so late already, that I am sure the rest of the party will be tired of waiting."

Guess if her companion was loth to obey her.

They moved on for some time almost in silence. Cecil's thoughts were busy with a picture, too—not the less vivid because only her own imagination had painted it. Her deep dreamy eyes passed over the landscape actually before them without catching one of its details : they were looking on a desolate stony plain, cracked and calcined by a

fierce Indian sun—a few plumy palms in the background, and the rocky bed of a river half dried up
—in the foreground a crowd of wild barbaric sol-
diery, with savage swarthy features, bareheaded or
white-turbaned; mingled with these were horsemen
in the uniform of our light dragoons, sabring right
and left mercilessly. In the very centre of the
mêlée was one figure round which all the others
seemed to group themselves as mere accessories.
She saw, very distinctly, the dark, determined face,
set, every line of it, in an unspeakable ferocity,
with a world of murderous meaning in the gleaming
eyes—so distinctly that it drove out the remem-
brance of the same man's face, expressive of
nothing but passionless indifference, though she
looked upon it but a few minutes since under the
grey branch of the olive. She almost heard his
clear imperious tones, cheering on and rallying his
troopers, when a ruder voice broke her reverie.

"*Halte là !*"

If there was one thing that miserable muleteer-
boy ought to have known better than another, it
was the insuperable objection entertained by the
Provençal peasant to anything like trespass on his
territory (the touchiness of the *propriétaire* bears
generally an inverse ratio to the extent of his possessions); yet, to make a short cut of about two
hundred yards, he had led his party through a gap
in the low stone wall over a strip of ground belong-

ing to the very man who was least likely to over-look the intrusion. Jean Duchesne had a bad name in the neighbourhood, and deserved it thoroughly; he was surly enough when sober (which was the exception), but when drunk there were no bounds to his blind, brutish ferocity, and his great personal strength made him a formidable antagonist. He was not an agreeable object to contemplate, that gaunt giant, as he stood there in his squalid, tattered dress, with rough matted hair, and face flushed by recent intemperance, and flecked with livid stains of past debauches. You may see many such, crowding round the guillotine or the tumbril, in pictures of the French Revolution.

It is very odd that one cannot write or read those two words without a boiling of the blood, a tingling at the fingers' ends, and a tightening of the muscles of the forearm—ineffably absurd when excited by a recollection seventy years old! Yet so it is. You may talk of oppression till you are tired; you may catalogue all the wrongs that *Jacques Bonhomme* endured before his day of re-taliation came; you may bring in your pet illus-tration of "the storm that was necessary to clear the atmosphere;" but you will never make some of us feel that the guilt of an Order—had it been blacker by a hundred shades—palliated the Mas-sacre of its Innocents. If the *Marquis* and

Mousquetaire only had suffered, they might have laid down their lives cheerfully, as they would have done the stake of any other lost game; and, as for the priests, it was their privilege to be martyrs. But think of those fair matrons, and gentle girls, and delicate *mignonnes,* that had been petted from their childhood, cooped up in the foul courts of the Abbaye and La Force, with even the necessaries of life begrudged them, till the light died in their eyes and the gloss faded from their tresses; and then brought out to die in the chill, misty *Brumaire* morning, howled at and derided by the swarm of blood-suckers, till they cowered down, not in fear, but sickening horror, welcoming Samson and his satellites as friends and saviours. Remember, too, that there was scarcely an exception to the rule of patient courage, calm self-sacrifice, and pride of birth that never belied itself. Dubarry might shriek on the scaffold, but the Rohans died mute. Reading of the atrocities of the Jacquerie, we have at least this consolation—that the savage peasants were slaughtered like wild swine by the good lances of the Count de Foix, from noon till the sun went down on a long summer's day; but that accursed *canaille* of '89 paid no penalty that we know of. Of course we all agree with the claptrap of the stage-sailor, that nothing can be too bad for the man who would strike a woman under any circumstances

(will the policemen of Ratcliff Highway endorse it?)
—but this scarcely applies when we think that five
years out of the middle of one's life would not
have been a high price to pay for the privilege of
riding straight down on a crowd of the *dames de la
halle* and their bullies, with a hundred troopers at
our back who could give point and edge fairly.
The word for the day should have been "Lam-
balle" and under such circumstances, Mr. Carlyle,
we might have dispensed with the Hammer of
Thor.

Of all the digressions we have indulged in, this
is perhaps the most unwarrantable; and though it
has relieved me unspeakably, I hereby tender a
certain amount of contrition for the same. *Revenons
à nos moutons*—though there was very little of the
sheep in the appearance of Jean Duchesne, whose
demeanour (when we left him) you will recollect
was decidedly aggressive. It was evident that the
mule-boy thought mischief was brewing, for he
twisted his features—irregular and tumbled enough
already—into divers remarkable contortions expressive of remorse and terror.

"Who, then, dares to trespass on my lands? Do
you think we sow our crops for your cursed mules
to trample on?"

He spoke in a hoarse thick voice (suggestive of
spirituous liquors), and in the disagreeable Provençal dialect, which must have altered strangely since

M

the time of the *troubadours:* brief as his speech
was, it found room for more than one of those ex-
pletives which are nowhere so horribly blasphemous
as in the south of France.

Cecil had started slightly at the first interjection,
which broke her day-dream, but she was not other-
wised alarmed or discomposed: she seemed to
regard the *propriétaire* simply as an unpleasant
obstacle to their progress, and glanced at Mr
Fullarton, as if she expected him to clear it away.
The latter was not good at French, but he did
manage to express their sorrow, if they had done
any harm unconsciously, and their wish to retire
instantly. "Not before paying," was the reply.
" Quinze francs de dedommagemens; et puis, filex
aux tous les diables ! "

Women are not expected to carry purses, or any
other objects of simple utility; but why, Mr. Fullarton should have left his at home on this particular
day is between himself and his own conscience.
The party very soon realized the fact that they
could muster about a hundred and fifty centimes
among them.

Even kings and kaisers, when *incogniti*, have
ere this been reduced to the extremest straits of
ignominy from the want of a few available pieces
of silver; and in ordinary life, five shillings, ready
at the moment, are frequently of more importance
than as many hundreds in expectancy. There lives

even now a man who missed the most charming
rendezvous with which fortune ever favoured him,
because he rode a mile round to avoid a turnpike,
not having wherewithal to pay it. Since that disas-
trous day he is ever furnished with such a weight
of small change that, had Cola Pesce carried it, the
strong swimmer must have sunk like a stone—in
penance, probably, even as James of Scotland wore
the iron belt. At a pause in the conversation you
may hear him rattling the coppers in his pocket
moodily, as the spectres in old romances rattle
their chains; but his remorse is unavailing. A
fair chance once lost, Whist and Erycina never
forgive. The beautiful bird, that might *then* have
been limed and tamed, shook her wings and flew
away exultingly : far up in air the unlucky fowler
may still sometimes hear her clear mocking carol,
but she is too near heaven for his arts to reach,
and has escaped the toils for ever.

On the present occasion Katie Fullarton " flashed "
her one half-franc with great courage and confidence; but the display of all that small capitalist's
worldly wealth did not mollify Jean Duchesne. He
had been lashing himself up, all along, into such
a state of brutal ferocity, that he would have been
disappointed if his extortion had been immediately
satisfied ; so he broke in savagely on the Chaplain's
confused excuses and promises to settle everything
at a fitting season :

"Tais toi, blagueur! On ne me flone pas ainsi avec des promesses; je m'en fiche pas mal. Au moins, on me laissera un gage."

His bloodshot eyes roved from one object to another, till they lighted on the parasol that Miss Tresilyan carried: it was of plain dark grey silk, with a slight black lace trimming, but the carvings of the ivory handle made it of some real value. Before any one could divine his intention he had plucked it rudely from her hand.

Almost with the same motion, Cecil set Katie down, and sprang herself from the saddle. In her eyes there was such intensity of anger that the drunken savage recoiled a pace or two, and for the first time in his life felt something like self-contempt: to have saved her soul she could not have spoken one word, but her silence was expressive enough as she turned to Mr. Fullarton. It is difficult to say what line she expected him to take—not the voie de fait, certainly; at least, if the hypothesis had been put to her when she was cool enough to consider it, she would utterly have repudiated such an idea. Perhaps she had a right to look for moral support if not for active championship.

We will not enter into the vexed question of physical courage and cowardice: it is a truism to say that the latter may co-exist with great moral firmness, which is, of course, far the superior

quality. They will tell you that, when confronted
with mere personal peril, a butcher, or grenadier
may match the best of us. Possibly: I am not
going to dispute it. Only remember that there are
occasions (very few in these civilized days) when
the most refined of *bas-bleus* would rather see a
strong, brave, honest man at her side, than an ab-
struse philosopher, a clever conversationalist—ay,
even than a perfect Christian whose nerves are
not to be depended on; when Parson Adams would
be worth a bench of Bishops. We cannot all be
athletes; and, with the best intentions, some of us
at such times are liable to defeat and discomfiture.
The most utterly fearless man I ever knew, had a
biceps that his own small fingers could have spanned.
No woman, however keeping the attributes of her
sex would think the worse of her champion for
being trampled under foot, when he had done his
best to defend her. You know, their province is to
console, and even pet the vanquished: they make
up lint for the wounded as readily as they weave
laurels for the conquerors. But when they have
once seen a man play the coward, the silver tongue,
with all its eloquent explanation and honeyed
pleadings, will hardly banish from their eyes the
peculiar expression, wavering betwixt compassion
and contempt. They may forgive cruelty, or insolence, or even treachery—in time; but they can
find no palliation, and little sympathy, for that one

unpardonable sin. Truly, transgression in this line, beyond a certain point, may scarcely be excused; for weakness may be controlled, if not cured : if we cannot be dashingly courageous, we may at least be decently collected : not all may aspire to the cross of Valour; but it is not difficult to steer clear of courts-martial.

A man is not pleasant to contemplate when terror has driven out all self-command; so we will not draw Mr. Fullarton's picture : he could scarcely stammer out words enough to suggest an immediate retreat. It was painful—*not* ludicrous—to see how justly his own child appreciated the position : the little thing left her father's side instinctively, and clung for protection to Cecil Tresilyan. The latter saw instantly how matters stood; and if the glance she cast on the aggressor was not pleasant to meet, far more unendurable was that which fell upon her unlucky companion : it was piercing enough to penetrate the armour of his wonderful self-complacency, and to rankle for many a day. She struck her small foot on the ground, with a gesture of imperial disdain. Even so the Scythian Amazon might have spurned the livid head of Cyrus the Great King.

" I will not stir, till I see if no one will come who can take my part. Ah—I would give——"

" Don't be rash, Miss Tresilyan. You might be taken at your word."

Cecil turned quickly, with a delicious sense of confidence and triumph thrilling through every fibre of her frame: on the top of the rock that rose ten feet high, like a wall, on the right, stood Royston Keene. A more pacific character would have dared a greater danger for the reward and the promise of her eyes.

He took in the whole scene at a glance (perhaps he had heard more than he chose to own), and swinging himself lightly down, strode right across the *potager* with a disregard of the proprietor's interests and feelings, refreshing to see.

"It seems to me that the ancient positions have been reversed. You have been spoiled by the Egyptians, Miss Tresilyan. Shall we try the secular arm? You have scarcely been safe under the protection of the church—*militant.*"

There was a pause before the last word, and it was unpleasantly emphasized. Then he advanced a step or two towards the Frenchman, without waiting for a reply, and spoke in a totally different tone—brief and imperative,—"Tu vas me rendre ça?"

Duchesne had been rather startled by the apparition of the new-comer, and if he had been cool enough to reflect, would not have fancied him as an antagonist; but his passion blinded him, and strong drink had heated his brutal blood above boiling point; he ground his teeth, as he answered, till the foam ran down—

"Le rendre—à toi—chien d'Anglais? je m'en garderai bien. Si la belle demoiselle veut le ravoir, elle viendra demain, me prier bien gentiment; et elle viendra—seule."

Now, Royston Keene was thoroughly impregnated with the bitterest of aristocratic prejudices : no man alive more utterly ignored the doctrines of liberty, equality, and fraternity; besides this, he had acquired, to an unusual extent, the overbearing tone and demeanour, which the habit of having soldiers under them is supposed to bring, too commonly, to modern centurions. He actually experienced a "fresh sensation" as he heard the insult levelled by those coarse plebeian lips at the woman he delighted to honour. His swarthy face grew white down to the lips, whose quivering the heavy moustache could not quite conceal ; and he shivered from head to foot where he stood. Jean Duchesne thought he detected the familiar signs of a terror he had often inspired.

"Tu as puer donc ? Tu tressailles déjà, blanc-bec ! Tonnerre de Di ! tu as raison."

Not a trace of passion lingered in the Major's clear cold voice, that fell upon the ear with the ring of steel.

"On ne tressaille pas quand on est sur de agner. Regarde donc en arrière."

Involuntarily the Frenchman looked behind him, expecting a fresh adversary from that quarter. As he turned his head, Keene sprang forward, and plucked the parasol from his grasp; in one second he had laid it lightly in its owner's hand; in the next, he had returned to his position, and stood, ready for the onset, motionless as the marble Creugas.

He had not long to wait. Even a well-conditioned Gaul does not like being outwitted; and the successful *ruse* exasperated Duchesne into insanity. Roaring like a wild beast that had missed its spring, he rushed in to grapple. Royston never moved a finger till the enemy was well within distance; then, slinging his left hand straight out from the hip, he let him have it, fairly between the eyes.

One blow—only one—but a blow that, had it been struck in the days of Olympian and Nemean contests—where Pindar and his peers were reporters—might well have earned a Dithyramb; a blow that would have gladdened the sullen spirit of the old gladiator who trained the Cool Captain, if the prophet had lived to see his auguries fulfilled; or if sights and sounds from upper earth could penetrate to the limbo of defunct athletæ. Nothing born of woman could have stood before it; and it was small blame to Jean Duchesne that he dropped like a log in his tracks. In another instant his conqueror had one knee on the chest of the fallen man, and both hands were griping his throat.

His own face was fearfully changed. It wore an expression that has been very often seen in the sixty centuries that have passed since Cain struck his brother down, but has very seldom been described; for the dead tell no tales beyond what their features, stiffened in hopeless terror, may betray. It has been seen on lost battle-fields—in the streets of cities given up to pillage, when the storming is just over, and the carnage begun— on desolate hill-sides—in dark forest-glades—in chambers of lonely houses, strongly but vainly barred—in every place where men in the death-agony have " cried and there was none to help them." It was full time for some one to interfere, when the devil had entered into Royston Keene.

From the moment that affairs had assumed such a different aspect, Mr. Fullarton had gradually been recovering his composure, and by this time was quite himself again. He advanced confidently, and, laying his hand on the Major's shoulder, with an imposing air, and with his best pulpit manner, enunciated, " Thou shalt do no murder ! " The latter, as we have already said, was utterly beside himself; but even this cannot excuse the abrupt, impatient movement that sent such an eminent divine reeling three paces back. The rigid lips only twisted themselves into an evil sneer, and the cruel fingers tightened their gripe, till the features of the prostrate wretch grew convulsed and black.

The whole scene had passed so quickly, though it takes so long to describe (some of us never *can* succeed in stenography), that Cecil felt perfectly lost in a whirl of conflicting emotions, till she saw the face in life before her, that she had been fancying ever since last night. A great fear came over her, but she overcame it, and her woman's instinct told her what to do. She laid her little hand upon Keene's arm before he was aware that she was near, and whispered so that only he could hear, "For *my* sake." Only these three simple words; but the exorcism was complete.

Again a shiver ran all through the hardy frame; and for once Love was more powerful than Hate. He loosed his hold—slowly though, and reluctantly —and rose to his feet, passing his hand over his eyes in a strange, bewildered way; but in five seconds his wonderful self-command asserted itself, and he spoke as coolly as ever.

"A thousand pardons. One does forget one's self sometimes, when the *canaille* are provoking; but I ought to have remembered what was due to *you*."

Though she could not speak, she tried to smile; but strong reaction had come on. In the pale woman that trembled so painfully, it was hard to recognise proud Cecil Tresilyan. Royston was

watching her narrowly; and his tone softened
till it made his simple words a caress.

"Don't make me more angry with myself than
I deserve. Indeed, there is nothing more to alarm
or distress you. If you would only forgive me!"
He helped her into the saddle as he spoke, and she
submitted passively. But the happy feeling of
perfect trust in him was coming back fast.

Jean Duchesne had somewhat recovered from
his stupor, and was leaning on one arm, panting
heavily, still in great pain; but he was inured to
all sorts of broils, and evidently would soon recover from the effects of this one, though he had
never been so roughly handled. It was sheer
terror that made him lie so still; he dared move
no more than a whipped hound while in the presence
of his late opponent.

The others turned slowly homewards; for it is
needless to say the wild-flowers and the rendezvous
were forgotten. As they turned the corner which
cut off the view of Duchesne's ground, Royston
looked back once, longingly. It was well for
Cecil's nerves, in their disturbed state, that she
did not catch that Parthian glance. Ah! those
ungovernable eyes! They were gleaming with the
expression that Kirkpatrick's may have worn—
when he turned into the chapel where the Red
Comyn lay—growling "I mak sicker."

None of the party were much disposed for con-

versation; for even Mr. Fullarton did not feel equal
to "improving the occasion" just then. Cecil
broke the silence at last; it was where the road
was so narrow that only two could walk abreast;
Royston never left her bridle-rein.

"You must fancy that I have thanked you: I
cannot do so properly now. It is strange, though,
that you should have come up so very opportunely
Was it a presentiment that made you follow us?"

The answer was so low that she had almost to
guess at it from the motion of his lips—"Have
you forgotten Napoleon's last rallying-cry—' Qui
m' aime me suit?'"

No wonder that his pulse should throb ex-
ultantly, as he saw the bright beautiful blush
that swept over his companion's cheek and brow!
They had almost reached home when he spoke
again,

"You would have been liberal in your promises
twenty minutes ago if I had not stopped you, Miss
Tresilyan. I *should* like to have some memorial of
to-day. Very childish, is it not? Will you give
me *this*? I deserve something for saving—that
pretty parasol."

He touched the glove she had just drawn off—
a light riding-gauntlet, fancifully cut, and em-
broidered with silk. Cecil hesitated, though she
would have been loth to refuse him anything just
then. She felt, as most proud, sensitive women

feel, the first time they are asked for what may be interpreted into a *gage d'amour.* The tribute may be nominal, and the suzerain may be lenient indeed; but none the less does it establish vassalage.

Royston interpreted her reluctance aright, and went on, with an earnestness very unusual with him : for once it was honest and true : " Pray trust me. The moment I cease to value that *souvenir* as it deserves, on my honour I will return it."

He was fated to triumph all through that day. When Cecil was alone she put something away with a very unnecessary carefulness; for surely nothing can be more valueless than a glove that has lost its mate.

CHAPTER XIII.

I AM almost ashamed to confess how deeply the scene she had witnessed affected Cecil Tresilyan. The exhibition of Keene's fierce temper ought certainly to have warned if it did not disgust her. She could only think—"It was for my sake that he was so angry; and he yielded to my first word."

There is rather a heavy run just now against the "physical force" doctrine. It seems to me that some of its opponents are somewhat hypercritical. For many, many years, romancists persisted in attributing to their principal heroes every point of bodily perfection and accomplishment; no one thought then of caviling at such a well-understood and established type. That most fertile and meritorious of writers, for instance, Mr. G. P. R. James, invariably makes his *jeun premier* at least moderately athletic: so much so, that when he has the villain of the tale at his sword's-point, we feel a comfortable confidence that virtue will triumph as it deserves. As such a contingency is certain to occur twice or thrice in the course of the narrative, a nervous reader is spared much anxiety and trouble of mind by this satisfactory arrangement. *Nous avons changé tout cela.* Modern refinement requires that the chief character shall be made interesting in spite of his being dwarfish, plain-featured, and a victim to pulmonary or some more prosaic disease. Clearly we are right. What is the use of advancing civilization if it does not correct our taste? What have we to do with the manners and customs of the English in the eighteenth century, or with the fictions that beguiled our boyhood? Let our motto still be "Forward;" we have pleasures of which our grandsires never dreamt, and inventions that they were inexcusable in ignoring. We are so great that we can afford to be generous. Let them sleep well, those honest but benighted Ancients, who went down to their graves unconscious of "Aunt Sally," and perhaps never properly appreciated caviare!

It is true that there are some writers—not the weakest—who still cling to the old-fashioned mould. Putting Lancelot and Amyas out of the question—I think I would sooner have stood up to most heroes of romance than to sturdy Adam Bede. It can't be a question of religion or morality: for "muscular *Christianity*" is the stock-sarcasm of the opposite party; it must be a question of good taste. Well, ancient Greece is supposed to have had some floating ideas on *that* subject; and she deified Strength. It is perfectly true, that to thrash a prize-fighter unnecessarily, is not a virtuous or glorious action; but I contend that the *capability* of doing so is an admirable and enviable attribute. There are grades of physical as well as of moral perfection; and, after all, the same Hand created both.

Have I been replying against the critics? *Absit omen!* They are more often right, I fear, than authors are willing to allow; for it *is* aggravating to have one's pet bits of pathos put between inverted commas for the world in general to make a mock at (we could hardly write them down without tears in our eyes), and to have our story condensed into a few clever pithy sentences (all in the present tense), till its weakness becomes painfully apparent. More than this, our candid friends are impalpable. Real life can furnish us with enough substantial opponents for us not to trouble ourselves about Junius. Neither in war nor love is it expedient to grasp at shadows? Ah! Mr. Reade, why were you not warned by Ixion?

One thing is certain: however sound your arguments in depreciation of personal prowess may be, you will never gain a unanimous feminine verdict. It must be an extraordinary exhibition of mental excellence that will really interest the generality of our sisters, for the moment, as deeply as a very ordinary feat of strength or skill. It is

N

not that they cannot thoroughly appreciate rectitude of feeling, brilliancy of conversation, and
distinguished talent; but remember the hackneyed
quotation—

> Segnius irritant animum demissa per aures
> Quam quæ sunt oculis subjecta fidelibus.

If you want a proof of the correctness of Horace's
opinion, go up to " Lord's " this month, and
watch the flutter among the fair spectaters, just
after a " forward drive " over the Pavilion ; or
better still, the next time the " Grand Military "
comes off at Warwick, mark the reception that the
man who rides a winner will meet with in the
Stand. Conventionality has done a good deal,
but it has not refined away all the frank, impulsive
woman-nature yet. The knights are dust, and
their good swords rust ; but dame and demoiselle
are very much the same as they were in the old.
days, when the Queen of Scots could sing—

> How they revelled thro' the summer night,
>   And by day made lanceshafts flee,
> For Mary Beatoun, and Mary Seatoun,
>   And Mary Fleming, and me.

Will this long, and rather rash *tirade* in the
least excuse Cecil Tresilyan ? Of course not. My
poor heroine ! It was very unnecessary—that

advertisement that she was not superior to the weaknesses of her sex; for it seems to me, with every chapter, she has been growing more fallible and frail. She was utterly incapable of being at all demonstrative or "gushing;" but her preference for Royston Keene was now quite undisguised.

Mrs. Danvers was bitterly exasperated. It would be unjust to deny that she was greatly actuated by a sincere interest in her *ci-devant* pupil's welfare; but other feelings were at work.

It is very remarkable how a perfectly well-principled woman will connive at what she cannot approve, so long as she is taken unreservedly into confidence; but when once one secret is kept back, the danger of her antagonism begins: the magic draught that has lulled the vigilant Gryphon to sleep loses its potency; the guardian of the treasure awakes—more savage because conscious of a dereliction in duty—and woe to the Arimaspian! The cold, pale, chaste Moon comes forth from behind the cloud, determined to reveal every iota of transgression; no further chance of concealment here—*Reparat sua cornua Phœbe.*

So, to the utmost of her small powers, Bessie did endeavour to thwart and counteract the adversary. Her line was consistently plaintive. In season and out of season, she whined and wept profusely. This was the last resource of her simple strategy: when the enemy was getting too strong to be met in open field, she adopted the Dutch plan of opening the sluices and trying to drown him. It is painful to be obliged to state that the inundation did not greatly avail. As she had done from the first, Cecil declined to make any confidences, or indeed to discuss the question at all.

Mr. Fullarton, too, felt keenly the defection of a promising proselyte. Since that unfortunate afternoon, Miss Tresilyan had been perfectly civil, but always very cold; and he could not but be aware that he had lost ground then that he never could hope to regain. The divine must have been very desperate, when he ventured to attack that impracticable brother. It was not a judicious move; nor would any one have tried it who knew Dick Tresilyan. It was not only that he liked and admired Royston Keene, but he had a blind confidence in his sister that nothing on earth could disturb: the evidence of his own senses would not have affected it in the least. "Whatever *she* does is right," he thought; and he clung to that idea, as many other true believers will do to a creed that they cannot understand. So when the question was broached he was not very angry (for he did *more* than justice to the Chaplain's sense of duty), but he stubbornly declined to enter upon it at all. Mr. Fullarton was so provoked that he was goaded into a taunt that he ought to have been ashamed of.

"Perhaps you are right," he said ; "Major Keene is so formidable an adversary, that it is hardly safe to interfere with him." (These " men of peace,"—*quand ils s'y prennent !* I believe the most exasperating man in Egland, at this moment, to be an influential Quaker.)

Dick Tresilyan took a long time (as was his wont) in finding out what was meant; when he did, even his limited intellect appreciated its bad taste and absurdity. A hundred sarcasms would not have disconcerted the Pastor so completely as his honest hearty laugh.

"Ah! you think I'm afraid of him? No—they don't breed cowards where I come from. I never heard that idea but once before : that was at the Truro fair. I wasn't in very good company, and they 'planted' a big miner on me at last. He wanted me to wrestle, and when I wouldn't, he said—just what you did. But I remember all the others laughed at him. They know *us* in those parts, you see. He'd better have kept quiet; for though he puzzled me at first with a ' back-trick ' he had, I knew more than he did, and he got an awkward fall : I don't think he'll ever do a good day's work again."

He paused, and his brow darkened strangely, and all his face changed, till it resembled more closely than it had often done the portraits of some of the "bitter, bad Tresilyans."

"I suppose you mean well, Mr. Fullarton, but I'm not going to thank you. We can manage our affairs without your meddling; and if you're wise you'll leave us alone."

It will be seen that the Chaplain did not take much by his motion.

Neither was Fanny Molyneux well satisfied with the turn affairs had taken lately. That poor little "white witch" was really alarmed by the unruly character of the spirit that she had been anxious to raise; she did not know the proper formula for sending it back to its own place : and, if she had, the stubborn demon would only have mocked at her simple incantations. Though she loved Cecil dearly, she was too much in awe of her to venture upon remonstrance or warning; indeed, the few mild hints that she *did* throw out had not met with such success as to tempt her to follow them up. So she was, perforce, reduced to an unarmed neutrality.

Her husband was perhaps the most thoroughly uncomfortable of the party. He knew the circumstances and bearings of the question better than any one else, and would have sacrificed a good deal ("his right hand," I believe is the proper phrase) to have averted the probable result. But he had not sufficient strength of mind to take the

decided measures that might have been of some
avail; in fact, he had a vague idea, that to act on
the offensive against his old comrade would be
unpardonable treachery. Arguing with the latter
was simply absurd; for this reason, if for no other,
that from the moment his feelings became really
interested, no amount of diplomacy would have
induced him to enter upon the subject. Harry
went about with a miserable, helpless sense of
complicity weighing him down, which was much
aggravated by a few words which dropped one
morning from Dick Tresilyan.

Dick had been dining *tête-à-tête* with Keene,
on the previous evening, after a hard day's snipe
shooting, and bore evident traces about him of a
heavy night—a fact which he lost no time in
alluding to, not without a certain pride, like the
man in Congreve's play, who exults in having
"been drunk in excellent company."

"We had a very big drink," he said, confiden-
tially, "and the Major got more than his allowance.
He didn't know what he was talking about at
last; and he told me more of his affairs than most
people know, I think : of course, I'm as safe as
a church;" and Dick made a gallant but abor-
tive attempt to wink with one of his swollen
eyelids.

Molyneux shrank away from the speaker, with

something very like a suppressed groan—he had heard *that* said before, and remembered what came of it. Credulity was as dangerous when men thought Royston Keene had lost his head, as when women flattered themselves he had lost his heart.

CHAPTER XIV

IF you will be good enough to look back on the one Romance in which, like the rest of the world, you probably indulged yourself, you will remember, perhaps more distinctly than any other feature, the *presentiment* which haunted you from the very beginning. We were absurdly sanguine and hopeful in those days—full of chivalrous resolves and unlimited aspirations; but still the feeling would come back—if indeed, it ever left us—that in the dim background there was difficulty and danger. We were not surprised when the small white speck rose out of the sea, and it needed no prophet to tell us then, that the heavens would soon be black with clouds, and that there would be a great rain (which indeed was the case, for there ensued a long continuance of wet weather; it was a very tearful season). Oddly enough, that same presentiment did not make us particularly melancholy or uncomfortable, but seemed rather to give a zest to our simple pleasures, relieving them from any tinge of sameness or insipidity. When the *dénouement* came we did not exactly see things in the same light certainly, and it took some time to settle thoroughly down into our present theory, that "it was all for the best."

It is the old story of Thomas the Rhymer over and over again (we were all Rhymers once). The lover knows that there is peril in the path, but not the less joyously he strides on by the side of the beautiful Queen. How sweetly they ring the silver bells on the neck of the milk-white palfrey; not so sweetly though as her low, musical tones. So on they fare, till the world of realities is left far behind, and they find themselves at their journey's end. It is very happy, that year spent in Her kingdom; but so like a dream, that he does not appreciate its pleasures so well at the moment as he will in the weary after-years. Yet the waking came too soon. The sojourner had not half grown tired of his resting-place, the bloom has not faded on the wondrous fruits and flowers, the strangely sweet wine has not lost its savour, when it is time for him to be gone; for a dreadful whisper runs through the company, that to-morrow the teind to Hell must be paid. Well, the black Tax-gatherer is baulked by a day, and the wanderer is back at Ercildoune again. Very dreary looks the grey, bare moorland. Do they call that foliage on the stunted fir-trees? It is only the ghost of a forest. The trim parterres have no beauty or fragrance for one that has lingered in more glo-

rious gardens and plucked redder roses. Tabret
and viol jangle harshly in the ears that have rioted
in melodies made by fairy harpers. The village
maidens may be comely, but they are somewhat
clumsy withal ; the earthen floor trembles under
their feet when they lead their simple dances ; very
different are their steps from those that kept time
to a wild, weird music, stirring but scarcely
bending the grass blades. There is no colour in
their flaxen locks, and little light in their mild
pale eyes; they will not bear comparison with the
smooth braided tresses that glistened like blue-
black serpents, or the glances that rained down
liquid fire through the twilight of the forests of
Elf-land. Slowly the discontented dreamer realizes
the fact that the spell is still upon him—riveted
when he stole that first fatal kiss in despite of his
mistress' warning. Nothing is left for him now,
but to expiate his folly in the loneliness of the grey
old tower, and to look forth, hoping to see the
grass-green robe gleam again against the setting
sun, and to hear the silver bells chime once more
in the still evening air. Vain—worse than vain.
With stiffened limbs and grizzled hair, we are not
worth beguiling.

This is essentially a masculine illustration, and
only applies to Cecil Tresilyan—thus far. She was
sensible of the influence that strengthened its hold
upon her every day, and did not now wish or try to

resist it, but she grew proportionately doubtful and
uneasy about the event. A feeling, very strange
and new to one of a temperament like hers, began
to creep over her now and then. At such times
she owned that her eyes were the more eagerly
and steadfastly fixed on the Present, because they
did not dare to look into the Future. Yet, as
far as she knew, there was no ground for much
apprehension.

It is always so. Only when we are carrying
something rare and precious do we appreciate the
possible perils of the road. How much steeper the
hills are now, how much deeper and darker the
ravines, how much more frequent the crags that
might so easily conceal a marauder, than when we
passed them some months ago, chanting the reckless roundelay of the *vacuus viator*.

We said, you remember, before, that Miss Tresilyan had one subject of self-reproach, for which
she had never gained her own absolution. The
whispers that had never been quite silenced, began
to make themselves heard unpleasantly often ; and
now they just hinted at—Retribution. As our
poor Cecil must come to confession some time or
another, it seems to me this is a convenient season.

At the country-house where she was spending
Christmas, three years before the date of our story,
she met Mark Waring. She knew his antecedents:
how, when sudden troubles came upon his family,

he gave up diplomacy, which he had entered upon, and took up the law—hating it cordially—simply because a fair opening was given him there of securing to his mother and sisters something better than bread. He never pretended to feel the slightest interest in his profession, but went on slaving at it resolutely and successfully. He made no merit of it, either; but always spoke, and I believe thought of it, as the merest matter of course—the right thing to do under the circumstance.

There was a hardihood of principle about all this which Cecil rather admired; and his frank bold bearing, and simple straightforward way of putting thoughts that were worth listening to into terse, strong language, aided the first favourable impression. She determined to make Mark like her; and when she had a fancy of this kind she was apt to carry it out without much consideration for the comfort or convenience of the person destined to the experiment. She had no deliberate intention of doing anybody any harm; but those innocent little whims and projects of amusement do more mischief sometimes than the most systematic machinations of Devil-craft.

Why, when you begin even to *write* a chapter, it is very difficult to say where it will end; when you begin to talk it or act it, it is harder still to prophesy aright. A character, or a sentence, or an idea, which looked quite insignificant at first, assumes perfectly portentous dimensions and importance before we have done with it; so that the alternate effect is nearly as startling when realized as that produced by Alice's conjuration—

> She crossed him thrice, that lady bold ;
> He rose beneath her hand,
> The fairest knight on Scottish mold,
> Her brother, Ethert Brand.

So while Cecil was drawing on Mark Waring to talk about his daily life—sympathizing with him about his hard distasteful work, and pitying his loneliness, she never guessed how her words were being branded, one by one, on the earnest, steadfast heart, that her own lofty nature was not worthy to understand. In a week after their first meeting she had drawn from him all the love he had to give; and men of Mark Waring's mould can only find room for one love in a lifetime.

Such characters are exceptional, fortunately : for they are very impracticable and difficult to get on with ; and their antiquated notions are perpetually contrasting and conflicting with the established prejudices of polite and well-organized society— sometimes even checking the same, for an instant, in its easy conventional flow. They *won't* see, that, of all ways of spending time and thought, the most absurdly unprofitable is to waste them on a Memory. Yet—O mine excellent friend and

cynical preceptor! to whom, for sage instruction,
I owe a debt of gratitude that I never mean to
repay—I beseech you, consort not too much with
these misguided men. They are not likely to
infect you with their pestilent doctrines and principles; but they may, in an unguarded moment,
make you do violence to your favourite maxim—
Nil admirari.

With all his strong common sense, Mark was
lamentably deficient in worldly wisdom. He never
saw the obstacles that would have daunted others.
Could anything be more improbable than that the
most triumphant beauty of the season should seriously incline to share the long up-hill struggle of a
rising barrister? Those dull Temple Chambers are
lucky enough if the sun condescends to visit them
at rare intervals in his journey westward. But
Waring's own singleness of purpose beguiled him
more effectually than the most inordinate vanity
could have done. Putting character out of the
question, he thought a woman could only derogate
by allying herself to one of inferior birth; and he
knew his own blood to be nearly equal to Miss
Tresilyan's. He was right so far—if she had only
loved him, she would have subscribed readily to
every article of his simple, knightly creed. The
last idea that entered his mind was, that she could
have stooped so low as to trifle with him. It was
the old mistake. We measure other people's feel-

ings by the intensity of our own, and think it hard
when we meet with disappointment. Yet a certain
misgiving, that he did not like to analyze, kept
him from bringing the question to an issue till the
day before his departure. Then he told her frankly
what his prospects were, and asked her to share
them.

Now, " the Refuser " was so used to seeing men
commit themselves in this way on the very shortest
notice, and without the faintest encouragement,
that the situation had ceased to afford her much
excitement : a proposal no more made her nervous,
than file-firing does a thoroughly broken charger.
For once, however, she felt uncomfortable and
vexed with herself, though she did not guess the
extent of the harm she had done. Nothing could
be kinder or gentler than her answer, but nothing
could be more decisive. On the cold smooth rock
there was not a cleft or a trailing weed for despair
to cling to in its drowning agony. So the hope
of Mark Waring's life went down there, without a
cry or a struggle—as it is fitting the hope of a
strong heart should die—into the depths of the
Great Sea that never will give up its dead.

The lover of the present day is rather a curious
study, immediately after he has encountered a
defeat or disappointment. Sometimes the phase
is a mild melancholy. I remember a case of this
sort not very long ago. The reflections on things

in general that flowed constantly from that man's lips for the space of about a fortnight were incredible to those who knew him well. They were so calmly philosophic—so pleasantly ironical, without a tinge of bitterness—so frequently relieved by the flashes of keen humour—that to listen to them (the weather being intensely hot) was soothing and refreshing in the extreme. Everybody was sorry when he was consoled; for, since that time he has never made an observation worth recording. She was a very clever woman who reduced our friend to this abnormal state, though she grossly maltreated him; and from close association, some of her conversational talent, perhaps insensibly, had got into his constitution; but it could not thrive in such an uncongenial soil, where there was nothing to nourish it. Some men, again, take the reckless and boisterous line, plunging for awhile into all sorts of demoralization, with an evident contentment in having a fair excuse for the same in their disappointment. Certainly it is rather a luxurious state of things—to satisfy one's vengeance whilst gratifying one's appetites—and to know that people are saying all the time—" Poor Charlie! He's very much to be pitied. It's entirely Fanny Grey's fault. He is dreadfully altered since she behaved to him so shamefully." Others —probably the majority—go for complete indifference; and succeed creditably on the whole. A few, *very* few, know that their happiness has got its death-wound, and are able to take it bravely and silently. It is of one of these last we are speaking.

Mark Waring was too honest to affect insensibility; he was not of the stuff out of which accomplished actors are made. He walked quickly to the window, that his face might not betray him, and did not turn round till he thought he had disciplined it thoroughly. It was but a half-victory after all; for when Cecil met his eyes, her cheek became the paler of the two. She read there enough to make her wish that she could give up all her former triumphs, and undo this last success. She tried to tell him that she was deeply grieved and repentant; but the words would not come. Mark forgot his own sorrow when he saw large drops hanging ready to fall on the dark, long eyelashes.

" Pray do not distress yourself," he said, quite steadily; " such presumption as mine deserves harsher treatment than it has met with from you. You are not answerable for my extravagant self-delusions. I would ask you to forgive me for having been so precipitate—only I know, now, that if I had waited seven years, your answer would have been the same. Let us part in kindness; it will be very long before we meet again; but I do not think I shall forget you; and I hope you will remember me if you ever want a hand or head to carry out any one of your wishes or whims. It would make me very happy if I could so serve you. Now, good-bye. It is only going this afternoon instead of to-morrow. I must try and make up for lost time, too, by working a little harder."

The smile that accompanied those last words haunted Cecil for many, many days. She knew already enough of Waring to be certain that he would never sink into maudlin sentimentality; it saddened her inexpressibly to fancy him—alone in his gloomy chambers, when the night was waning, chained to those crabbed law-papers from a dreary sense of duty, but without a hope or an interest to cheer him on: he had given up ambition long ago. (There are many clocks that keep time to a second, when their striking part is ruined utterly.) She felt angry, then and afterwards, that she could find no words to say the least appropriate or expressive: she held out her hand timidly, pleading for forgiveness with her eyes. He just touched it with his lips before he let it go. That kiss of peace was a more precious tribute, than any of her hundred vassals had offered to the proud Tresilyan. So they parted.

Cecil's conscience was disagreeably uncompromising, and for a long time, declined to admit any valid excuse for the mischief she had done; but time and change are efficient anodynes; and her penance was nearly completed when she came to Dorade. Of late, however, the reproachful vision had presented itself oftener than ever. She realized more completely the pain that Mark Waring must have endured, as she guessed what would be the bitterness of her own feelings if it should prove that she had mistaken Royston Keene. That sor-rowful Memory seemed to rise before her like a warning spectre, waving her back from the path she had begun to tread. Truly, Cecil Tresilyan *was* different from the generality of her sex; or when her own heart was sorely imperilled, she would never have found time to think so often, and so regretfully, of one that she had broken.

But, when a woman has once determined to set her whole fortunes on the turn of a die, where is the monitor that will teach her prudence or self-restraint? She will hardly be persuaded "though one rose from the dead."

CHAPTER XV

ROYSTON KEENE had indeed good reason to augur ill of the ending of his love-dream; but it was in his nature, always to walk straight on to the accomplishment of his purpose, overlooking the obstacles that lay between and the dangers that lay beyond. This partly accounted for his utter insensibility to ordinary inconveniences and annoyances.

His own words to Molyneux one day, when the latter remarked on this peculiarity, though somewhat allegorical, expressed his theory and practice fairly : " Hal, when we are travelling, we always remember where we change our large notes ; but life is not long enough to recollect how the thalers and piastres go." His companion thought this rather a brilliant illustration, especially as it squared with his own ideas of existence. But in reality, between the two men there was a marked distinction. A genial kindliness in the one, and a hard unscrupulous determination in the other, worked out nearly the same results.

Royston liked Cecil Tresilyan better than any woman he had ever seen, and he made up his mind to win her. It is more than doubtful if he took the probable consequences to either into consideration at all. Foot by foot he was gaining ground till he felt almost sure of success; but this confidence never made him for an instant less vigilant in watching the chances, less careful in scoring every point of the game. He had played it long enough to know these right well.

Yet to him, too, the Past brought its warning. He was rarely troubled or favoured with dreams; but one night was an exception to the rule. To understand it you must look back once more, and bear with me while we moralize yet again. *Excusez du peu.*

There is a regret that has power to move and torment the coldest Stoic that vegetates on earth: it comes when our own hand or act has slain the one living thing that loved us best of all. We may have done the deed unwittingly or unwillingly; we may have been unconscious of the love that was borne us till it was too late for acknowledgment; we may never in thought or word or act have injured our victim before that last wrong of the death-blow;—well for those who can plead so fair an excuse; yet even this, with all the rest, the inexorable Nemesis laughs to scorn. I wonder that poets and dramatists have not oftener selected this saddest theme. It may be true that the last murmur from the lips of the Llewellyn, when his life

was ebbing away in the Pass of the Ambush, syllabled the name, not of wife or child or friend, but of
a stanch wolf-hound; and perhaps tears less bitter
have been shed over the graves of many exemplary
Christians than those that sprinkled the turf under
the birch-trees where Gelert was sleeping. It could
not free the ancient mariner from the remorse that
clung to him like a poisoned garment till it made
him a "world's wonder," because, when he shot the
albatross, he thought he was benefiting his fellows.
Not less accusingly did the voices of the sea wail in
the ears of the desolate Viking, because, when the
bitter arrow went aside, he was fighting hard to
save Oriana. Nothing could be more correct than
the conduct of Virginius, or more creditable to a
Roman Father; but, when he harangued in the
Forum in after days, I doubt if the commons
thronged so densely, as to shut out from the
demagogue a vision of fair hair dabbled in blood,
gleaming awfully in the sunlight, and of dark-blue
eyes turned upon him in a wondering horror till
that look froze in them for evermore. I doubt if
the cheers of his partisans were so noisy, as to
drown the memory of a certain choked shivering
moan : in the long, lonely winter nights at least, be
sure those sights and sounds visited the Tribune's
hearth, often enough to satisfy the savage spirit of
the doomed Decemvir.

It was this remorse which had stricken Royston

Keene sorely, even through his armour of proof, as
he knelt, not very long ago, by the side of a death-
bed. A woman lay there, scarcely past girlhood,
and fair enough to have been the pride of any English household, as daughter or sister or wife. You
shall not read unnecessarily an episode of sin and
bitter sorrow, and of shame that was not less heavy
to bear because the eyes of the world were blinded
and saw it not. It is enough to say that the blood
of Emily Carlyle was as certainly on her tempter's
head as that of any one of those whom he had slain
in open fight with shot or steel. This is what she
answered when he asked her to forgive him :—

"My own, I have forgiven you long ago! I
could not help it if I would. I cannot reproach you
either, for though I have tried hard to repent, I
fear, if all were to come over again, I should not
act more coldly or wisely. But listen! I know you
will be able, if you choose it, to make others love
you nearly as well as I have done—and you *will*
choose it. Darling, promise me that for my sake
you will spare *one*. I could die easier if I thought
my intercession had saved another's soul, though I
was so weak in guarding my own. It might help
me too, perhaps—if anything can help me—where
I am going."

Even Royston Keene shivered at the low terror-
stricken whisper in which these last words were
spoken. He gave the promise though, and remem-

bered it occasionally—till tho time for keeping it came.

The Major had been spending the evening with Cecil Tresilyan, making arrangements for a picnic that was to take place two days later. He had had a passage of arms or two with Mrs. Danvers, wherein that strong-principled but weak-minded enthusiast had been utterly discomfited, and routed with great slaughter. Altogether it was very pleasant entertainment; and he went to his rest in a state of great contentment and satisfaction. He woke (or seemed to wake) with a sudden start and shudder; for he was aware of the presenee of Something in the room, that was not there when he laid down.

Out of the blaek darkness a face slowly defined itself, bending over the pillow, and creeping close to his own—only a face—he could not distinguish even the outline of a figure. He knew it very well; and the eyes too—but there was an upbraiding there that, while she lived, he had never seen in those of gentle Emily Carlyle; and a reproach eame from the white lips, though they did not move to give it passage. " All forgotten ! I—the promise, too. And yet—I suffer—I suffer always." The sad, pleading expression of tho face and eyes vanished then ; and a strange, palo glare, not liko the moonlight, that seemed to come from within, lighted them up—fixed and rigid, yet eloquent, of unutter-

able agony: there was written plainly the self-
abhorrence of a heart conscious of the coils of the
undying worm—the despair of a soul looking far
into Futurity, yet seeing no end to the wrath to
come. Then the darkness swallowed up all; and,
before Keene thoroughly roused himself—with a
smothered cry—he knew that he was alone again.

A cold dew lingered on the dreamer's forehead,
as if a breath from beyond the grave had lately
passed over it; but terror was not the predomi-
nating feeling. He had ruled that timid, trusting
girl too long and too imperiously, to quail before
her disembodied spirit. But a strange sadness
overcame him as he pondered upon all that she had
endured—and might still be enduring—for his
sake: a glimmer of something like generosity and
compassion flickered for a brief space over the surface of the cast-steel heart. He rose, and leant
forth into the steady, outer moonlight, musing, for
several minutes, and then began muttering aloud.

"It would be as well to clear off one debt at
least. I did pass my word. She deserves this
sacrifice, if it were only for never complaining: let
her have her way. By G—d I'll go off to-morrow
evening; and I'll tell Cecil so, as soon as I can see
her. Bah! what is a man worth if he cannot forget? Besides, I don't know——" The rest of his
doubts and scruples he confessed—not even to the
stars.

Climate has a great deal to answer for. A sudden tempest, or an opportune mist, has turned the scale of more battles than some of the most successful generals would have liked to own. If the next morning had broken sullenly, things might have gone far otherwise. But it was one of those brilliant days that make even the invalids not regret, for a moment, that they have given up all English comforts and home pleasures for the off-chance of wringing another month or two of life out of the wreck of their constitution. Everything looked bright and in holiday guise, from the wreaths of ivy glistening on the brows of the shattered old castle, down to the ἀνηρίθμον γελάσμα of the turquoise sea. Under the circumstances, it was very unlikely that Royston would keep to his virtuous resolutions. The first half of them he carried out perfectly: he did go straight to Cecil Tresilyan, and tell her of his intentions to depart. She did not betray much of her disappointment or surprise; but argued with so fascinating a casuistry against the necessity of such a sudden step, that it was no wonder if she soon convinced her hearer of the propriety of, at least, delaying it. In a case like this, an excuse of "urgent private affairs," that would suffice for the most rigid martinet that ever tyrannized over a district or a division, sounds absurdly trivial and insincere. When a proud beauty does condescend to plead, a man who really

cares for her must be very peculiarly constituted if
he remains constant in denial.

The vision of the night had faded away already.
Those poor ghosts ! ,They have no chance—the
mystics say—against embodied spirits, if the latter
only keep up their courage, and choose to assert
their supremacy. Besides, they must, perforce, fly
before the dawn.   And what dawn was ever so
bright as the Tresilyan's smile, when she guessed
from Royston's face, without his speaking, that she
had won the day ?

So the picnic came off according to arrangement.
The weather and everything else looked so promising, that even the vinegar in Bessie Danvers'
composition was acidulated : and, when Keene
greeted her at the place of *rendezvous*, she favoured
him with just such a smile as one of the grim
Puritan dames, in a rare interval of courtesy, may
have granted to Claverhouse or Montrose—the
right of reprobation being reserved.   It is greatly
to be feared that the Malignant did not appreciate
the condescension : his attention was so entirely
taken up in another quarter.

Cecil Tresilyan was perfectly dazzling in the
splendour and insolence of her beauty : the calm
self-possession that usually distinguished her
seemed changed into almost reckless high spirits :
even her dress betrayed a certain intention of
coquetry ; and her splendid violet eyes flashed ever

and anon with a mischievously mutinous expression that made their glance a challenge. Such a frame of mind the Scotch describe, when they speak of a person being "fey," holding it to be a sure presage of impending disaster.

O guileless maidens! be warned, and trust not to attractive appearances. Lo! there is not a cloud in the sky that smiles over the Nysian vale; all round the roses and lilies are blooming, till the air is faint with their perfume; merry and musical rings the laugh of Persephonë as she goes forth with her comrades a-Maying: but worse things than serpents lurk beneath the waving grass. We, who have read the ancient legend, listen already for the roll of the nether thunder: we know that, in another minute, the earth will disgorge Aïdoneus, the swart ravisher, with his iron chariot: then will come a struggle of the dove in the clutch of the falcon—a cry for help drowned in a hoarse growl of triumph—shrieks and wild disorder amongst the flying nymphs: but the loveliest of the band will rejoin them never any more. Demeter (like other careful chaperones), when she is most wanted is far away, tending her corn-lands, or revelling in the odours of sacrifice. Finding her after long-baffled search—she will hardly recognise her innocent child in the pale Queen of Shades, who seems worthy of her awful throne far-gleaming through the leaden twilight. The little hand that used to

weave garlands so deftly, sways the golden sceptre
right loyally; but the deep, solemn eyes have forgotten how to smile. She who once wept bitterly
over her pet-bird when it died, listens, unmoved, to
the clank of Megæra's scourge, and to the wail of a
million spirits in torment. Her beauty is more
magnificent than ever; but it is tinged with the
austere and dreary majesty that befits the consort
of the King of Hell. Ah, woeful mother! desist
from intercession, and dry those unavailing tears;
it is too late now to tempt her to follow you, even
if Hades will let its Empress depart for a season;
the pure, natural fruits of your upper earth have
lost all savour for the lips that once have tasted the
fatal pomegranate.

Mr. Fullarton and his family completed the
party, which was confined to the Molyneux's set.
The Chaplain was strangely nervous, fussy, and important: it seemed as if the possession of some
weighty secret that he was eager, yet afraid, to
divulge, had disturbed his phlegmatic complacency.
He took the first opportunity of beseeching Miss
Tresilyan to be allowed to act as her escort: it was
customary on all these expeditions that each dame
and demoiselle, besides the professional muleteer,
should be attended by at least one "dismounted
skirmisher." Cecil was rather puzzled by the petition, and by the earnest way in which it was preferred; but she was too happy to deny anybody

anything just then; besides which she felt conscious
of having visited her Pastor of late with a certain
amount of neglect, not to say contumely. So she
consented, graciously; but the sidelong glance at
Keene, asking for his sympathy, did not escape her
reverend cavalier.

It was evident that Mr. Fullarton had something
on his mind that he intended to impart to his companion; but it was equally clear that he did not see
his way to the confidence. The path turned abruptly across the line of hills; and while he was
hesitating and looking about for a fair opening, it
got so steep and rugged that it soon left him no
breath for the disclosure. Before they had gone
half a league the divine was decidedly in difficulties;
he rolled hither and thither, panting painfully, like
one who has already endured all the burden and
heat of the 'day. Still he clung obstinately to
Cecil's bridle-rein, rather assisted than assisting,
till they reached a point where the road resembled
greatly a flight of garret stairs, without any regu-
larity in the steps thereof. The mule and its leader
stumbled together; the former recovered itself
cleverly, after the fashion of its kind; but such a *tour
de force* far exceeded the exhausted energies of the
pursy pastor. He was fairly "down upon his head."

Since the cavalcado started, Major Keene had
not attempted to disturb the order of march; at
first he walked by the side of Fanny Molyneux, and

did his best to amuse her; when the path became too narrow for three abreast, he resigned the charge to Harry (who never, willingly, when *en voyage*, abdicated the charge of his *mignonne*), and went on by himself, just in the rear of Miss Tresilyan and her clerical escort. He presented, in truth, a striking contrast to that over-tasked pedestrian — going easily within himself, without a quickened breath, or a bead of moisture on his forehead. *Shikari* of the Upper Himalayas, gillies of Perthshire and the Western Highlands, chamois-hunters of the Tyrol, and guides of Chamounix or Courmayeur, could all have told tales of that long, level stride, to which hill or dale, rough or smooth, never came amiss; before which even the weary German miles were swallowed up like furlongs. He sprang quickly forward when he saw the mishap of his front rank; Miss Tresilyan was quite safe, so he only gave her a smile in passing, and then raised the fallen ecclesiastic, with a studied and ostentatious tenderness that would have aggravated a saint.

"I hope you are not severely hurt, Mr. Fullarton? You really should be less rash in over-exerting yourself. The spirit is willing, but the flesh is— somewhat 'short of work.' May I relieve you of your responsibility till you have recovered your wind?"

In spite of his own sacred character, and the

proprieties of time and place, had Keene been weak and of small stature, it is within the bounds of possibility that the Pastor might have assaulted him, there and then.

If it had not been for that unfortunate sense of the ridiculous which was perpetually offering temptations to Miss Tresilyan, she would have undoubtedly on this occasion espoused the losing side; but she exhausted all her powers of self-control in expressing (with decent gravity) her sorrow that her guide should have come to grief in her service. She had none left wherewith to concoct a rebuke for the Cool Captain. Considering the circumstances, Mr. Fullarton's laugh, and attempt at a jest on his own discomfiture, did him infinite credit. With the smothered expression that half escaped his lips, as he fell to the rear, the chronicler has no earthly concern.

As the other two moved onwards, Royston spoke, his dark eyes glittering scornfully.

" I wonder if women will ever get tired of deriding us, or we of ministering to their amusement ? It must have been a great satisfaction to Anne of Austria to see Richelieu dance that saraband. (But Mazarin paid her off for it. I am very glad that the Cardinal was avenged by the *charlatan*.) Now, how could you allow the Shepherd to be so rash ? Consider that he has a large and increasing family totally dependent on him for support. If I were

Mrs. Fullarton, I would bring an action against
you. It is a necessity that his successor should
quote *something;* and he really did bring to my
mind the description of the White Bull of Dun-
craggan, who started up-hill so vigorously—

> But steep and flinty was the road,
> And sharp the hurrying pikeman's goad,
> And when we came to Dennan's Row,
> A child might scatheless stroke his brow.

I shouldn't like to be the child, though," he added,
meditatively, with a backward glance at the object
of his remarks, who indeed did present a very
" dissolving view."

The tone and manner of his speaking showed
how much, within the last few weeks, the relations
of the two had altered: the scale was already
wavering, and ere long might be foretold a change
in the balance of power.

His beautiful companion shook her head, till the
soft curling plumes that nestled round her hat
danced again; but the effect of the reproving
gesture was quite spoilt by the laugh that followed
it, suppressed, though clear as a silver bell.

" I will not be made an accomplice in your irreverent comparisons; I don't admit the resemblance;
if there were one, it was too bad of 'the pikemen'
not to be more considerate. You always try to
impute malicious motives to the most innocent.

How could I guess that Mr. Fullarton would suffer
so for his devotion to my interests? I will give
you back your quotation in kind. See—if I were
as mischievous as you insinuate—

> My loss may pay my folly's tax ;
> I've broke my trusty battleaxe."

The ivory handle of her parasol (the same that
had been rescued from Duchesne) chanced to be
entangled in the bridle when the mule stumbled,
and the jerk snapped the frail shaft in two. Keene
took the fragments from her, and looked at them
for an instant.

"Poor thing!" he said, compassionately; "so
it was fated to be short-lived? It was hardly
worth while saving it from the wrath of the sinner,
if it was to be sacrificed so soon to the awkward-
ness of the saint."

"Not at all," Cecil replied. "It was my fault,
for being so heedless. But I cannot afford another
misadventure to-day. Will you take great care of
me?"

Her soft caressing tones thrilled through Royston's veins till the blood mounted to his forehead:
but he made no answer in words, only looking up
earnestly into her face with his rare smile.

I have tried throughout to avoid inflicting on
you a dialogue that does not bear in some way on
the incidents of our tale; on this principle we will

not record the conversation that occupied those two till they reached the crown of the pass. It was probably interesting to *them*, for it was long before either forgot a word that was spoken. But the imagination or the memory of the reader will doubtless fill up a better fancy-sketch than the one omitted here.

There was a general halt on the brow of the hill. Indeed, the view was worth a pause. From below their feet, the track of low woodland rolled right down to the edge of the sea, like a broad toss-ing river; swelling into great billows of grey, or dark green, where the taller olives or fir-trees grew, and broken here and there with islets of many-coloured stone. With the rest came up the Chaplain, who had recovered by this time his breath, and, to a certain extent, his equanimity While the others stood silent, he saw one of those openings for improving the occasion professionally of which he was ever so ready to avail himself. So, casting his hand abroad theatrically, he de-claimed,

How glorious are thy works, Parent of Good !

The words came oozing out in the oiliest of his unctuous tones; and the elocutionist's expansive glance fell, first on the landscape patronizingly, then on the bystanders encouragingly. It was as though he said, "You may fall to, and admire now. I have

asked a blessing." Nothing more occurred worthy
of note till they reached their destination in
safety.

Of course, "there never was such a place for a
picnic;" but as that has been said of about three
hundred different spots in every civilized country
of Europe, it is certainly not worth while describing this particular one. The luncheon went on
very much as such things always do when the
arrangements are perfect, the commissariat unexceptionable, and the guests hungry and happy.

Mr. Fullarton, however, applied himself so assidu-
ously to the champagne-cup, that his sober-minded
helpmate (the only person who took much notice
of his proceedings) was filled with an uncomfortable wonder. At last, during a pause in the
general conversation, he addressed Royston abruptly—there was a strange huskiness in his voice,
and his lower lip kept trembling,—

"I heard from Naples this morning. My friend
mentions having met Mrs. Keene there."

The Major looked up at the speaker with the
cool, indifferent glance that had often irritated him.
"Indeed! I was not aware that my mother had
got so far south yet. She wrote last from Rome."

The other tossed off his glass with an unsteady
hand, and set it down sharply. "I never heard of
your mother, sir," he said; "I was speaking of—
your wife."

CHAPTER XVI.

TO quarrel with a man over his cups, or in any-wise to molest him in his drink, is an offence against the proprieties, that even the goodnatured Epicurean cannot find it in his easy heart to palliate or pardon. On this point he speaks mildly, but very firmly :—

> Natis in usum lætitiæ scyphis
> Pugnare, Thracum est. Tollite barbarum
> Morem : verecundumque Bacchum
> Sanguineis prohibete rixis.

The ghost of Banquo was an uncivilized spectre, or—strong as was the provocation—it would have confronted Macbeth in any other place sooner than the banqueting-hall. The worst deed in the life of a cruel, false king was the setting on of the black bull's head before the doomed Douglases; and perhaps Pope Alexander, though singularly exempt from all vulgar prejudice, found it hard to obtain his own pontifical absolution for the poisoned wine in which he pledged the Orsini and Colonna. In these, and a hundred like instances, there was certainly the shadowy excuse of political expe-

diency or necessity ; but what shall we say of that
individual who interrupts the harmony of a meeting
solely to gratify his own private pique or pleasure ?
Truly, with such enormities, Heaven "heads the
count of crimes." I consider the most abominable
act of which Eris was ever guilty was the selection
of that particular moment for the production of
the golden apple. If she was bound to make
herself obnoxious, she might have waited till the
Olympians were sitting in conclave, or, at least, at
home again; it was infamous to disturb them
while doing justice to the talents of Peleus's *cor-
don-bleu.* I wish very much that injured and
querulous Œnone had met her somewhere on
the slopes of Ida, and "given her a piece of
her mind."

On these grounds, I venture to hope that all
well-regulated readers will concur with me in
pronouncing Mr. Fullarton's conduct totally indefensible. It would have been so easy to have
communicated his intelligence to any that it might
concern, discreetly, at a fitting place and time,
instead of casting it into the midst of a convivial
assembly like a fulminating ball. Under other
circumstances he would probably have taken the
quieter course; but he had been smarting for
some time under a succession of provocations,
real and fancied, from Royston Keene, and his
own misadventure that morning had filled the cup

of irritation brimful. It was the old exasperating
feeling—

Earl Percy sees my fall.

Whatever might be the cost, he could not make
up his mind to let slip so fair a chance of embar-
rassing his imperturbable enemy: there is no
saying what he would have given to see that
marvellous self-command for once thorougly break
down. It is unfortunate that the best laid plans
cannot always ensure a triumph. The Chaplain
certainly did succeed in producing a " situation,"
and in reducing most of the party to that uncomfortable frame of mind which is popularly described as "wishing oneself anywhere;" but the
person who seemed most completely unconcerned
was the man at whom the blow was levelled.

The Major shook his head with a quick gesture
of impatience, just as if some insect had lighted
on his forehead; beyond this, for any evidence of
his being annoyed by it, Mr. Fullarton's last remark
might have related to missionary prospects or
Chinese politics. The steady colour on his swarthy
face neither lost nor gained a shade; there was not
a sign of anger, or shame, or confusion in his clear,
bold eyes; and when he answered, there was not
one fresh furrow on the brow that, at lighter provocation, was so apt to frown.

"I give you credit for being utterly ignorant of

what you are talking about, Mr. Fullarton. You could not possibly guess how disagreeable the subject would be to me. As it can't be in the least interesting to any else, suppose we change it ? "

Just the same cold, measured voice as ever, with only a slight sarcastic inflexion to vary the deep, grave tones : but a very close observer might have seen his fingers clench the handle of a knife while he was speaking, as if their gripe would have dinted the ivory.

It was hardly to be expected that the rest of the party would emulate the *sang-froid* of the Cool Captain. Sailing under false colours is a convenient practice enough, and productive sometimes of many prizes; but divers penalties attach to its detection on land as well as on sea. Indeed it involves the necessity of *somebody's* appearing as a convicted impostor. On the present occasion—as the actor for whom the character was cast utterly declined to play it—the part fell to poor Harry Molyneux, who certainly looked it to perfection. In all his little difficulties and troubles, when hard pressed, he was wont to fall back upon the reserve of *la mignonne,* sure of meeting there with sympathy, if not with succour. He dared not do so now. He dared not encounter the reproach of the beautiful, gentle eyes that had never looked into his own otherwise than trustfully, since they first told the secret that she loved him dearly. The half-smothered cry that broke from Fanny's lips when the Chaplain made his disclosure, went straight to the heart of her treacherous husband; he felt as if he deserved that those pretty lips should never smile upon him again.

O all my readers!—masculine especially—whose patience has carried you thus far, remark, I beseech you, the dangers that attend any dereliction from the duty of matrimonial confidence. What right have we to lock up the secrets of our most intimate friends, far less our own, instead of pouring them into the bosom of the βαθύκολπος ἄκοιτις, which is capacious enough to hold them all, were they ten-fold more numerous and weighty? Such reticence is rife with awful peril. In our folly and blindness we fancy ourselver secure, while the ground is mined under our guilty feet, and the explosion is even now preparing, from which only our *disjecta membra* will emerge. Of course some cold-hearted caviller will begin to quote instances of carefully planned and promising conspiracies, which mis-carried solely because the details reached a feminine ear. It may have been so; but I don't see what business conspiracies have to succeed at all. Long live the Constitution!

Truly, such delightful confidences must be some-thing one-sided; for the mildest Griselda of them all would be led as a "Martha to the Stakes," sooner than concede to her husband the unrestricted supervision of her correspondence. I have indeed a dim recollection of having heard of *one* bride of seventeen, who, during the honeymoon, was weak and (*selon les dames*) wicked enough to submit to profane male eyes epistles received from the friends of her youth, in their simple entirety, instead of reading out an expurgated edition of the same. She had been brought up in a very dungeon of decorum by a terrible grandmother, a rigid moralist whom no man ever yet beheld without a shiver; and during those first few weeks after her escape she was probably intoxicated by the novel sense of freedom; besides which she was perfectly infatuated about "Reginald;" but all this could not exculpate her when arraigned before her peers. She lived long enough to repent, and to reassert, to some extent, her lost matronly dignity; but she died very young — let us hope in fair course of nature. She had violated the first law of a guild more numerous and influential than that of the Freemasons: examples are necessary from time to time; and though the *Vehmegericht* may pity the offender, it may not therefore linger in its vengeance. Nevertheless, my brethren, our course is clear. Let us resign to the châtelaine the key of the letter-bag and the censorship thereof. If, after due warning, our light-minded friends *will* write to us in terms that mislike that excellent and

punctilious inspectress, they must abye it in the
cold looks and bitter inuendoes which will be their
portion when they come to us in the next hunting
season. Our conscience, at least, will be pure and
undefiled, and we shall pass to the end of our
pilgrimage *sans peur*, though, perchance, even then
not *sans reproche*. "Servitudes," as Miggs, the
veteran vestal, remarked, "is no inheritance;" but
there are natures who thrive rarely in this tranquil
and inglorious condition. Such men live, as a rule,
pretty contentedly, to a great old age, and die in
the odour of intense respectability. Salubrious, it
seems, as well as creditable to the patient, is a
régime of moderate hen-pecking; only it is necessary that he should be of the intermediate species
between Socrates and Georges Dandin.

Mrs. Danvers would certainly have indulged
openly in that immoderate exultation to which
all minor prophets are prone when their predictions chance to be verified, but this was checked
by her constitutional timidity. She was horribly
afraid of the effect that the revelation might
have on her patroness. Therefore, what precise
meaning was implied by the complicated contortions of her countenance, no mortal can guess or
know. Her sensations probably resolved themselves into an access of admiration for the Pastor
in his new character of a denouncer of detected
guilt and champion of imperilled innocence : added

to which was a vague desire to launch her own
Anathema Maranatha at Royston Keene.

Dick Tresilyan took the whole thing with remarkable coolness, not to say complacency. He
nodded his head, and smiled, and winked cunningly aside at Molyneux, as if to intimate that
he had known all about it long ago ; and indeed
so far he had been admitted into the Major's
confidence on the night when the latter was
supposed to have "lost his head." By what
sophistries Royston had succeeded in masking
his purpose and making his case good, even to
such an unsuspicious mind and easy morality, the
Devil could best tell, who in such schemes had
rarely failed him.

We have left Cecil to the last. My proud,
beautiful Cecil—was she not born for better things
than to be made the prize of all those plottings
and counter-plottings—to surrender the key of
her heart's treasures to one who was unworthy to
kiss the hem of her robe—and now, to have her
self-command tried so cruelly, to gratify the
wounded vanity of a weak, shallow enthusiast ?

She did not flinch or start when Mr. Fullarton's
words caught her ear, but a heavy, chill faintness
stole over her, till she felt all her limbs benumbed,
and everything before her eyes grew misty and
dim. The numbness passed away almost immediately, but still the figures around her appeared

distorted and fantastically exaggerated; they
seemed to be tossing and whirling round one
steadfast centre, as the dead leaves in winter
eddy round the marble head of a statue; that
single centre-object remained, throughout, distinct
and unaltered in its aspect, while all else was confused and uncertain—the face of Royston Keene.

The sight of that face—not defiant or even
stern, but immutable in its cold tranquillity—acted
on Cecil as a magical restorative; it seemed as
though he were able, by some mesmeric influence,
to impart to her a portion of his own miraculous
self-control. Before his reply to the Chaplain was
ended, she threw back her proud head with the
old imperial gesture, as if scorning her own momentary weakness; no mist or shadow clouded the
brilliant violet eyes; she might speak safely now,
without risking a false note in the music. It was
no light peril that she escaped; the betrayal of
emotion under such circumstances would have
weighed down a meeker spirit than the Tresilyan's
with a sense of ineffaceable shame : for remember
—however marked her partiality for Keene might
have been—there had been no suspicion of an
engagement between them. Had she broken down
then, she would not have forgiven Royston to her
dying day; she never *did* forgive the Chaplain.
As it was—by a strange anomaly—at the very
moment when she became aware of having been

deluded and misled, in intention if not by actually spoken words—when she had most reason to hate or despise the "enemy who had done her this dishonour"—she felt his hold upon her heart strengthened, as though he had justified his right to command it.

Not to women alone, but to all beautiful, wild creatures, the ancient aphorism applies : the harder they are to discipline, the better they love their tamer. Cecil thought, "There is not another man alive whose eyes could meet mine so daringly;" and the haughty spirit bowed itself, and did obeisance to its suzerain. Different in many respects as Good can be from Evil—in one, those two were as fairly matched as Thiodolf and Isolde. Who can tell what wealth of happiness might have been stored up for both, if they had only not met—too late?

These two words seem to me the most melancholy of any that are written or spoken. They strike the key-note of so many human agonies, that they might form a motto, apter than Dante's, for the gates of Hell. Very few may hear them without a melancholy thrill; well—if they do not bring a bitter pang. Like those awful conjurations that blanched in utterance the lips of the boldest Magi, they have a fearful power to wake the dead. Lo! they are scarcely syllabled, when there is a stir in the graveyard where sad or guilty memories lie buried; the air is alive with phantoms; the watcher may close his eyes if he will, not the less is he sensible of the presence of those pale ghosts that come trooping to their vengeance. Many, many hours must pass, before the spell is learned that will send them back to their tombs again.

Not long ago I heard a story that bears upon this. The man of whom it was told lost his love, after he had fairly wooed and won her. It matters not what suspicion, or misconception, or treachery parted them; but parted they were for eight miserable years. Then the lady repented or relented, and came to her lover to make her confession. When she had done speaking, she looked up into his face; she saw no light of gladness or welcome there—only a deepening and darkening of the weary look of pain; the arms whose last tender clasp she had not forgotten yet, never opened to draw her to his breast. He bent his head down upon his shaking hands, and the heavy drops that are sometimes wrung from strong men in their agony began to trickle through his fingers. In old days, he could never bear to see her sad for a moment; now—he sat as though he heard her not, while she lay at his feet, wailing to be forgiven. When he could perfectly control his voice, he answered—

"More than once, in my dreams, I have seen you *so*, and I have heard you say what you have said to-day. I answered then as I answer now—

I never can forgive you. I do not know that you would not regain your old ascendancy; I believe you are as dangerous, and I as weak, as ever. But I do know that the more fascinating I found you, the harder it would be to bear. Thinking of what I had missed through that accursed time of famine, would drive me mad soon. I have got used to my present burden : I won't give you the chance of making it heavier. Those tears of mine were selfish as well as childish; they were given to the happiness and hope that you killed eight years ago. Stay—we parted with a show of kindness then : we will not part in anger now."

He laid his lips on her forehead as he raised her up—a grave, cold, passionless kiss, such as is pressed on the brow of a dear friend lying in his shroud. They never met alone again.

It is exasperating to think how long I have taken to describe events and emotions that passed in the space of a few minutes; but to place all the *dramatis personæ* in their proper positions does take time, unless the stage-manager is very experienced. Will you be good enough to imagine the picnic broken up (*not* in confusion), and the "strayed revellers" on their way to Dorade? Nothing worthy of note occurred on the spot; a commonplace conversation having been started and maintained, in a way equally creditable to all parties concerned.

Q

CHAPTER XVII.

A LL the inquiries that the Chaplain had "felt it his duty" to make respecting the antecedents of Royston Keene had failed to elicit anything more discreditable than may be said of the generality of men who have spent a dozen years in rather a fast regiment, keeping up to the standard of the corps. Doubtless graver charges might have been imputed to him, if the whole truth had been known; but the living witnesses who could have proved them had good reasons for their silence. Whether successful or defeated, the Cool Captain was not wont to take the world into his confidence. As for betraying his own or another's secrets—his lips were about as likely to do *that* as those of an effigy on a tombstone.

Naples was a cover that the reverend investigator had not drawn; so he was considerably startled by the following words in a letter from thence, received that morning: "I meet a lady constantly in society here, of whose history I am curious to know more. She is the wife of Major Keene, the

famous Indian *sabreur*; but has been separated from
him for several years. She never makes an allusion to his existence ; it was by the merest chance
that I heard this, and also that her husband is
spending the winter at Dorade. Perhaps you can
throw some light on the cause of the separate
maintenance ? People are not particular here, and
have no right to be : still, one would like to know.
I fancy it cannot be her fault : she is perfectly
gentle in her manner, but rather cold—very
beautiful, too, in a placid, statuesque style." It
is not worth transcribing the writer's further
speculations. If a silent, but ultra-fervent benediction can at all profit the person for whom it is
intended, very few people have been so well paid
for epistolary labour, as was then Mr. Fullarton's
correspondent. The reason why has already been
explained.

Well, he had made his great *coup* without carefully counting the cost—that financial pleasure was
still to come. He could not help feeling that it
had been rather a *fiasco*. The man whom he had
purposed utterly to discomfit had throughout been
provokingly at his ease; the best that could be
made of it was, a drawn battle. A disagreeable
consciousness crept over the Chaplain, of having
made himself generally obnoxious without reaping
any equivalent advantage, or even satisfaction.
No one seemed to look kindly or admiringly at

him since the disclosure, except Mrs. Danvers, and, glutton as he was of such dainties, the adulation of that exemplary but unattractive female began rather to pall on his palate. He was clear-sighted enough to be aware that Miss Tresilyan was probably offended with him beyond hope of reconciliation, but this did not greatly trouble him. He had been sensible for some time of the decay of his influence in that quarter. Last of all rose on his mind, with unpleasant distinctness, Cecil's warning, "If I were a man, I should not like to have Major Keene as my enemy." He had thrown the lance over that enemy's frontier, and it was now too late to talk of truce; a dread of the consequences overcame him as he thought of the reprisals that might be exacted by the merciless and unscrupulous Guerilla. True, it was not very evident what harm the latter could do him; nevertheless, he could not shake off a vague, depressing apprehension. More and more, as he strolled on moodily musing, far in the rear of the rest, he felt inclined to appreciate the wisdom of the ancient proverb, "Let sleeping dogs lie." Years afterwards, he remembered with what a startled thrill, raising his eyes at a sharp angle of the path, he found himself face to face with Royston Keene.

For some seconds they contemplated each other silently—the Priest and the Soldier. A striking

contrast they made. The one heated and excited
and nervous, both in appearance and manner,
looking more like a culprit brought up for judgment than a pillar of the Established Church ; the
other outwardly as undemonstrativo as the rock
against which he leant—just a shade of paleness
telling of the sharp mental struggle from which he
had come out victorious,—his whole bearing and
demeanour precisely what might have been expected if he had been sitting on a court-martial.

The absurdity of the position struck the Chaplain as soon as he collected himself from the first
surprise. It never would do for *him* to look as if
he had anything to be ashamed of ; so, summoning
to his aid all the dignity of his office and his own
self-importance, with a great effort he spoke
steadily—

" I presume you wish to talk to me, Major Keene ?
I shall be glad to hear anything that you may
have to communicate or explain. It is my duty
as well as my desire to be useful to any member
of my congregation, however little disposed they
may be to avail themselves of their privileges.
Interested, as I must be, in the welfare of all committed to my charge, I need hardly say that the
course you have chosen to pursue here has caused
me great pain and anxiety,—I own not so much for
your sake as that of others, to whom your influence
was likely to be pernicious. What I heard this

morning makes matters look still worse : I wish I could anticipate any satisfactory explanation."

The old *ex cathedrâ* feeling came back upon him while he was speaking : his tone, gradually becoming rounder and more sonorous, showed this. Was he so besotted by sacerdotal confidence as to fancy that he could win that grim penitent to come to him to be confessed or absolved ?

Since the Chaplain first saw him, Royston had never changed his attitude. He was leaning with his shoulder against the corner of the rock round which the path turned, standing half across it, so that no one could pass him easily. The dense blue cloudlets of smoke kept rolling out from his lips rapidly but regularly, and his right hand twined itself perpetually in the coils of his heavy brown moustache. That gesture to those who knew his temper well, was ever ominous of foul and stormy weather. He did not reply immediately; but, taking the cigar from his mouth, began twisting up the loose leaf in a slow, deliberate way. At last he said,

" You did that rather well this morning. How much did you expect to get for it ? My wife is liberal enough in her promises sometimes, when she wants to make herself disagreeable; but she don't pay well. You might have driven a better bargain by coming to me. I would have given you more to have held your tongue." His tone was such as the other had never heard him use—

such as most people would be loth to employ towards the meanest dependent. No description can do justice to the intensity of its insolence; it made even Mr. Fullarton's torpid blood boil resentfully.

"How dare you address such words to me?" he cried out, trembling with rage; "if it were not for my profession——"

"Stop!" the other broke in, rudely, "you need not trouble yourself to repeat that stale claptrap. You mean to say that, if I were not safe from your profession, I should not have said so much. It isn't worth while lying to yourself, and I have no time to trifle. The converse is the truer way of putting it. You know better than I can tell you that, if you had been unfrocked, you would never have ventured half what you have done to-day. You don't stir from hence till this is settled. Do you suppose I'll allow my private affairs to be made, again, an occasion for indulging your taste for theatricals?"

The Chaplain flushed apoplectically: he just managed to stammer out—

"I will not remain another instant to listen to your blasphemous insults. If you mean to prevent me from passing, I will return another way."

Scornfully
He turned; but thrilled with priestly wrath, to feel
His sacred arm locked in a grasp of steel.

A bolder man might have got nervous, finding himself on a lonely hill-side, face to face with such an adversary; reading, too, the savage meaning of those murderous eyes. Remember, that Mr. Fullarton held Royston capable of any earthly crime. His own short-lived anger was instantly annihilated; the sweat of mortal terror broke out over all his livid face; his lips could hardly gasp out an unintelligible prayer for mercy.

The Soldier's stern face settled into an expression of contempt; in his gentlest moods, he could find little sympathy for purely physical fear.

"Don't faint," he said; "there is no occasion for it. Do you think I shall 'slay you as I slew the Egyptian yesterday'? Well, I have scanty respect for your office, especially when its privileges are abused. If it were not for good reasons, I would serve you worse than I did that drunken scoundrel who frightened you almost to death, down there among the vines. But that don't suit my purpose. Listen—if you dare to interfere again, by word, or deed, or sign, in the affairs of me and mine, I know a better way of making you repent it."

As soon as he saw that there was no real danger to life or limb, the Chaplain's composure began to return; he launched forth immediately into a gallant, though incoherent defiance. Royston's features never for an instant changed, or softened in their scorn.

"Fair words," he retorted, "but I'll make your bubbles burst. You don't monopolize *all* the resources of the Private Inquiry Office;" and, stooping down, he whispered a dozen words in the other's ear.

They related to a charge brought against Mr. Fullarton, years ago—so circumstantial and difficult to disprove, that, with all the advantages of counter-evidence at hand, it had wellnigh borne him down. He knew right well that if it were once revived here abroad, where the lightest suspicion is caught up and used so readily, the consequences would be nothing short of utter ruin. He was a poor man, with a large family: no wonder if he quailed.

"You know—you know," he gasped, "that it is a vile, cruel falsehood." To do him justice, he spoke the simple truth there.

With a cold, tranquil satisfaction, the Major contemplated his victim's agony.

"I choose to know nothing about it, except that it carries more probability than most stories one hears. The world in general is, fortunately, not incredulous, and I have seen a man 'broke' on lighter evidence. Well, you will take your own course; and I shall take mine. I fancy we understand each other—at last."

By a superhuman effort the unlucky ecclesiastic did contrive to mutter something about his "determination to do his duty." Royston listened to him with his worst smile.

"I'll take my chance about that," he said; "I feel tolerably safe. Now, I'll leave you to settle the affair between your interest and your conscience."

He turned on his heel, and strode away without another word. Long after he was out of sight, the Chaplain stood fixed in the same attitude of panic-stricken, helpless despondency. By my faith! even in these degenerate days we have petrifying influences left, that may match the Head of the Gorgon.

Meanwhile, the others were wending slowly homeward; truly, in a very different mood from that in which they had gone forth that morning. Even as no man can be pronounced happy till the hour of his death, so can no excursion or entertainment be called successful till night has fairly closed in; caprice of climate is only one of the many sources of disappointment; and the event justifies so seldom our sanguine predictions that we have little right to complain of false and fallible barometers.

It is worthy of remark, how often these trifles illustrate that trite and time-honoured simile of Life. The vessel starts gaily enough; heeling over

gracefully to the land-wind, in the old approved
fashion, " Youth at the prow, and Pleasure at the
helm," there is not a misgiving in the heart of
any one of the passengers; they cannot help pitying
those left behind on the shore; what a cheery
adieu they wave to the friends who come down to
wish them "good speed." After a voyage more or
less prolonged, the same ship drifts in slowly
shorewards, over the harbour-bar, under the calm
of the solemn sunset. Even the deepening twilight
cannot disguise the evidences of a terrible "sea-
change." Not a trace of paint or gilding remains
on the wave-worn shattered timbers; sails rent,
and cordage strained, tell-tales of many storm-
gusts, or, perchance, of one tornado; and, see—
her flag is flying half-mast high; the corpse of the
Pilot is on board. Let us stand aside, lest we
meet the passengers as they land: it were worse
than mockery to ask how the yachting trip has
sped.

Miss Tresilyan rode somewhat in advance of the
rest, under her brother's escort. Dick was a model
in his own line, and other brothers-of-beauties
might well imitate his moderation and discretion.
He never thrust himself into the conversation or
into her presence when there was a chance of his
intrusion being ill-timed; but was always at hand
when he was wanted: the slightest sign, or even
a glance from Cecil, brought him to her side; and

there he would march for hours, in silent but
perfect satisfaction. On the present occasion he
seemed disposed to be unwontedly talkative, and to
indulge in certain speculations relative to the
intelligence they had just heard. It was true, he
knew it before; but nothing had been disclosed to
him beyond the simple fact that Royston was
married, and married unhappily. Cecil checked
him gently, but very decidedly

"I had rather not hear or say one word on the
subject: it ought not to interest either of us. In
good time, I suppose, we shall be told all that it is
fitting we should know; meanwhile, it would be
very wrong to make conjectures. No one has any
right to pry into Major Keene's affairs if he chooses
to keep them secret. I do not believe any one
ever did so, even in thought, without repenting it.
I dare say Mr. Fullarton will find this out soon;
and I shall not pity him in the least. A person
ought to be punished who tries to startle people in
that disagreeable way. Did you hear Fanny's
little shriek? I have not had time to laugh at her
about it yet; the path is too narrow for two to ride
abreast."

The light tone and manner of her last words
might have deceived a closer observer than honest
Dick Tresilyan. He lapsed into silence; but, after
some time, his meditations assumed a cheerfully
roseate hue, as they resolved themselves into the

fixed idea that Royston was lingering behind "to
have it out with the parson."

Some distance in the rear walked Harry Molyneux, holding dutifully his wife's bridle-rein. It
was very touching to see the diffidence and humility
with which he proffered his little attentions, which
were accepted, as it were, under protest. The
truth was, that *la mignonne* had forgiven him
already, and it was with great difficulty she refrained from telling him so, by word or smile. Her
soft heart melted within her at the sight of the
criminal's contrition, and decided that he had done
penance enough during the last half-hour to atone
for a graver misdemeanour. But she deferred
asking for explanations till a more convenient
season, when there should be no chance of interruption; and meanwhile, on grounds of stern
political necessity, *elle le boudait.* (If any elegant
scholar will translate that Gallicism for me literally,
I shall feel obliged to him.)

Fancy the sensations of a man fighting his frigate
desperately against overwhelming odds, when he
sees the outline of a huge "liner," with English
colours at the main, looming dimly through the
smoke, close on the enemy's quarter; or those of
the commander of an untenable post, when the first
bayonets of the supporting force glitter over the
crest of the hill; and you will have a fair idea of
Harry's relief as he looked back, and saw Keene

gaining on them rapidly. As he fell out and yielded his post to Royston, this was written so plainly on his face that the latter could not repress a smile; but there was little mirth in his voice when he addressed Fanny—she had never heard him speak so gently and gravely.

"I know that you are angry with your husband as well as with me for keeping you in the dark so long. I must make his peace with you, even if I fail in making my own. He could not tell you one word without breaking a promise given years ago: if he had done so, in spite of the excuse of the strong temptation, I would never have trusted him again. Ah, I see you have done him justice already: that is good of you. Now for my own part: why I did not choose to let you into the secret as soon as I began to know you well, I can hardly say. Hal will tell you all about it; and you will see that for once I was more sinned against than sinning. So I was not afraid of your thinking worse of me for it. Perhaps the last thing that a man likes to confess is his one arch piece of folly, especially if he has paid for it as heavy a price as attaches to most crimes. I think I am not sorry that you were kept in the dark till now: the past has given me some pleasant hours with you that might have been darkened if you had known all. I wish you would forgive me. We have always been such good friends; and, in your sex at least, I can reckon so few."

If he had spoken with his ordinary accent, Fanny would scarcely have yielded so readily; but the strange sadness of his tone moved her deeply. A mist gathered in her gentle eyes, as she looked at him for some moments in silence, and then held out a timid little tremulous hand.

"I should not have liked you worse for knowing that you had been unhappy once," she whispered; "but I ought never to have been vexed at not being taken into confidence. I don't think I am wise or steady enough to keep secrets; only I wish —I do wish—that you had told Cecil Tresilyan."

He answered her in his old cool provoking way : "I know what you mean to imply; but you do Miss Tresilyan less than justice, and me too much honour. What right have you to infer that I look upon her in any other light than a very charming acquaintance, or that she feels any deeper interest in to-day's revelation than if she had heard un-expectedly that any one of her friends was married? Surprises are seldom agreeable, especially when they are so clumsily brought about. I am sure she has not told you anything to justify your sus-picions."

Fanny was the worst casuist out. She was seldom certain about her facts, and when she happened to be so, had not sufficient pertinacity or confidence to push her advantage. Her favourite argument was ever *ad misericordiam*. "I wish I

could quite believe you," she said, plaintively;
"but I can't, and it makes me very unhappy.
You must see that you ought to go."

Her evident fear of him touched Royston more
sharply than the most venomous reproach or the
most elaborate sarcasm could have done; but he
would not betray how it galled him.

"Three days ago," he replied, "I had almost
decided on departure; now it does not altogether
depend on me. But you need not be afraid. I
shall not worry you long; and while I stay, I have
no wish, and, I believe, no power, to do any one
any harm.

She looked at him long and earnestly, but failed
to extract any further confession from the impenetrable face. Keene would not give her the chance
of pursuing the subject, but called up Harry to
help him in turning the conversation into a different channel, and keeping it there. Between
the two they held the anxieties and curiosities of
the oppressed *mignonne* at bay, till they entered
Dorade.

They were obliged to pass the Terrasse on their
way home : there, alone, under the shadow of the
palms, sat Armand de Châteaumesnil. The invalid's
great haggard eyes fixed themselves observantly on
Cecil Tresilyan as she went by. He laid his hand
on the Major's sleeve when he came to his side,
and said, in a hoarse whisper, " Qu'as tu fait donc,

pour l'atterrer ainsi?" The other met the searching gaze without flinching—"Je n'en sais rien; seulement—on dit que je suis marié." If the Algerian had been told, on indisputable authority, that Paris and its inhabitants had just been swallowed up by an earthquake, he would only have raised his shaggy brows in a faint expression of surprise, exactly as he did now. "Tu es marié?" he growled out. "A laquelle donc des deux doit on compâtir— Madame ou Mademoiselle?" Yet he did not like Keene the worse for the impatient gesture with which the latter shook himself loose, muttering— "Je vous croyais trop sage, M. le Vicomte, pour vous amuser avec ces balivernes de romancier."

Fanny Molyneux and Cecil passed the evening together tête-à-tête. That kind little creature had a way of taking other people's turn of duty in the line of penitence and apology. On the present occasion she was remarkably gushing in her contrition, though her own guilt was infinitesimal; but she met with scanty encouragement. She had found time to extract from Harry all the details of the matrimonial misadventure, and wished to give her friend the benefit of them. Miss Trosilyan would not listen to a word. She did not attempt to disguise the interest she felt in the subject, but said that she preferred hearing the circumstances from Royston's own lips. With all this her manner had never been more gentle and caressing: she

R

succeeded at last in deluding Fanny into the belief that everybody was perfectly heart-whole, and that no harm had been done, so that that night *la mignonne* slept the sleep of the innocent, no misgivings or forebodings troubling her dreams.

Those brave women!—when I think of the pangs that they suffer uncomplainingly—the agonies that they dissemble—I am inclined to esteem lightly our own claims to the Cross of Valour. How many of them there are who, covering with their white hand the dagger's hilt, utter with a sweet, calm smile, and lips that never tremble, the falsehood holier than most outspoken truths— *Pœte, non angit!*

When Cecil returned home, Mrs. Danvers was waiting for her, ready with any amount of condolence and indignation. She checked all this, as she well knew how to do ; and at last was alone in her own chamber. Then the reaction came on ; with natures such as hers, it is a torture not to be forgotten while life shall endure.

There were not wanting in Dorade admirers and sentimentalists who were wont to watch the windows of The Tresilyan as long as light lingered there. How those patient, unrequited astronomers would have been startled, if their eyes had been sharp enough to penetrate the dark recess where she lay writhing and prone—her stricken face veiled by the masses of her loosened hair—her slender hands clenched till the blood stood still in their veins, in an agony of stormy self-reproach and fiery longing and injured pride; or if their ears had caught the sound of the low, bitter wail that went up to heaven like the cry from Gehenna of some fair, lost spirit, " My shame—my shame !"

Under favour of the audience, we will drop the curtain here. One of our puppets shall appear to-night no more. When a heroine is once on the stage, the public has a right to be indulged with the spectacle of her faults and follies, as well as of her virtues and excellences ; yet I love the phantasm of my queenly Cecil too well to parade her, discrowned and in abasement.

CHAPTER XVIII.

OTHER eyes besides Cecil's kept watch through
the night that followed that eventful day.
Royston's never closed till the dawning. Sometimes sitting motionless, sunk in his gloomy meditations, sometimes walking restlessly to and fro,
and cooling his hot forehead in the current of the
fresh night-air, he kept his mind on a perpetual
strain, calculating all probable and improbable
chances; and the dull red light was never
quenched that told of perpetually renewed cigars.

I fancy I hear an objection, springing from lips
that are wont to be irresistible, levelled against
such an atrocious want of sentiment. Fairest critic!
we will not now discuss the merits or demerits of
nicotine, considered as an aid to contemplation or an
anodyne; but do you allow enough for the force of
habit? Putting aside the case of those Indian
captives who are allowed a pipe in the intervals of
torment (for these poor creatures have had no advantages of education, and are beyond the pale
of civilized examples), do you not know that men
have finished their last weed while submitting to
the toilette of the guillotine? We are told that a

Spaniard has begged of his confessor a light for his *papelito* within sight of a freshly dug grave, when the firing party was awaiting him, a hundred paces off, with grounded arms.

Only when the sky was grey did Royston lie down to rest; but he slept heavily late into the morning. His first act, when he rose, was to send a note to Cecil Tresilyan, begging her to meet him at a named place and time. She did not answer it: nevertheless, he felt certain she would come. Assignations were no novelties to him; but he had gone forth to bear his part in more than one stricken field, where the chances of life and death were evenly poised, without any such despondency or uncertainty as clung to him then on his way to the appointed spot. He arrived there first; but he had not waited long when Cecil came slowly along the path that led into the heart of the woodland. As she drew near, Keene could not help thinking of the first time his eyes had lighted on her, mounting the zigzags of the Castle-hill. There was still the same elasticity of step, the same imperial carriage of the graceful head; but a less observant eye would have detected the change in her demeanour. The pretty petulance and provocative manner, which, contrasting with the royalty of her form and feature, contributed so much to her marvellous fascinations, had departed, he feared, never to return.

Many instances occur daily where that same

painfully unnatural gravity exasperates us, when its cause cannot be traced up to either guilt or sorrow. Ah, Lilla! there are many who think that your wild-flower wreath was a more becoming ornament than that diamond circlet—bridal gift of the powerful Baron. Sweet Eugenia! faces that were never absent from your *levées* in old times, you have missed at your court since you wedded Cæsar.

Both were outwardly quite calm; but who can guess which of those two strong hearts was most conscious of tremor and weakness, when Royston and Cecil met? His hand at least was the steadier, for her slight fingers quivered nervously in his grasp. He did not let them go till be began to speak.

"Whatever your decision may be after hearing me, I shall always thank you for coming here. It was like you—to give me the chance of speaking for myself. At least no falsehood or misconception shall stand between us. Will you listen to my story?"

"I came for no other purpose," Cecil said, and she sat down on the trunk of a fallen olive: she knew there would be need to husband all her strength. Thinking of these things in after days, she never forgot how carefully he arranged his plaid on the branches behind her, so as to keep off the gusts of wind that ever and anon blew sharply. At that very instant, as if there were some strange sympathy in the elements, the sun plunged into the bosom of a dull leaden cloud, and there came a growl of distant thunder.

"I shall not tax your patience long," Royston went on. "It shall only be the briefest outline. But do not interrupt me till I have ended; it is hard enough to have to begin and go through with it. I cannot tell you why I married. Many people asked me the question at the time, and I have asked it of myself often since; but I never could find any satisfactory answer. The woman I chose was, then, very beautiful, and it was not a disadvantageous match; but I had seen fairer faces and fortunes go by without coveting them. I think a certain obstinacy of purpose, and an absurd pleasure in carrying off a prize (such a prize!) from many rivals, was at the bottom of it all. In six months I began to appreciate the inconveniences of living with a statue; but I can say it truly, I never dreamt of betraying her. Yet I had temptations: remember I was not yet twenty-two, and one does not bear disappointments well at that age. We had not been married quite a year, when an officer in a native regiment died, up in the Hills, of *delirium tremens*. Do you know that, under such circumstances, there is always a commission appointed to examine the dead man's papers? I could not help seeing that, for some days past, my wife's manner had been strangely sullen and cold; but I had no suspicion of the truth.　I don't think I have ever been so surprised as when the president of the commission brought me a bundle of her letters.　I never saw her paramour : he must have been more fool than scoundrel to have kept what he ought to have burned.　I did not thank the man who gave me those papers, and I never spoke to him again. I only read one of them—it was written soon after our marriage.　I went to my wife with *this* in my hand.　She listened to me in her own icy way, not denying or confessing anything ; but she defied me to prove actual infidelity, either before or after my authority began.　I could not do it, whatever I might think.　I could only prove a course of lies and *chicanerie*, worked out by her and all her family, that would have sickened the most unscrupulous schemer alive.　I told her I would never sleep under the same roof with her again.　She laughed —if you could hear her laugh, you would excuse me for more than I have done—and said, ' You can't get a divorce.'　She was right there.　So it was settled that we were to live apart without any public scandal.　But her people would not accept their position.　They sent a brother to bully me.　It was an unwise move.　My temper was wilder in those days, and I had strong provocation ; yet I repent that I did not keep my hands off the throat of that wretched, blustering civilian.　It was all arranged peacefully at last, and I have not seen her since, though I hear of her from time to time, as I did yesterday This happened eleven long years ago, and she has never given me a chance of ridding myself of her since. She is always carefully circumspect, and so works out a patient revenge, though I believe I did her no wrong. You have heard all I dare to tell you, and all the truth. Judge me now."

For the last few minutes a great battle had been waging in Cecil Tresilyan's heart. Can the wisest of us—before the armies meet—prophesy aright as to the issue of such an Armageddon ?

Twice she tried to speak, and found her voice rebellious; at last she answered, in a faint, broken tone, " I cannot say how I pity you."

He threw back his lofty head, in anger or disdain.

" I will not accept groundless compassion, even from you. Do not deceive yourself. I have learnt how to bear my burden ; it scarcely cumbers me now. It has fretted me more in the last three weeks, than it has done for years. I only wish you to decide whether I did very wrong in keeping back the knowledge of all this from you ; and, if I have offended unpardonably, what my punishment shall be."

There was something more than reproach in the glance that flashed upon him out of the violet eyes; for an instant, they glittered almost scornfully; her lip, too, had ceased to tremble; and the silver in her voice rang clear and true :

"You are not afraid to ask that question—remembering many words addressed to me, each one of which was an insult—from you ? You dare not, yet, dishonour me in your thoughts so far as to doubt how I should have acted *at first*, if I had known your true position. Or are you amusing yourself still at my expense ? I had thought you more generous."

The gloom on Royston's face deepened sullenly. Though he had schooled himself up to a certain point of humility, even from her he could ill brook reproof.

" Those insults were not premeditated, at least," he retorted. " Have you not got accustomed, yet, to men's losing their heads in your presence, and then talking as the spirit moved them ? And you think I am amusing myself now. *Merci !* there runs something in my veins warmer than ice-water."

His accent was abrupt, even to rudeness; yet Cecil felt a thrill of guilty triumph as she heard it, and marked the shiver of passion that shot through his stalwart frame from brow to heel. A more perfect specimen of womanhood might not have been insensible to that mute acknowledgment of her power. But she shook her head in sorrowful incredulity.

"You do less than justice to your self-control.
But it is too late for reproaches. I forgive you for
any wrong that you may have done me, even in
thought or intention. I wish tho past could be
buried. For the future, I can only say this—wo
must part, and that instantly; it is moro than timc."

Keene had expected some such answer, and it
did not greatly disconccrt him. After pausing a
second or two, he said,

"I did not ask you for your decision without
meaning to abide by it. But it would be well to
pause before you make it final. Remember—we
shall not part for days, or months, if you send me
away now. At least, you need not fear persecution.
Yet it is difficult to reconcile oneself to banish-
ment. Will you not give me a chance of making
amends for the folly you complain of? I cannot
promise that my words shall always be guarded,
and my manner artificial; but I think I would
rather keep your friendship than win the love of
any living woman; and I would try hard never
to offend you. Let us finish this at once. You
have only to say 'Leave me,' and I swear that
you shall be obeyed to the letter."

On that last card hung all the issue of the game
that he would have sold his soul to win; yet he
spoke, not eagerly, though very earnestly; and
waited quietly for her reply, with a face as calm
as death.

Cecil ought not to have hesitated for an instant: we all know that. But steady resolve and stoical self-denial, easy enough in theory, are often bitterly hard in practice. It is very well to preach to the wayfarer that his duty is to go forward, and not tarry. Fresh and green grow the grasses round the Diamond of the Desert; pleasantly over its bright waters droop the feathery palms. How drearily the grey arid sand stretches away to the sky-line! Who knows how far it may be to the next oasis? Let us rest yet another hour by the fountain.

From any deliberate intention to do wrong, Cecil was as pure as any canonized saint in the roll of virgins and martyrs; but if she had been a voluptuary as elaborate as La Pompadour, she could not have felt more keenly that her love had increased tenfold in intensity since it became a crime to indulge it. The passionate energy that had slumbered so long in her temperament was thoroughly roused at last, and would make itself heard, clamorously enough, to drown the still, small voice, that said, "Beware and forbear." Her principles were good, but they were not strong enough to hold their own. O pride of the Tresilyans! that had tempted to sin so many of that haughty house, when you might have saved its fairest descendant, was it the time to falter and fail? She looked up piteously in her great extremity; there was a prayer for help in her eyes; but between them and Heaven was interposed a stern bronze face, not a line of it softening.

At length the faint, broken whisper came—" God help me! I *cannot* say it."

There was a pause, but not a stillness, for the beating of her companion's heart was distinctly audible. Then Cecil spoke again in her own natural caressing tones.

" You will be good and generous, I know. See how I trust you! "

The thought of how their continued intimacy might touch her fair fame never seemed to suggest itself for an instant. Yet, remember, The Tresilyan was no longer a guileless, romantic girl, believing and hoping all things. She knew right well what scandals and jealousies lurk under the smooth surface of the society in which she had borne so prominent a part; she knew that there were women alive who would have given half their diamonds to have her at their mercy and torment her at their will. Was it likely that such would let even a slander sleep?

Let the *Rosière* of last season lay this reflection to her heart, to temper the immoderation of triumph—" For every one of my victories, I have made one mortal enemy." Not only while in supremacy is the potentate obnoxious to conspiracies; the dagger is most to be dreaded when the dignity is laid down. All dethroned and abdicating Dictators have not the luck of Sylla.

Silently and unreservedly to accept such a sacrifice, while the offerer was resolved not to count the cost, transcended even the cynicism of Royston Keene. He grasped her arm as though to arrest her attention, and almost involuntarily broke from his lips words of solemn warning:

" Let me go on my way alone, while there is time. It is hard to touch pitch and keep undefiled. Child, you are too pure to estimate your danger. If you remained as innocent as one of God's angels, the world would still condemn you."

Her slender fingers twined themselves round his wrist,—so tenderly!—and she bent down her soft cheek, till its blush was hidden on his hand. Then she looked up in his face with a bright, trustful smile.

" Great happiness cannot be bought without a price. I fear no reproach so much as that of my own conscience. Do not think I delude myself as to the risk I am incurring. But if I am innocent, I shall never hear or heed what the world may say; if I am guilty—I have no right to complain of its scorn."

Hardened unbeliever as he was, Royston could have bowed himself there, and worshipped at her feet. But he would not confess his admiration; still less betray his triumph. He raised the little white hand that was free, gently, to his lips. Not with more reverent courtesy could he have done homage to an Anointed Queen.

"I wish I were worthier of you," he murmured; and no more was said then.

As they walked slowly homewards, the sullen clouds broke away from the face of the sun; but a weather-wise observer could have told that the truce was only treacherous. The tempest bided its time.

CHAPTER XIX

IT is not pleasant to stand by and assist at each step of an incantation that draws down a star from heaven, or darkens the face of the moon. Let us be content to accept the result, when it is forced upon us, without inquiring too minutely into the process. Not with impunity can even the Adepts gain and keep the secrets of their evil Abracadabra. The beard of Merlin is grey before its time : premature wrinkles furrow the brow of Canidia : though the terror of his stony eyes may keep the fiends at bay, the death-sleep of Michael Scott is not untroubled ; the pillars of Melrose shake ever and anon, as though an earthquake passed by, and the monks cross themselves in fear and pity, for they know that the awful wizard is turning restlessly in his grave.

As we are not writing a three-volume novel, we have a right, perhaps, not to linger over this part of our story. For any one who likes to indulge a somewhat morbid taste, or who happens to be keen about physiology, there is daily food sufficient in those ingenious romances *d'Outre-mer.*

It is hardly worth while speculating how far Cecil deluded herself, when she thought that she was safe in trusting to her own strength of principle, and to the generosity of Royston Keene. All this seems to me not to affect the main question materially. Does it help us—after we have yielded to temptation—that our resolves, when it first assailed us, should have been prudent and sincere, if such a plea cannot avert the consequences or extenuate the guilt? The grim old proverb tells us, how a certain curiously tesselated Pavement is laid down. Millions of feet have trodden those stones for sixty ages; yet they may well last till the Day of Judgment—they are so constantly and unsparingly renewed.

It is more than rashness for any mortal to say to the strong, treacherous ocean, "Thus far shalt thou go, and no further;" it is trenching on the privilege of Omnipotence. The dykes may be wisely planned and skilfully built; but one night, a wilder wind arises than any that they have withstood; the legions of the besieging army are mustering to storm. At one spot in the sea-wall, where patient miners have long been working unseen, a narrow breach is made, widening every instant; it is too late now to fly; the wolfish waves are within the entrenchments, mad for sack and pillage. On the morrow, where trim gardens bloomed, and stately palaces shone, there is nothing but a waste of waters strewn with wrecks, and blue, swollen corpses. The Zuyder Zee, rolls, ten fathom deep, over the ruins of drowned Stavoren.

So we will not enter minutely into the details of poor Cecil's demoralization—gradual, but fearfully rapid. It was not by words that she was corrupted; for Royston was still as careful as ever to abstain from uttering one cynicism in her presence; but none the less was it true, that daily and hourly some fresh scruple was swept away, some holy principle withered and died. The recklessness which ever carried him on straight to the attainment of a purpose, or the indulgence of a fancy, trampling down the barriers that divide good from evil, seemed to communicate itself to Cecil contagiously. She seldom ventured on reflection now —still less on self-examination; but she could not help being herself sensible of the change; thoughts that she would have shrunk back from in horror, not so long ago (if she could have comprehended them fully), had ceased to startle or repel her as she looked them in the face. Do not suppose, for an instant, that there was a corresponding alteration in her outward demeanour, or that it displayed any wildness or eccentricity. Melodrama may be

very successful at a transpontine theatre, but it is
unpardonably out of place in our *salons*. The
Tresilyan understood the duties of her social, if not
of her moral position (so long as the first was not
forfeited), as well as the strictest duenna alive;
though she might choose to defy the world's censure, she never dreamt of giving an opening to its
ridicule ! she was less capable of a *gaucherie* than
of a crime. In her bearing toward others she was
just the same as ever; if anything, rather more
brilliant and fascinating; and, if crossed or interfered with, perhaps a shade more haughtily independent.

Only when alone with Royston did she betray
herself. It was sad to see how completely the
stronger and worse nature had absorbed the
weaker and better one, till all power of volition
and free agency vanished, and even individuality
was lost. She was not sentimental or demonstrative in his presence (on the contrary, at such
times, that loveliest face was very apt to put on
the delicious *mine mutine*, which made it perfectly
irresistible), but the idea seemed never to enter
her mind that it would be possible to resist or
controvert any seriously expressed wish of her—
lover.

There—the word is written : and, woe is me !
that I dare not erase it : it must have come sooner
or later, and it is as well to have got it over.

According to all rules for such cases laid down and provided, Cecil's life ought to have been spent in alternations between feverish excitement and poignant remorse. But, the truth must be told—she was unaccountably happy. The simple fact was, that she had no time to be otherwise. Even when entirely alone, her conscience could find no opportunity of asserting itself. Her thoughts were amply occupied with recalling every word that Royston had said, and with anticipating what he would say at their next meeting.

It is idle to suppose that remorse cannot be kept at arm's length for a certain time; but the debt, recklessly incurred, must generally be paid to the uttermost farthing. Life, if sufficiently prolonged, will always afford leisure for reflection and retrospect; and, at such seasons, we appreciate in full force the tortures of "solitary confinement." The criminal may go on pilgrimage to a hundred shrines, and never light on the purification that will scare the Erinnyes.

In this instance, the victor certainly did not abuse his advantage, and was anything but exacting in his requirements. It was strange how his whole manner and nature altered when alone with his beautiful captive. The more evident became her subjugation, the more he seemed anxious to treat her with a delicate deference. They talked, as a rule, on any subject rather than

their own feelings; and he spoke on all such indifferent topics honestly, if not wisely. For the
rest of the world, his sarcasm and irony were
ready as ever : he kept all his sincerity and
confidence for Cecil Tresilyan. This is the secret
of the influence exercised by many men, at whose
successes we all have marvelled. Sweet, as well
as disenchanting experiences, are sometimes gained
behind the scenes ; none but those who have tried
it, can appreciate the delight of finding in a
manner, that the uninitiate call cold and repellant,
an ever-ready, loving caress. But in Royston's
case there was no acting; it was only that he
allowed Cecil to see one phase of his character that
was seldom displayed.

The subordinates in the drama betrayed much
more outward concern and disquietude than the
principals. When Fanny Molyneux found that
Royston did not intend to evacuate his position,
she tried the effect of a vigorous remonstrance on
her friend. The latter heard her patiently, but
quite impassively; declining to admit any probability of danger, or necessity to caution. La
mignonne was not convinced; but she yielded.
She wound her arm round Cecil's waist, as
they sat and whispered, nestling close to her
side—

"Dearest, remember this; if anything should
happen, I shall always think that some blame

belongs to me, and I will never give you up—
never."

The Tresilyan bent her beautiful swan-neck, as
though she were caressing a dove nestling in
her bosom; and pressed her lips on her companion's cheek, long and tenderly.

"I could not do *that*," she said, "if I were
guilty."

Neither had Harry refrained from lifting up his
testimony against what he saw and suspected. The
Major would take more from him than from any
man alive; he was not at all incensed at the interference.

"My dear Hal," he said, "don't make an old
woman of yourself by giving credit to scandal
or inventing it for yourself. If you choose
to be worried before your time, I can't help it,
but it is more than unnecessary. Una can take
care of herself, perfectly well, without your playing
the lion. Besides—what is the brother there for?
You know there are some subjects I never talk
about to you; and you don't deserve that I should
be communicative, now. But listen—you shall
not think of Cecil worse than she is; up to this
time, I swear, even her lips are pure from me.
Now—I hope you are satisfied; you have made
me break my rule, for once : drop the subject, in
the devil's name.

Though fully aware of his friend's unscrupulous

character, Harry was satisfied that nothing *very* wrong had occurred so far. Royston never lied.

"I'm glad that you can say so much," he replied; "the worst of it is, people will talk. I wonder that obnoxious Parson has not made himself more disagreeable already. I didn't go to church last Sunday afternoon, because I felt a conviction that he was going to be personal in his sermon."

The Major laughed his hard, unpleasant laugh. "Don't let that idea disturb your devotions another time. He is not likely to bite, or even to bark very loud: he don't get my muzzle off in a hurry."

Indeed, it was profoundly true that since the disclosure the Chaplain's reticence had become remarkable. When his own wife questioned him on the subject (very naturally), he checked her with some asperity, and read her a lecture on feminine curiosity that moved the poor woman, even to weeping. Mrs. Danvers was greatly surprised and disconcerted by the decision with which Mr. Fullarton rejected her suggestion, that he should aid and abet in thwarting Keene's supposed designs. "He had thought it right," he said, "to make Miss Tresilyan, and others, aware of the real state of the case; but he did not conceive that further interference lay within the sphere of his duty." It was odd how that same once arbitrarily elastic sphere had contracted since the prophet met the lion in the pathway !

Dick Tresilyan—the only other person much interested in the progress of affairs—did not seem to trouble himself much about them. He was perpetually absent on shooting expeditions ; but when at home it was observed that he drank harder than ever, getting sulky sometimes without apparent reason, and disagreeably quarrelsome.

Royston had only stated the simple fact when he said that Cecil was free from any stain of actual guilt or dishonour. Whether the credit of having borne her harmless was most due to her own prudence and remains of principle, or to her tempter's self-restraint, we will not, if you please, inquire. It is as well to be charitable now and then. Her escape was little less than miraculous, considering how often she had trusted herself unreservedly to the mercy of one who was wont to be as unsparing in his love as in his anger. Let not this immunity be made an excuse for credulous confidence, or induce others to emulate her rashness. The Millennium will not come in our time, I fancy ; and, till it arrives, neither child nor maiden may safely lay their hand on the cockatrice's den. The ballad tells us that Lady Janet was happy at last : but she paid dearly through months of sorrow and shame for those three red-roses plucked in the Elfin Bower. The precise cause of Keene's forbearance it would be very difficult to explain : more than one feeling probably had to do with it.

If Memory has any pleasures worth speaking of (which many grave and learned doctors take leave to doubt), certainly amongst the purest is the recollection, of having once been endowed with the whole love of a rare and beautiful being, which we did not abuse or betray. This is the only sort of lost riches on which we can look back with comfort out of the depths of present and pressing poverty; the pearl is so very precious that it confers on its possessor a certain dignity which does not entirely pass away, even when the jewel has slipped from his grasp, following the ring of Polycrates. Alas, alas ! less generous than the blue Ægæan are the sullen waters of the Mare Mortuum. Only on these grounds can that wonderful self-possession be accounted for, which enables men, seemingly ill-fitted for the situation, to confront the world in all its phases with so grand a calmness. It is refreshing to see how even coquetry recoils from that armour of proof, and to fancy how the dead beauty might triumph over the defeat of her living rivals, laughing the seductions of their loveliness to scorn. Even in crises of graver difficulty, where sterner assailants are to be encountered than Helen's magical smile, or Florence's magnetic eyes, the invisible Presence seems to inspire her lover with supernatural valiance. Remember the story of Aslauga's Knight; when once through the cloud of battle-dust gleamed the golden tresses, horse and man went down before him.

Royston was not half good enough to appreciate all this; yet some shadowy and undefined feeling, allied to it, may have helped to hold him back from pushing his advantage to the uttermost. Another and more selfish presentiment worked probably more powerfully. There was one phantom from which the Cool Captain never could escape; for years it had followed close on the consummation of all his crimes, and was, in truth, their best avenger: his Nemesis was satiety. He knew too well how the sweetest flowers lost their colour and fragrance, so soon as they were plucked and fairly in his grasp, not to shrink before the prospect of a certain disenchantment. This curse attaches to many of his kind: the instant the prize is won there arise misgivings as to its value; and defects develop themselves hourly in what seemed fault-less perfection before. It is boy's play to simulate being *blasé;* but the reality makes mature man-hood disbelieve anything sooner than inevitable retribution. Very often the thought forced itself upon Keene's mind,—"If I were to weary of *her* too?"—and made him pause before he urged Cecil to the step that must have linked him to her fate for ever.

Under other circumstances his patience might

have held out still longer; but there were number-
less difficulties and obstacles in the way of their
meeting, and the perpetual constraint fretted Royston sorely   His principle always had been not
openly to violate conventionalities, without gaining
an adequate equivalent; so he was more careful of
Cecil's reputation than she was inclined to be, and
amongst worse lessons, taught her prudence. They
met very seldom alone.   When Mrs. Danvers was
present, she made it her business to be as much as
possible in the way; and her awkward attempts at
interference   were   sometimes   inexpressibly provoking.   On one particular evening she had been
unusually pertinacious and obtrusive.   The Major
stood it tolerably well up to a certain point, but his
savage temper gradually got the better of him; his
face grew darker and darker, till it was black as
midnight when he rose to go, and his lips were
rigid as steel. It was evident he had come to some
resolution that he meant to keep.   When he was
wishing Bessie " good night," he held her hand
imprisoned for a moment without pressing it.

" You are so good a theologian," he said, " that
perhaps you can tell me where a text comes
from that has haunted me for the last hour. It
speaks of some one who ' loosed the bands of
Orion.' "

His manner, and the sudden address, disconcerted Mrs. Danvers so completely as to incapaci-

tate her from reply: she suffered "judgment to go by default;" and left Royston under the impression that she had never read the Book of Job.

The next day he asked Cecil to elope with him.

She listened without betraying either terror, or anger, or disdain; but she raised her beautiful eyes to his with a sad, searching inquiry, before which many men would have quailed.

"Have you counted the cost to yourself and to me?"

"I have done both," replied Keene, gravely. "I cannot say that you will never repent it; but I know that I shall never regret it."

There were no promises or vows exchanged; but a silence for two long minutes; and, when these were past, the sweet, pure lips had lost their virginity

So, with a few more words, it was finally arranged; and the next day Royston left Dorade, to make preparations all along the road of their intended flight. Their plan was to take boat at Marseilles for the East, making their first permanent resting-place one of the Islands of the Grecian Archipelago. Both were most anxious to evade any possibility of interception, more especially of collision with Dick Tresilyan.

On that evening Cecil was alone in her own room (Mrs. Danvers had gone out to a sort of love-feast at the Fullartons', where the company were to be entertained with weak tea and strong doctrine *à discretion*). She had rejected the offer of Fanny's companionship on the plea, not altogether false, of a tormenting headache. *La mignonne* was too innocent to suspect the reason, that made her friend shudder in their parting embrace, half averting her cheek, though Cecil's arms clung round her as though they would never let her go. The saddest feeling of the many that were busy then in the guilty, troubled heart, was a consciousness, that in a few hours the gulf between them would be deep and impassable, as the chasm dividing Abraham from Dives.

Miss Tresilyan had taken unconsciously an attitude in which you saw her once before—half-reclined, and gazing into the fire : outwardly still remained the same pensive, languid grace; but very different was the careless reverie that had stolen over her then, from the wild chaos of conflicting thoughts that involved her now.

Her whole being was so bound up in Royston Keene's that she felt without him there would be nothing worth living for; neither had she the faintest misgiving as to the chances of his inconstancy. There had descended to her some of the stability and determination of purpose which had made many of her race so powerful for good or evil; in the pursuit of either they would never admit a doubt or listen to a compromise. When

Cecil believed, she believed implicitly, and, not even with her own conscience, made conditions of surrender. So long as *his* strong arm was round her, she felt that she could defy shame, and even remorse; but how would it be, if that support should fail? He had not been away yet twenty hours, and already there came creeping over her a chilling sense of helplessness and desolation. She knew her lover's violent passions and haughty temper, impatient of the most distant approach to insolence or even contradiction from others, too well not to be aware that such a man walked ever on the frontier-ground betwen life and death. Suppose that he were taken from her?—her spirit, dauntless as it was, quailed before the ghastly terrors of imagined loneliness. An evil Voice that had whispered perhaps in the ear of more than one of the "bitter, bad Tresilyans," seemed to murmur, " You, too, can die :" but Cecil was not yet so lost as to listen to the suggestion of the subtle fiend. She wasted no regrets on the past, and the wreck of all its brilliant promises ; she was resolute to meet the perils of the future; nevertheless, her heart was heavy with apprehension. Remember the answer that the stout Catholic made to Des Adrets, when the savage baron taunted him with cowardice for shrinking twice from the death-leap on the tower, " *Je vous le donne, en dix.*" So, it is not in womanhood—however ruined in principle or reckless of the consequences—to venture deliberately, without a shudder, on the fatal plunge from which no fair fame has ever risen unshattered again. Even prejudices may not be torn up by the roots without stirring the earth around them.

She might have sat musing thus for about an hour: so deep in thought that she never heard the *portière* slowly drawn aside that divided the room from an antechamber. The Tresilyan had her emotions under tolerable control, and at least was not given to screaming; but she could hardly repress the startled cry that sprang to her lips when she raised her eyes.

The reproachful spectre that had haunted her for years — till very lately, when a stronger influence chased it away — assumed substance of form and feature, as the dark doorway framed the haggard, pain-stricken face of Mark Waring.

CHAPTER XX.

IT is not very easy to confront, with decorous composure, the sudden apparition of the person on earth that one would have least liked to see. All things considered, Cecil carried it off creditably, and greeted her unexpected visitor with sufficient cordiality. Mark took her offered hand gravely, without eagerness, not holding it an instant longer than was necessary. Then he spoke—

"They told me I should find you alone. I was so anxious to do so as soon as possible, that I ventured to break in upon you, even at this unseasonable hour. You will guess that I had powerful reasons?"

The Tresilyan threw back her haughty head, as a war-horse might do at the first blast of the trumpet—she scented battle in the wind.

"Will you be good enough to explain yourself?" she said, as she took her own seat again, and motioned him into another; "I am sure you would not trifle with me, or vex me unnecessarily?"

Waring did not avail himself of the chair indi-

cated, but crossed his arms over the back of it, and
stood so, regarding her intently

"You only do me justice there," he replied; " I
will speak briefly, and plainly too. I came here
from Nice to ask you how much truth there is in
the reports that couple your name with Major
Keene's?"

No one likes to give the death-blow to the loyalty
of a faithful adherent, be he ever so humble; and
Cecil was bitterly pained that she could not speak
truly, and satisfy him. Her face sank lower and
lower, till it was buried in her hands. Nothing
more was needed to convince Waring that his
worst fears were realized. For a moment or two
he felt sick and faint. No wonder; he had given
up hope long ago, but not trust and faith; now
these were blasted utterly. In any religion,
whether true or false, the fanatic is happier, if not
wiser, than the infidel; if you cannot replace it
with a better, it is cruel to shake the foundation of
the simplest creed. Mark's voice—hollow, and
hoarse, and changed—could not but betray his
agony.

"God help us both! Has it come to this—that
you have no words to answer me, when I dare to
hint at your dishonour?"

She looked up quickly, flushing to the brow,
rose-red with anger.

"I will not endure this, even from you. Understand at once—I deny your right to question me."

The clear blue eyes met the violet ones with a steady, judicial calmness, undazzled by their ominous lightning.

"Listen to me quietly, two minutes longer," he said, "and then resent my presumption as much as you will. Three years ago it pleased you to make me the subject of an experiment. How far you acted heedlessly, and in ignorance of the consequences, I have never stopped to inquire—it would be wasting time; the sophistries of coquetry are too subtle for me. I only know what the result has been. Before I met you I could have offered to any woman who thought it worth her acceptance, a healthy, honest love; now—even if I could conquer my present infatuation—I could only offer a feeling something warmer than friendship: to promise more would be base treachery. Do you think I would stand by God's altar with a worse lie than Ananias' on my lips? Is it nothing that, to gratify your vanity or your whims, you should have condemned a man, whose blood is not frozen yet, to something worse than widowhood for life? My religion may be a false and vain idolatry; but it is all I have to trust to. I will not stand patiently by, and see the image that I have bowed down to worship, pilloried for the world to scorn. Now— do you deny my right to interfere?"

His words had a rude energy, though little eloquence; but they came so evidently from the depths of a strong, troubled heart, that they caused a revulsion in Cecil's feelings; returning remorse bore down her stubborn pride. Very low and plaintive was the whisper, "Ah! have mercy— have mercy; you make me so unhappy!" but there came a more piteous appeal from her eyes. In Mark's stout manhood was an element of more than womanish compassion and tenderness; he never could bear to see even a child in tears;—no wonder if his anger vanished before the contrition of the one being whom he loved far better than life. He lost sight of his own wrongs instantly, but *not* of the object he had in view.

"Forgive me for speaking so roughly; I ought to have declined your challenge. I behaved better once, you remember. But be patient while I plead for the Right,—though, if you would but listen to them, prudence and your own conscience could do that better than I. When infatuation exists, it is worse than useless to prove the object of it unworthy: so I will not attempt to blacken Major Keene's character; besides, it is not to my taste to attack men in their absence. I fear there are few capitals in Europe where his name is not too well known. From what I have heard, I believe his wife was most in fault when they separated; but the life he has led since deprives him of all right to complain of her, or condemn her. Recollect, you have only heard one side. But it is not a question of his eligibility as an acquaintance. There is the simple fact—he is married; and your name being connected with his, involves disgrace. You cannot have fallen yet so far as to be reckless about such an imputation? In my turn I say, ' Have mercy!' Do not force me henceforth to disbelieve in the purity of any created thing."

Cecil could only murmur, "It is too late—too late!" The ghastly look of horror that swept over Waring's face showed that his thoughts had gone beyond the truth. "I mean," she went on, blushing painfully, "that I have promised."

"Promised!" Mark repeated, in high disdain; "I have lived too long when I hear such devil's logic from your lips. You know full well there is more sin in keeping than in breaking such engagements. I will try to save you, in spite of yourself. Listen. I do not threaten; I know you well enough to be certain that such an argument would be the strongest temptation to you to persevere in taking your own course. I only tell you what I will do. I shall speak to your brother first; if he cannot understand his duty, or shrinks from it, I will carry out what I believe to be mine. I utterly disapprove of and despise the practice of duelling; but, at any risk, I *will* stand between you and Major Keene. He shall not gain possession of you while I am alive. When I am dead—if you touch his hand you shall know that my blood is upon it, and the guilt shall rest on your own head. I believe that, in keeping you apart, I should act kindly towards both. I do him this justice—it would make him miserable to see you pining away. There are limits to human endurance, and you are too proud to bear dishonour."

Cecil felt that every word he had spoken was good and true, and that he would not waver in his purpose for an instant. She remembered how, when they were returning together, four days ago, the sidelong glance of a matronly Pharisee had lighted on her in a spiteful triumph; and how, though neither of them alluded to it afterwards, the dark-red flush of anger had mounted to Royston's forehead. She had ceased to care for herself; but could she not save *him*, while yet there was time? And more—had she not wrought wrong enough to Mark Waring without having his murder on her soul?—for she never doubted as to the result, if those two should meet as foes.

They talk of hair that has grown grey in the briefest space of mental anguish. It is all a delusion and an old wife's fable; when Cecil rose the next morning there was not a silver line in her tresses. Outward signs of the mortal struggle, while it lasted, there were none, for her clasped

hands veiled her face jealously : when she raised it,
her cheek was paler than death, and wet with an
awful dew : and when she spoke, her voice retained
not one cadence of its wonted melody.

"You have prevailed, as the Truth always ought
to prevail. Now tell me what to do."

Mark Waring would have drained his heart's
blood, drop by drop, to have lightened one throb
of her agony; but he never thought of flinching
from his purpose.

"There are perils where the only safety lies in
flight. You must leave this before Major Keene
returns; and he returns to-morrow."

Perhaps I have failed in making you understand
one hereditary peculiarity of the Tresilyans.
When their hand was fairly laid on the plough,
they were incapable of looking back. Had Mark
come ten hours later, when Cecil's purpose was
absolutely fixed, all his arguments would have been
futile. As it was, once having decided finally
on the line she was to take, it never occurred to
her to make further objections. "Yes, I will go,"
she said; "but I must write to him."

"I think you ought to do so," answered Waring;
"and if you will give me the letter I will deliver
it myself."

Every vestige of the returning colour faded
from Cecil's cheek. "You do not know him : I
dare not trust you."

He misinterpreted the cause of her terror. " I promise you that, however angry Major Keene may be, I will bear it patiently, and never dream of resenting it. He is safe from me now."

She smiled very sadly, yet not without a dreary pride; she could have seen Royston pitted against any mortal antagonist, and never would have feared for *him*. "You scarcely understand me; I was not anxious for his safety, but for yours."

Mark was too brave and single-hearted to suspect a taunt, even had such been intended. "Then there is nothing more to be settled," he said, quietly, "but the time and manner of your departure. I will leave you now; I shall see you before you go."

Cecil Tresilyan rose and laid her hand on his arm—her beautiful face fixed in its resolve, like that of one of those fair Norse Valas, from whose rigid lips flowed the bode of defeat or victory, when the Vikings went forth to the Feast of the Ravens.

"I am not angry with one word you have said to-night; you have only expressed what my own cowardly conscience ought to have uttered. Nevertheless, to-morrow sees our last meeting. All your account against me is fairly balanced now. I do not know what I may have to suffer; but I do know, that I *will* be alone till I die. Perhaps some day I may thank you in my thoughts for what you have done ; I cannot—now."

With a heavy heart, Waring owned to himself that her words were bitterly true. In curing such diseases the physician must work without hope of reward or fee ; it will be long before the patient can touch without a shudder the hand that inflicted the saving cautery.

Her tone changed, and she went on murmuring, low and plaintively, as if in soliloquy, and unconscious of another's presence :

" I could not help loving him, though I knew it was sin ; if there is shame in confessing it, I cannot feel it yet. I wish I had told him *once*—how dearly I loved him ; I shall never be able to whisper it to him now, and I dare not write it. No, he will not forget me as he has forgotten others ; but he will hate me, and call me false, and fickle, and cold. Cold—if he could only read my heart ! I never read it myself till now, when we must be parted for ever."

Is it pleasant, think you, to listen to such words as these, uttered by the woman that you have worshipped, even if it be hopelessly, for years ? Men have gone mad under lighter tortures than those that Mark Waring was then forced to endure. But he knew that it was the extremity of her anguish that had hardened, for a season, Cecil's generous nature, and made her heedless of the pain she in-

flicted. So he answered in a slow, steady voice,
such as we employ when trying to calm the ravings
of a fever-fit,

" Hush ! you speak wildly. My presence here
does you no good. You may think of me as hardly
as you will ; perhaps time will soften your judgment ; if not—I shall still not repent to-night's
work. I will come for your letter at the moment
of your departure. Good-night ; I pray that God
may help you now, and guard you always."

He raised her hand and just touched it with his
lips, with the same grave courtesy that had marked
his manner when they parted last, three years ago;
and in another second Cecil was alone again.

She was not long in recovering from her bewilder-
ment ; and when Mrs. Danvers returned, she was
perfectly collected and calm. It is not worth while
recording Bessie's noisy expressions of astonishment and delight, nor describing Dick Tresilyan's
way of receiving notice of the sudden change in
their plans. His stolid composure was not greatly
disturbed thereby ; he muttered, under his breath,
some sulky anathemas on " women who never
knew their own minds ; " but this was only because he considered a growl to be the form of
protest suitable to the circumstances, and due to
his masculine dignity   On the whole, he was
rather glad to go. It had become evident, even
to his dull comprehension, that great mischief was

brewing somewhere; and for days past he had been in a state of hazy apprehension—as he expressed it, "not seeing his way out of it at all." So he set about his part of the preparations for their exodus with a right goodwill. Neither will we give the details of Cecil's parting with *La Mignonne*. The latter was so rejoiced at the idea of her friend's being out of harm's way, that she did not question her much as to the reasons for such an abrupt departure: it was not till afterwards that she learnt that it had been brought about by the influence of Waring. It is unnecessary to mention that the adieus were not accomplished without a certain amount of tears; but they were all shed by Fanny Molyneux. Cecil dared not yet trust herself to weep. She took a far more formal farewell of Mr. Fullarton, and the Chaplain did not even venture on a parting benediction.

The heavy travelling chariot, with its hundred cunning contrivances, is packed at last; and Karl, the accomplished courier, wiping from his blonde moustache the drops of the stirrup-cup, touches his cap with his accustomed formula—"Zi ces dames zont brêtes?" Mark Waring leans over the carriage door to say "Goodbye:" the hand he presses lies in his grasp, unresponsive and unsympathetic as a splinter from an iceberg. His sad, earnest look pleads in vain, for there is no softening or kindness in Cecil's desolate, dreamy

eyes. The road on which they are to travel is the
same for some leagues as that along which Royston
Keene must return; and she is thinking, divided
betwixt hope and fear, if there may not be a
possibility of their meeting. The wheels move,
and hasty farewells are waved; and Mark stands
there half-stupefied, unconscious of anything but a
sense of lonely wretchedness. The one solitary link
that still binds him to Cecil Tresilyan will be
severed when the letter is delivered that he holds
in his hand.

As the carriage swept round the corner of the
terrace, it passed close to the spot where Armand
de Châteaumesnil sat, basking in the sunshine.
The invalid lifted his cap in courteous adieu; but
his face grew dark and his shaggy brows were
knit savagely.

"On l'a triché donc, après tout," he muttered;
"Sang dieu! les absens ont diablement tort."

Sunk as she was at that moment in gloomy
meditations, Cecil never forgot that the last object
on which her eyes lighted in Dorade, was the
wreck of the crippled Algerian.

Molyneux and his wife stood silent till their
friends were quite out of sight; then Harry turned
slowly round and gazed at his *mignonne*. He
knew that the same thought was in both their
minds, for her sweet face was paler than his own.
(Neither of them guessed at the truth; and they

saw in Mark Waring nothing more than an old
acquaintance of the Tresilyans.)

"Royston will be here in four hours," he said
"and who will tell him this ?   I dare not."

Fanny feigned a carelessness that she was far
from feeling :

"I don't know how that is to be managed; but
I believe it is all for the best.   He can't kill either
of us; that is some comfort."

Harry did not smile ; his countenance wore ar
expression of grave anxiety, such as had seldom
appeared there.

"No, he will not hurt us ; but I fear he will have
some one's blood, before all is done."

CHAPTER XXI

IT was past nightfall when Major Keene returned
to Dorade. As he drove past the hotel where
the Tresilyans lodged, he looked up at the windows
of their apartments, and was somewhat surprised to
see no light there; but no suspicion of the truth
crossed his mind. He had made all preparations
for the intended flight with his habitual skill and
foresight. The Levantine steamer left Marseilles
early on the third morning from this; and relays
were so ordered along the road as to prevent the
possibility of being overtaken, and just to hit the
hour of the vessel's sailing. So far everything
seemed to promise favourably for the accomplishment of his purposes; and Royston could not have
explained even to himself the reason of his feeling
so moody and discontented. He went straight to
his own rooms, without looking in at the Molyneux's; for he was heated and travel-stained; and
under such circumstances was wont to postpone
the greeting of friends to the exigencies of the
toilette. This was scarcely concluded when his
servant brought him Mark Waring's card, with a
request pencilled on it for an immediate interview

Even the Cool Captain started perceptibly
when he read the name : he was well acquainted
with the episode connected with it ; for Cecil had
kept back none of her secrets from him, and this
was among the earliest confidences. *Then* he had
felt no inclination to sneer ; but now his lip began
to curl cynically.

" *Caramba !*" he muttered ; " the plot begins to
thicken. What brings the old lover *en scène ?*
I hope he does not mean to make himself disagreeable. I haven't time to quarrel just now ,
and besides, it would worry Cecil. Well—we'll
find out what he wants. Tell Mr. Waring that I
am disengaged, and shall be happy to see him."

Royston advanced to meet his visitor, with a
manner that was perfectly courteous, though it
retained a tinge of haughty surprise.

" I cannot guess to what I am indebted for this
pleasure," he said. " Pardon me if I ask you to
explain your object as briefly as possible. I have
much to do this evening, and my time is hardly my
own."

Waring gazed fixedly at the speaker for a few
seconds before he replied. Like most of his profession, he was an acute physiognomist ; and in
that brief space he fathomed much of the character
of the man who had rivalled him successfully. He
confessed honestly to himself that there were
grounds, if not excuse, for Cecil's infatuation ; but

he shrank from thinking of the danger which she had escaped so narrowly.

"Yes, I will be as brief as possible," Mark answered, at length. "Neither of us will be tempted to prolong this interview unnecessarily. I have promised to deliver a letter to you; and when you have read it, I shall have but very few words to say"

A stronger proof than Keene had ever yet given of superhuman control over his emotions, was the fact that, neither by quivering of eyelid, change of colour, or motion of muscle, did he betray the faintest astonishment or concern, as he took the letter from Waring, and recognized Cecil's hand on the cover. It was not a long epistle, for it scarcely extended beyond two sides of a note-sheet: the writing was hurried, and in places almost illegible: it had entirely lost the firm, even character which usually distinguished it, from which a very moderate graphiologist might have drawn successful auguries. Perhaps this was the reason that Royston read it through twice, slowly. As he did so his countenance altered fearfully; the deadly white look of dangerous passion overspread it all; and his eyes began to lighten. Yet he spoke calmly—

"You knew of this being written?"

"I am happy to say I was more than passively conscious of it," Mark replied; "I did all in my power to bring about the result that you are now made aware of; and I thank God that I did not fail."

While the other was speaking, Royston was tearing up the paper he held into the smallest shreds, and dropping them one by one. The act might have been involuntary, but seemed to have a savage viciousness about it, as if a living thing were being tortured by those cruel fingers. (The poor letter!—whatever its faults might have been, it surely deserved a better fate: it was doubtless not a model of composition; but some of the epistles which have moved us most in our time, either for joy or sorrow, might not in this respect emulate Montagu or Chapone.) Still he controlled himself with a mighty effort, enough to ask, steadily, "Were you weary of your life to have done all this, and then come here to tell me so?"

Waring laughed drearily.

"Weary? So weary that, if it had not been for scruples you cannot understand, I would have got rid of it long ago. But I need not inflict my confidences on you; and I don't choose to see the drift of your question."

The devil had so thoroughly by this time possessed Royston Keene, that even his voice was changed into a hoarse, guttural whisper.

"I asked because I mean to kill you."

Mark's gaze met the savage eyes that gleamed like a famished panther's, with an expression too calm for defiance, though there might have been perhaps a shade of contempt.

"Of course I shall guard my own life as best I may, either here or elsewhere; but I do not apprehend it is in great danger. There is an old proverb about 'threatened men;' they are not killed so easily as women are betrayed. Beyond the simplest self-defence, I warn you that I shall not resent any insult or attack. I will not meet you in the field; and as for any personal struggle, I don't think that even you would like to make Cecil Tresilyan the occasion for a broil that might suit two drunken peasants."

Though shorter by half a head, and altogether cast in a less colossal mould, as he stood there, with his square, well-knit frame, and bold Saxon face, he looked no contemptible antagonist to confront the swarthy giant. In utter insensibility to fear, and carelessness of consequences (so far as they could affect a steady resolve), the Cool Captain had met his match at last. Even then, in the crisis of his stormy passion, he was able to appreciate a hardihood so congenial to his own character; pondering upon these things afterwards, he always confessed that at this juncture, and indeed all throughout, his opponent had very much the best of it. Ferocity and violence seemed puerile and out of place when contrasted with that tranquil audacity. He covered his eyes with his hand for a moment or so, and when he raised his face it had recovered its natural impassibility, though the ghastly pallor still remained. Besides, the truth of Waring's last words struck him forcibly. He muttered under his breath, " By G—d, he's right *there,* at all events ; " then he said aloud—

" Well, it appears you won't fight; so there is little more to be said between us. You think you can thwart my purposes, or mould them as you like. We'll try it. I told you I had many things to do to-night: I have one more than I dreamt of on hand. I wish to be alone."

Mark gazed wistfully at the speaker, without stirring from his seat.

" I know what your intention is, perfectly well. You mean to follow her. I believe it would be quite in vain ; you have misjudged Cecil Tresilyan, if you fancy that she would alter her determination twice. But you might give her great pain, and compromise her more cruelly than you have done already. There are obstacles now in your way that you could not encounter without causing open scandal. Her brother's suspicions are fairly roused by this time, and he cannot help doing his duty: he may be weak and credulous, but he is no coward. There is no fear of further interference from me: my part is played. But I do beseech you to pause. Supposing the very worst—that you could still succeed in persuading Cecil to her ruin—are you

prepared deliberately to accept the consequences of
the crime? You are far more experienced in such
matters than I: do you know a single instance of
such guilt being accomplished, where *both*, before
the year was ended, did not wish it undone? I do
not pretend to be interested about your future;
but I believe I am speaking now as your dearest
friend might speak. You both delude yourselves
miserably, if you think that Cecil could live under
disgrace. I do you so much justice—you would
find it unendurable to see her withering away day
by day, with no prospect before her but a hopeless
death. In God's name, draw back while there is
time. It is only a sharp struggle, and self-command
and self-denial will come. Loneliness is bitter to
bear: *I* know that; but what is manhood worth, if
it cannot bear its burdens? I have put everything
on the lowest grounds; and I will ask you one
question more—you might guard her from some
suffering, by hiding her from the world's scorn—
could you guard yourself against satiety?"

He spoke without a trace of anger or animosity,
and the grave, kind tones made some way in
the winding avenues leading to Royston's heart.
Besides this, the last word struck the cord of the
misgiving that had haunted him ever since he proposed the flight, and had already made him half
repent it. But the fortress did not yet surrender.

"All this while, you have had some idea of improving your own position with Cecil. It is natural enough; yet I fancy you will find yourself mistaken there."

Instead of flushing at the taunt, Waring's face grew paler, and there shot across it a sharp spasm of pain.

"So, you cannot understand disinterestedness?" he said. "Before I ventured on interference, I was aware of the certain consequences, and weighed them all. Miss Tresilyan thought she had done me some wrong; and I trusted to her generosity to help me when I spoke for the Right. But I knew that the spell could only be used once, and that the cancelled debt could not be revived. I shall never speak to her—perhaps never see her—on earth again. Do you imagine I love her less for that? Hear this—I suppose I have as much pride as most men; but I would kneel down here and set your foot on my neck if I thought the humiliation would save her one iota of shame or sorrow."

Keene was fairly vanquished. He was filled with a great contempt for his own guilty passion, compared with the pure self-sacrifice of Mark's simple chivalry. He raised his eyes from the ground, on which they had been bent gloomily while the other was speaking, and answered without hesitation—

"I owe you some amends for much that has been said to-night; and I will not keep you in suspense a moment unnecessarily. I shall leave Dorade to-morrow; but it will not be to follow Cecil Tresilyan. More than this: if there is any chance of our meeting hereafter, on my honour I will avoid it. I wish many things could be unsaid and undone; but nothing has occurred that is past remedy. As far as any future intentions of mine are concerned, I swear she is safe as if she were my sister."

Waring drew a long breath, as if a ponderous weight had been lifted from his chest. "I believe you," he said simply: then he rose to go. He had almost reached the door, when he turned suddenly and stretched out his hand. It was a perfectly unaccountable and perhaps involuntary impulse; for he still could not absolve the other from dark and heavy guilt. The Major held it for a few seconds in a gripe that would have paralyzed weaker fingers; even Mark's tough joints and muscles were long in forgetting it. He muttered these words between his teeth as he let it go—" *You* were worthy of her."

So the interview ended—in peace.

Nevertheless, there was little peace that night for Royston Keene: he passed it alone; how, no mortal can know; but the next morning his appearance fully bore out the truth of the ancient aphorism, "There is no rest for the wicked." His face was set in the stoniest calmness; but the features were haggard and drawn, and fresh lines and furrows were there, deeper than should have been engraved by half a score of years. A violent, passionate nature does not lightly resign the one object of its aims and desires. Larches and firs will bear moving, cautiously; for they are well-regulated plants, and natives of a frigid zone; but transplanting rarely succeeds in the tropics.

Harry Molyneux came to his friend's apartments early on the following day, in a very uncomfortable and perplexed frame of mind. In the first place, he was sensible of that depression of spirits which is always the portion of those who are left behind, when any social circle is broken up, by the removal of its principal elements. There is no such nuisance as having to stay and put the lights out. Besides this, he was quite uncertain in what temper Royston would be found; and apprehended some desperate outbreak from the latter, which would bring things, already sufficiently complicated, into a more perilous coil.

Keene's first abrupt words, in part, reassured him. "Well, it is all over; and I am going straight back to England."

Harry felt so relieved that he forgot to be considerate : he could not repress his exultation. "Is it really all over ? I am so very glad ! "

"And I am not sorry," was the reply. The speaker probably persuaded himself that he was uttering the truth; but the dreary, hopeless expression of his stricken face gave his words the lic. It cut deep into Molyneux's kind heart; he felt more painfully than he had ever done the difficulty of reconciling his evident duty with the demand of an ancient friendship; on the whole, a guilty consciousness of treachery predominated. He was discreet enough to forbear all questions, and it was not till long afterwards that he heard an outline of part of what had happened in the past night; it was told in a letter from Miss Tresilyan to his wife. Had he been more inquisitive, his curiosity would scarcely have been gratified. Keene guarded the secrets of others more jealously than he kept his own; and he would have despised himself for revealing one of Cecil's, even to his old comrade, without her knowledge and leave. If the feeling which prompted such reticence was not a high and delicate sense of honour, it was, at least, a very efficient substitute for a profitable virtue.

"You go to England?" Molyneux went on, after a brief pause; "when do you start? and what do you mean to do?"

Royston looked up, and saw his own discontent reflected in the countenance of his faithful sub-altern; he knew he had found there the sympathy that he was too proud to ask of any living man.

"I start to-night," he replied; "so you see I have no time to lose. I can hardly tell you what I mean to do, Hal. Do you remember what we said about the best way of spending our resources? Well — I have broken into my last large note; and I suppose I must get rid somehow of the change."

Harry's answer was not very ready, nor very distinct when it came. "I wish—I wish I could help you!"

For one moment, there returned to Keene's disciplined face, a good, [natural expression, which had been a stranger there since the days of his hot youth; when he first went forth to buckle with the world, frank, and honest, and fearless; his voice, too, softened, almost to tenderness.

"Old friend, the time has come to say goodbye. Our roads have been the same—for longer than I like to think of: but henceforth they must lie so far apart that I doubt if they will ever cross again. You will see me off, I know; but I may not be able to say then a dozen words that I should be sorry to leave unsaid. I'll do you this justice— in no one instance have I ever seen you flinch when I wanted your help; though often you had no object of your own to serve. I believe no man ever had a cheerier comrade, or a better backer. I don't like you the worse for standing aloof during the last five weeks. I never had one unpleasant word from you; but if any of mine have vexed or offended you—see now—I ask your forgiveness from the bottom of my heart."

It is no shame to Harry's manhood that he could not answer intelligibly; but ten sentences of elaborate sentiment would hardly have been so eloquent as the pressure of his honest hand.

Later in the day, Keene went to take leave of *La Mignonne*. He did so with pain and reluctance. Men, utterly hard and merciless towards their own species, have been very fond of their pets, even when these last belonged to an inferior order of creation. Conthon would fondle his spaniel while he was signing a sheaf of death-warrants; and the Prophet, who could contemplate placidly a dozen cities in flames, and watch human hetacombs falling under the sword of Omar or Ali, cut off the sleeve of his robe rather than disturb a favourite cat in her slumbers.

Nevertheless, when two people agree to ignore, carefully, the one subject that is uppermost in the thoughts of both, the result must be an uncomfortable constraint and reserve. So the adieus, up to a certain point, were rather formal. But, just as he was going, the same impulse overcame Royston which had affected him in his interview with Harry Molyneux. Considering that the age of miracles is past, it was remarkable that, twice in one day, the Cool Captain should have approached so near to the verge of sentimentalism.

"I hope that I shall see you again before long," he said; "but nothing seems certain—not even the meeting of friends. I wish to thank you now for some pleasant days and evenings. You have brought a good deal of sunshine into my life, since I knew you first. I like to think that, neither in deed or intention, I have ever deliberately done you or Harry any harm. I hope you will go on taking as much care of him, and making him as perfectly happy, as you have done. Perhaps I have vexed you both lately; but all that is over; and I fancy the punishment will be proportionate to the offence, before it is ended. Farewell. Don't forget me sooner than you can help; and while you do remember me, think of me as kindly as you can."

He leant over her as he finished speaking, and his lips just brushed her smooth forehead. When Charles the Martyr embraced his children an hour before his death, they received no purer or more sinless kiss. A sob choked Fanny's voice when she would have replied; and the beautiful brown eyes were so dim with rushing tears, that they never saw him go.

Keene's last visit in Dorade was to the Vicomte de Châteaumesnil. The latter manifested no surprise at the sudden departure, and expressed his regrets with a perfectly calm courtesy. But, at the moment of leave-taking, he detained the other's hand for a second or so, and said, looking wistfully in his face,—

"Ainsi, vous partez—seul? Je ne l'aurais pas
cru; et, je l'avoue franchement, ça me contrarie.
N'importe; je connois votre jeu; et je ne vous
tiens pas pour battu, quand c'est manche à. Ce
serait une bêtise, de dire—' au revoir.' Adieu;
amusez-vous bien."

Royston shook his head impatiently; he was too
proud to save his credit by dissembling a defeat;
and his reply was quick and decisive:

"Vous me flattez, M. le Vicomte. Quand on
perd, on doit au moins l'avouer loyalement, et payer
l'enjeu. Cette fois j'ai tant perdu, que je ne pren-
drai pas la revanche."

Not another word was exchanged between them;
but Armand had accepted repulses in his time
with more equanimity than he could muster when
ruminating afterwards on the discomfiture of
Royston Keene.

Some days later the subject was discussed at the
Cercle; and one of the *habitués* hazarded several
cunning conjectures, and more than cynical surmises. (Did you ever hear a thoroughly profligate
Frenchman sneer a woman's character away? It
is almost worth while overcoming your disgust to
listen to the diabolical ingenuity of his inuendoes.
The scandal of our bitterest dowagers sounds
charitable by comparison.) The savage outbreak
of the Algerian's temper that every one had long
been expecting, came at last—with a vengeance.

"Tu mens, canaille! C'est le meilleur éloge de
M. Keene, que les manans, comme toi, ne puissent
le comprendre. Quand à Mademoiselle—elle vaut
mille fois tes sœurs, et ta mère. Si tu as le cœur
de pousser l'affaire, je te donnerai raison sur mes
béquilles. Pour le pistolet, ma main n'est pas
encore percluse."

He held it out, as steady and strong as it was in
the old days, when it could sway the sabre from
dawn to twilight, and never know weariness.

If the other persuaded himself that consideration for the invalid's infirmities made him patient
under the insult, his friends were less romantically
credulous : the stigma of that night cleaves to him
still. Brazen it out as he may, the hang-dog look
remains, telling us that the barriers have been at
least once broken down which separate the Man
from the Serf. There would be, perhaps, less mischief abroad, if slander were always so promptly
and amply avenged.

CHAPTER XXII

NOT long after the events here recorded, came a time that we all remember right well; when, without note of preparation, the war-trumpets sounded from the East and the North; when Europe woke up, like a giant refreshed, from the slumber of a forty years' peace, and took down disused weapons from the wall, and donned a rusted armour.

It was a time rife with romantic episodes; and, as such seasons must ever be, fraught with peril to the prudence of womankind. There was perpetual recurrence of the striking antithesis which happened at Brussels before Waterloo, when the roll of the distant cannon at Quatre Bras mingled with the music of the Duchess's ball. The coldest reserve is apt to melt rapidly, and the most skilful coquetry is brought to bay when opposed to pleading urged, possibly, for the last time. Those were days of rebuke and blasphemy to "the gentlemen of England who sate at home at ease;" and even the Foreign Office "irresistibles" could hardly hold their own. What chance have the honeyed words of the accomplished civilian against the simple eloquence of the soldier, who speak with his life in his hand? Truly there were many conquests then achieved of which the world knew nothing, for the victor never came back to claim his prize.

When the funeral of the Great Duke went by, it was easy to find fault with some of the details of that pretentious pageant; but which of us was cool enough to criticise, on the grey February morning, when the Guards marched out? There were practised veterans enough to be found in their ranks; and each of these, perhaps, could number some who loved him dearly; but none in the column won such hearty sympathy as those "trim subalterns, holding their swords daintily," who went forth to their doom gaily and gallantly, as if pestilence were not lying in ambush at fever-stricken Varna, and lines of hungry graves waiting for their prey in the bleak Chersonese. Surely there were sadder faces at home than any that lined the road; and the anxious crowd at the station represented very inadequately the "girls they left behind them."

When the first certain rumours of war prevailed, Royston Keene was shooting woodcocks in the Hebrides; he hastened back to town without a moment's delay. We know how quick and unerring, on such occasions, is the instinct of the Rapacidæ. His object was to get on the active service list as

soon as possible. With his powerful interest and
high reputation, this was not difficult; and he was
soon gazetted to a Light Calvary regiment. But
he did not go out with the first detachments, and
the summer was far advanced when he reached the
Crimea.

There was great jubilation at his coming. Many
out there knew him personally, well; and others
rejoiced at having the opportunity of judging for
themselves if he really deserved his fame. It
soon became apparent that the Cool Captain was
strangely altered. To be sure, the opportunities
for general conviviality were few; for mess-rooms
and ante-rooms were phantoms of the imagination,
or only pleasant memories; still there was a certain
amount of agreeable though select *réunions*, where
the vintages of Bordeaux and Burgundy were
sufficiently replaced by regulation rum. At these
Royston appeared rarely, and when he did show
there, was remarkably silent, and apt to let a
favourable opportunity, even for a sarcasm, go
by. He seemed to prefer the solitude of his own
tent to the most tempting inducements of society.
Men remembered afterwards how, if they went in
and found him alone, he was always busy with his
revolver, or playing with his sabre. He had
refused two advantageous offers of staff appoint-
ments, for no apparent reason, except the desire
not to be out of the way if any work were to be

done; and scarcely a day passed when he was not up at Head-quarters, trying to find out if there was any chance of a break in the long inaction of the Cavalry. Whether it was that the old blood-thirstiness had waked again in a congenial atmosphere, or whether a great weariness weighing on his spirits made him so impatient and restless—none can know for certain. Again I say, let us not sift motives too inquisitively.

It is the morning of the 25th of October, and a lull comes between the storm-gusts. The "Heavies" have just taken up their position, after that magnificent charge in which the Russian lancers were scattered like dead leaves in autumn when the wind is blowing freshly. There are murmurs of discontent running through the ranks of the Light Brigade: it seems as if *their* chance was never coming. One of his intimates grumbles as much to Royston Keene. The Cool Captain straightens a stray lock of his charger's mane, and answers with his old provoking smile—

"Don't fret yourself, George. I have a presentiment that we shall get rid of the 'fidgets' before we sleep. See—*that* looks like business."

It seemed as if a spirit of prophecy possessed him; for, even while he was speaking, the aide-de-camp came down at speed. There was a pause while that message was delivered, the exact words of which will never be known—for you cannot summon the dead as witnesses; then a brief hesitation, and a dozen sentences exchanged between the first and second in command; and then—every trooper in the Brigade understood what he had to do. Many drew true and evil augury from the cloud lowering on the stern features of the " Haughty Earl."

Keene had been under fire oftener than most there, and his practised eye took in and appreciated every item of the peril; nevertheless, his brow cleared, and all his face lighted up strangely.

" What did I tell you, young one ?" he said to the man who had addressed him just before : " it will be warmer work than the old Phœnix field-days; but one comfort is, it won't last so long."

Before the words were fairly uttered, the trumpets rang out; and, with a gayer laugh on his lip than it had worn for many a day, the Cool Captain led his squadron gallantly into Aceldama.

We will not describe the charge. Enthusiasts are not wanting who would rather have ridden in it than have won the highest distinction to which civilians can aspire. Who dares to object that it was not ultimately successful ? Such a taunt has never been weighed in the balance against the glories of Thermopylæ. I frequently meet in society one of the Paladins of that fatal Roncesvalles. In private life he has few peculiarities, except a tendency to engage in each and every game of chance, and a perfect monomania for waltzing. Yet I regard him with an immense respect and reverence, that the object of the feeling would be the last to understand. I think of the awful peril out of which the delicate, feminine face• has come without a scar; and I protest I would no more dream of speaking to him angrily or slightingly, than I would venture to discourse about the Derby to the Bishop of O——, or to offer to that dignified prelate the current odds against the favourite. Rely upon it, in many Homes of England (if the Manchesterians leave them standing), there will be one family portrait that our children will most delight to honour. Pointing out to strangers the crowning glory of their house, they will pass by grave effigies of lawyers, ecclesiastics, and statesmen, and pause opposite to a martial figure, dressed in the uniform of a Light Dragoon. All his ancestors shall give precedence to the simple soldier who rode that day in the van of the Six Hundred.

Yes, we will leave that charge alone. The most hackneyed of professional *littérateurs* might shrink from sitting down to his writing-desk, to make merchandize of such a " deed of *derring-do.*" Nevertheless, Royston Keene bore his part in it manfully; and the troopers talk yet of the feats of skill and strength wrought by his sabre.

The immunity from dangers of shot and steel,

for which he had been always remarkable, did not
seem to have deserted him; for he had come out
of the batteries without a scratch, and had fought
his way through more than one knot and peloton
of the enemy, with no scathe beyond a slight
flesh-wound. In one of these encounters he had
got separated from such remnants of his squadron
that still held together (you know even regiments
lost their unity in that terrible *mêlée*); the only
man who kept near him was his covering-sergeant.
All this while, the fire from the Russian guns on
the hill-side grew heavier and heavier, and the
cruel grape-shot ripped through the mingled
masses of friends and foes; making sudden un-
sightly gaps here and there, just as may be seen
in a field of ripe corn " laid" by the lashing hail.
The good horse on which Keene was mounted
had not been out from England long enough to
suffer materially in wind or limb; he was in very
fair condition, and had carried his master splen-
didly so far, with equal luck in escaping any
serious injury. Five hundred yards more would
have placed them in safety, within the position,
where the Heavy Brigade was already moving up
to cover the retreat of their comrades; when The
Templar, going at top speed, pitched suddenly
forwards, as a ship does when she founders; and,
after rolling once half-over his rider, lay still,
with limbs just faintly quivering. Two grape-shot,

making one wound, had crashed right into his chest, and through the heart.

His covering-sergeant was within three lengths of Royston when the latter went down: he pulled up and sprang down instantly, and was by his officer's side in a second, trying to extricate him.

"Hold up, Major," he said cheerily; "that's nothing. Take my horse. He'll carry you in; and I can manage well enough."

The strong soldier reeled, from sheer weakness, as he was speaking; for the blood was spouting in dark-red jets from a ghastly cut in his bridle-arm; yet he seemed to see nothing in his offer but a simple act of duty—though men have won a place in history for meaner self-sacrifice. One of the most remarkable peculiarities about the Cool Captain, was the hold he maintained over the affections and impulses of those with whom he was brought in contact, without any visible reason for such influence. He was the strictest possible disciplinarian, and his demeanour towards his subordinates was consistently dictatorial; yet the present case was only one instance of the enthusiasm with which they regarded him.

Keene looked up at the speaker wistfully, from where he lay; and his face softened in its set sternness.

" You're a good fellow, Davis," he said, "but I would not avail myself of your generosity if I could.

I can't take much credit for refusing it. My thigh is broken; and I am hurt besides. I couldn't keep the saddle for ten seconds. Draw my right gauntlet off, and take my ring; you deserve it better than the Cossacks. Keep it as long as you like ; it will always bring you a fifty, if you get hard up. And take *this* too." He put his hand into the breast of his uniform ; but drew it back quickly " No : it shall stay with me while I live."

His tone and manner were just the same as if he had met with a heavy fall, out hunting, and were answering some goodnatured friend who had stopped to pick him up.

The trooper took the ring; but he lingered still. Royston saw a knot of the enemy sweeping down on them, like ravens on a stag wounded to the death ; his voice resumed its wonted accent of irresistible command :

" Did you hear what I said ? I told you to go. Those devils will be down on us in less than a minute. I have not fired one barrel of my revolver, and I'm good for one or two of them yet."

The habit of obedience, more than the instinct of self-preservation, made Davis mount and ride away without another word. He looked back, though, as he did so. He heard three distinct reports from Keene's revolver : two of the enemy's skirmishers dropped to the shots, and the third wavered in his saddle; the rest closed round the fallen man with levelled lances. The stout sergeant looked back no more; but he set his teeth hard, and turned out of his way to encounter a stray Russian, and laid the foeman's face open from eyebrow to lip with an awful blasphemy.

The spot where Royston fell was so near to the British lines that those who slaughtered him dared not stay for plunder. Half an hour later, Davis and two more volunteers, went out and brought in the mangled body of the best swordsman in the Light Brigade.

CHAPTER XXIII.

NOT dead yet.

Though the bloody Muscovite spearmen thought they left a corpse behind them, and though the surgeons who examined him decided that he could not survive the night, the obstinate vitality in Royston Keene still lingered on, refusing to yield to wounds that might have drained the life out of three strong men. It seemed as if some strange doom were upon him, such as was laid on the Black Slave in the "Arabian Nights," loved by the enchantress-queen; or on Durindarte in the old romance, where the tortured spirit, enthralled by potent spells, was withheld for a season from departure, though its tenement was all shattered and ruined. His case from the first was utterly hopeless; and his bodily helplessness at times almost resembled catalepsy; yet his faculties were quite clear. He could recognize his friends, and talk with them quite composedly : cry or complaint never once issued from his lips. They sent him down to Scutari at last—not with any hope of his recovery, but wishing to ensure him all available comforts in his dying moments.

It was a rough passage (even on invalids the cruel Euxine had little mercy) : this, and the pain of transport through the few hundred yards that were between the vessel and the hospital, almost

exhausted the dregs of Royston's strength. When
they laid him down on the bed allotted to him, in a
small room off the main ward, of which he was to
be the sole tenant, none of the surgeons could have
told if they were dealing with life or death. Work
was so heavy on their hands at that dreadful season,
that they could not devote more than a certain
space of precious time to any one patient; so, after
trying all means and appliances of recovery in vain,
they left Keene for awhile in his swoon. It seemed
as if he never would open his eyes again.

They unclosed slowly at last, still dim with the
deathly faintness; his head was dizzy and confused,
and in his ears there was a dull, droning sound, like
the murmur of a distant sea. As objects and
sounds assumed more distinctness, he became
aware of the figure of a woman sitting on the
ground by the side of his couch—her head buried
in her hands—rocking herself ever to and fro, and
never pausing in her low, heartbroken wail. If old
tales speak truth, such a figure might be seen in
dark corners of haunted houses; and such a wail
might echo at dead of night through chambers
conscious of some fearful crime. Instinct, more
than reason, revealed to Royston the truth.

The lips that under the thrusts of Russian lances,
and through all subsequent tortures, had guarded
so jealously the secret of his agony, could not repress a groan, as they syllabled the name of—Cecil
Tresilyan.

It was so. The brilliant beauty who for two seasons had ruled the world in which she moved so imperiously—insatiate of conquest and defying rivalry—the delicate *aristocrate*, who from her childhood had been used to every imaginable luxury, and had appreciated them all—was found again, here, in the grey robe of a Sister of Charity, content to endure real, bitter hardships, and to witness, daily, sights from which womanhood, with all its bravery, must needs recoil.

The motives that had urged her to such a step would be hard indeed to define. The same weariness and impatience of inaction that have been alluded to in the case of Royston Keene may have had much to do with it; to this, perhaps, was added a feeling of wild remorse, seeking to vent itself in self-torturing penance, such as impelled kings and conquerors in old days to don the palmer's gown, and macerate their bodies by fast and scourge; there may have been, too, some vague, unacknowledged longing to seize the last chance of seeing her lost love once again. Might she not tend *him* as she nursed the other wounded, without adding to the weight of her sin? If she ever entertained such an idea, her punishment may well have atoned for her offence, when she came suddenly and unprepared into that sick chamber, and looked upon the mangled wreck lying senseless there.

Royston spoke first. "What brought you here?"

If it was possible that he could feel anything like terror, surely the hollow, tremulous voice betrayed it then.

Cecil Tresilyan sprang to her feet as if an electric shock had moved her, and stood gazing at him with her great, desolate, tearless eyes : all her misery could not make them hard or haggard, nor dispel their marvellous enchantment. Royston marked the impulse that would have drawn her to his side, and threw out one weak hand to warn her off; with the other he tried to cover his own scarred, ghastly face. "Don't come near me," he muttered ; "I can't bear it." Her woman's instinct fathomed his meaning instantly : he thought that even *she* must shrink from him. She laughed out loud (for her brain was almost turning) as she knelt down and raised his head on her arm, and smoothed his matted hair, and kissed the death-damp from his forehead, murmuring between the caresses, "You dare not keep me from you. Do you think that *I* fear you, my own—my own!"

The glory of a great triumph—grand, even if sinful—lighted up the face of the dying man; and intense passion made even his voice strong and steady.

"I believe *this* is better than the paradise we dreamed of in the island of the Greek Sea!"

Without a moment's pause, the sweet sad voice replied—

"Yes, it is better. *Then* I should have died first

and hopelessly. Now there is no guilt between us that may not be forgiven."

Silence lasted, till Royston gathered energy to speak again.

"You remember the glove? See—I have not parted with it yet." He drew from his breast a case of steel links hung round his neck by a chain: it held Cecil's gauntlet—stained and stiffened with his blood. That was the treasure he would not resign when he lay on the ground, waiting for the Russian lances. "You did not think that I should forget you, because I never answered your letter?"

As had happened once before, a portion of his fortitude and self-command seemed transfused into Cecil Tresilyan. She spoke quite steadily now.

"How could I misjudge your silence, when I begged you not to write? I have been very miserable, thinking how angry you would be; and yet I could not help what I did. But I never fancied you had forgotten me. Forgetting is not so easy. Now tell me about yourself. I have heard of that glorious charge. But those terrible wounds—how you must have suffered!"

Out of the dim, glazing eyes flashed, for one moment, a gleam of soldierly pride. "Yes, we rode straight, on the twenty-fifth—I amongst the rest. I suppose I have suffered some pain, but that is all past and gone. I am sensible of nothing but the happiness of holding your little hand once more. See—I can hold it without shame, for my fingers have not pressed those of any woman alive since we parted."

She saw how the utterance of those few words told upon him ; and refrained from the delight of listening longer to the voice, that was still to her inexpressibly dear. So she checked him, when he would have gone on speaking. Yet the silence that ensued was first broken by Cecil.

" My own ! I fear—I fear, that you are in great danger. How long we may *both* have to suffer, God alone can tell. But will you not see a clergy-man ? He might help you, though I am weak and powerless."

A shadow of the old sardonic scorn swept across Keene's emaciated face, and passed away as suddenly " It is somewhat late for any help that priests can bring. Besides, I cannot dwell now on any of my past sins, save one. All my thoughts are taken up with the wrong that I have done to you."

This was true. If there were reproachful phan-toms that had a right to haunt Royston's death-bed, the living presence kept them all at bay.

Cecil's eyes had never been more eloquent than they were then; but they spoke of nothing but despair.

" Ah, heaven ! cannot you see, that all *I* have to forgive has been forgiven long ago ? What is to become of me, if you die hardened in your sin ? Must I live on, *hoping* that we are parted for

...ver? If you are pitiless to your own soul—have mercy, at least, upon me!"

All Royston's former crimes seemed to him venial by comparison, as he witnessed the misery and abasement of the glorious creature on whom he had brought such sorrow, if not shame. The remorse that a strong will and hard heart had stifled so long, found voice at last in three muttered words—"God forgive me!"

A very niggardly and inadequate expression of contrition—was it not? conceded to a life whose sins outnumbered its years. Yet the slight thread of hope drawn therefrom has been able, since, to hold back Cecil Tresilyan from the abyss of utter desperation. She forbore to press him further then, seeing his increasing weakness, and trusting, perhaps, that a more favourable opportunity would come.

Indeed, there were a thousand things to be said about the past, in which both had borne a part, and the future, in which only one could share; but Royston had estimated rightly the extent of his remaining physical resources; and when he found how each syllable exhausted him, he became as chary of his words as a miser of his gold. His right hand still grasped hers, firmly; and her delicate cheek was pillowed on his shoulder; the fingers of his other hand played gently with a long, glossy chestnut tress that had escaped from the prison of the close cap she wore. So they

remained, for a long time — no sound passing
between them, beyond half-formed whispers of
endearment. No one came in to molest them:
there was work enough and to spare, that night
for all in Scutari. The thought of interruption
never crossed Cecil's mind for an instant. Always
careless and defiant of conventionality, or the
world's opinion, she was tenfold more reckless
now. Her head was bent down and her eyes
closed; so that she could not see how the hollows
deepened on her lover's face; nor how the pallor
of his cheek darkened rapidly to an ashen-grey.
But inward warnings of approaching dissolution
spoke plainly enough to Royston Keene. He
knew what he had to do.

He raised her head from where it rested, and
said—so gently—"If my time is short, there is
the more reason that I should be loth to lose
you, even for an hour. But you must have rest;
and I feel as if I could sleep. Do not try to
persuade me; but leave me now When you
think hereafter of this evening, remember what
my last words were—*I loved you best of all.*
Darling—wish me good-night; and come to see
me early to-morrow."   .

He guessed, full well, how long that Night
would last; and what sight would meet Cecil on
the morrow; but he was resolute to spare her one
additional pang; and so, endured alone the whole
burden of the parting agony. His life had been

full of deeds of reckless daring; but, in good truth, this achievement was its very crown of courage.

Now, as heretofore, Cecil was incapable of re-- sisting any one of his expressed wishes or com- mands; besides this, physical exhaustion was beginning to overcome her: and she, too, felt that it was time to go. She leant down, without speaking, and their lips met in a long, passionate kiss. So little of vitality lingered in Royston's, that they remained still iey-cold under the pressure of those ripe, red roses.

"I will come again, early," she whispered.

The last relies of a strength that had been super- human passed into the lingering pressure of the hand that bade her tenderly farewell. Half an hour later the surgeon came to Royston Keene. All that night shrieks and groans, and other sounds through which human agony finds a vent, had been ringing in his ears, till they were weary of the din; but the silence of that chamber struck the visitor yet more painfully. He looked, for a second, gravely at the motionless figure; and laid his ear against the lips; no breath issued thence that would have stirred a feather; then he drew very gently the sheet over the dead man's face—a quiet, stead- fast face—that, even in the death-throe, had retained its proud, placid calm.

When Cecil Tresilyan saw that same sight, the next morning, she did not scream or faint. Neither then nor afterwards did she prove herself unworthy of her haughty lover by demonstrating or parading her sorrows. Many others besides her have taken for their motto—"The heart knoweth its own bitterness;" and have carried it out to the end, unflinchingly. Verily, they have their reward. If there is little comfort on this side the grave, and only vague hope eyond it, it is something—to escape condolence.

We follow her fortunes no farther. It is needless to give all the details of the hospital service which occupied her till the conclusion of the war set her free; and we will not seek to penetrate into the retreat in the Far West, where she is dwelling still. That grey manor-house guards its secrets well, though it has witnessed, in its time, sorrows and sins that might have wrung a voice from granite. Conscious of many broken hearts and blasted hopes, is the home of the Tresilyans of Tresilyan.

I confess to a certain regret, as the graceful figure vanishes from the stage that never was worthy of her queen-like presence. Was it in dream-land that I saw the Original of the character and face that I have endeavoured, thus roughly, to portray? Perhaps so. But there are visions so near akin to realities, that one's brain grows dizzy in trying to disentangle the two.

It is unfortunate that the void created by any man's death is by no means proportionate to his intrinsic merits. So it happened that the loss of Royston Keene was felt more than he deserved.

Far and wide over the surface of the world's sea, the circles spread, from the spot where his life went down. He was missed not only by his old comrades in arms; men who scarcely knew him by sight spared some regret to the favourite hero of the Light Dragoons.

Mark Waring, in the loneliness of his dreary chambers, gnashed his teeth in bitterness of envy; for he guessed *who* would be the chief mourner. Armand de Châteaumesnil's remark was characteristic. Hearing that his old opponent had fallen in the front of the battle, he struck his hand impatiently on his crippled limbs, muttering, " Sang dieu !—Il avait toujours la main heureuse." Harry Molyneux cannot trust his voice to speak of him yet; and other beautiful eyes besides *La Mignonne's* were dim with tears when they read a certain death-gazette. Truly " great men have fallen in Israel," and saints have departed in the plenitude of sanctity, without winning such wealth of regrets as was lavished on the grave of that strong sinner. Only two women alive (and these he had never wronged) rejoiced over the news unfeignedly—Bessie Danvers, and his own wife.

Shall we pass judgment on Royston Keene? He had erred so often and heavily, that even the intercession of a penitent who never kneels before Heaven without mingling his name in her prayers, must probably be unavailing. Yet will we not cast the stone.

Y

All temptations, of course, can be resisted, and ought to be overcome. But there are men born with so peculiar a temperament, and who seem to have been so completely under the dominion of circumstances, that they might well be supposed to have been raised up for a warning. How far are such to be held accountable? Let us refrain from this subject, remembering how grave and learned theologians, earnest opponents of Predestinarianism, have been reduced to the extreme of perplexity when confronted with the ensample of Pharaoh.

It would neither be pleasant nor profitable to pry into the secrets of the black darkness that lies beyond Royston's death-bed; in it, few would be able to distinguish the faintest glimmer of light. But we have no more authority to fix limits to the long-suffering of Omnipotence, than we have to dispute the justice of its revenge. Let us stand aside, and hope

> That heaven may yet have more mercy than man,
> On such a bold rider's soul.

A strange doctrine, that; savouring perhaps of heterodoxy, and perilous to be adopted by such as cannot fathom it thoroughly. But if there be no germ of truth therein—it were better for some of us that we had never been born.

WYMAN AND SONS, PRINTERS, GREAT QUEEN STREET, LONDON, W.C.